THE GLOBAL
WARMING
CONSPIRACY

JOHAN FAUST

Charlotte and I met 45 years ago in Australia. A few years later we were married in Liverpool. We have travelled the world, changed careers, and lived charmed lives. If none of this had happened, we would have become different people today, and this book would not have been written.

Table of Contents

Preface

This is a fictional story, masquerading as a novel, about hypothetical events. The story's main characters include three individuals who decide that something has to be done about global warming. Some peripheral characters appear in order to establish a current context for the life experiences of the main characters. The peripheral characters are fictionalized versions of individuals who are known to most of us but play no roles in the subsequent plot. You will find them on the internet in Wikipedia and similar entries. They have been associated with issues that have changed recent global and regional history. I have attached views and ideas to these individuals that are consistent with their careers and are documented in the public domain. If I have misinterpreted the information in the public domain, I can only apologize and hope to be forgiven.

Two of the main characters are wholly fictional. I have endeavoured to link the plot to actual events and places. As well, I have described technologies and data that are familiar to me. In some instances, I have extrapolated from current economic and political trends and outcomes into the near future. It may not happen that way, but it seems plausible to me that the future could unfold in the manner I have imagined. I make no apologies for the way I have described the fictional characters. They are unusual constructs, but I have known individuals that could fit my descriptions, at least in part. The world is populated by unusual individuals, and there are bound to be some that recognize themselves, but no single person I have encountered should feel that they have been used as models.

Prologue

My story ends on yet another mild and showery late-spring day in 2025 on the banks of the Thames some miles north of Oxford. Recently there have been more than the usual number of such days: I should be pleased. Within a few days, I will no longer be with you. If my thinking is correct, you can look forward to an old-fashioned winter with a week or two of snow and ice, a late spring and a pleasantly mild summer. It would be a change from the climatic extremes of recent years. I will not be here to see the seasons unfold, but my hope is that you, the reader, will be here to enjoy the summers beyond 2025.

Being an elderly traditionalist, I would not expect any tale to begin with some serious finger-wagging and to end with my personal and private demise. But we live in interesting times. I fully expect to be judged, maybe kindly, a "strange" person by a few readers of the following narrative, so anything goes. I intend to say what needs to be said. Other readers will be outraged and will judge me along the lines of derangement or wilful criminality, but such feelings will have little to do with split infinitives and other similar blemishes in my prose. You might also recognize that English is not my native language and that I am not a habitual writer of fiction.

As you will see, the tale is communicated partly in the first person ('I'). I am talking to you as one person to another. There are sections in the book that will seem to be written by either a fly on the wall or by an omniscient observer. In some instances, I am looking at myself while guessing at my self. I hope that there will be an epitaph at the end and that this will be written by the person who was nearest and dearest to me.

Why am I writing this? In the beginning, the outcomes of events, to be described in later chapters, were hypothetical, or virtual, if you wish. There was a plan, constructed in my mind, but not existing outside my mind. If you think about an outcome, such as the firing of a bullet, getting a date with Rachel Welch or Johnny Depp, or becoming filthy rich from buying shares in Tesla, the outcomes remain hypothetical, and of no practical consequence, until the plans are executed. (Your prey/enemy is not shot. Rachel/Johnny is spared your attention, and you have not placed an order with your stock broker). It is only when the plan is executed that the outcome becomes real, and you have to live with the consequences.

* * *

Now I have to say something about the main character, who is the narrator. The personality, P, is all-important. I will use P_1 and P_2 to describe how I believe my mind works, but not necessarily as seen by an outside observer. I will do this because the hidden workings of a mind of a particular person cannot be divined. It is likely that the workings of my mind will have some bearing on the unfolding of the hypothetical tale. I will therefore tell you about P_1 and P_2. Such a mental state was once called a split personality. It is quite possible that if my mind had worked in a different way, there would not have been a story to tell.

I was an only child, as far as I am aware, and rarely lived in one place for very long. I never knew my parents. They seemed to have been absent from before I was capable of having lasting memories. Increasingly distant and reluctant relatives and strangers were enlisted as my carers. I felt unwanted and unable to make sense of the world in which I found myself. So, I took to talking to myself. It soon became apparent that in the days of my childhood, people who walk around and talk to themselves attract attention and find themselves in an institution. One way to avoid this fate, I thought, was to internalize the talking. There were then two voices of two personalities having a dialogue in my mind. The P_2 held forth about fear and apprehension, longing, empathy and love, yearning and wishing. The P_1 dealt with planning and scheming, analysis and problem-solving, how to make the best out of a bad situation, and how to anticipate consequences of choices and actions. Conversations between the two Ps over a period of many years went like these:

P_2: "Why do I have to go to another school again? I will have no friends. I look different, I speak another dialect. I will get beaten up, again. I want to run away."

P_1: "Running away is not going to work. They will find me, and I will end up in a school for bad children, where I will get beaten up every day. I think the trick is to be invisible, sit at the back of the class, say nothing unless asked, don't be a smarty-pants, stay close to the teacher on duty in the school yard, curl up into a ball, and don't fight back."

P_2: "Why was I sent away from my grandparents to a new home? Didn't they like me? I heard my uncle asking auntie why I was being dumped on them."

P_1: "I think I can understand what happened. Grandfather's heart problems got worse. I got pneumonia and went to the hospital. I remember Grandmother coming to see me. She had sad eyes. I don't think she was coping."

P_2: "I really like the cute girl with the blonde ponytail and the dimples. I bring her books that I think she would like to read, and I talk to her about how life can be difficult. I think she sort of likes to talk to me. I saw her in town the other day, walking hand-in-hand with a boy from the next higher grade. What is wrong with me?"

P_1: "I think it has something to do with hormones and early onset of facial hair growth. I will bide my time. Sooner or later, the bookworm will overtake the stud."

P_2: "I have to decide what I am going to do with my life. I have read every book in the local one-room library, and I have hated every mathematics assignment; I think I am best suited to study something in the arts or maybe the social sciences."

P_1: "I disagree, partly because I am clever and can do anything and partly because I want to have a solid basis to my existence, such as the laws of nature. Everything else is relative and fluid. So far, my life has been chaotic and meaningless. It can't go on like this."

P_2: "OK, I am convinced. Physics is security. My life is based on something reliable and substantial, and I can stop worrying about being useless and helpless."

This is how I came to do physics for most of the rest of my life. Each time I walked past an apple tree and saw apples fall down, P_1 was pleased that life had meaning. P_2 kept warning my other self from time to time that if P_1 ever saw an apple fall up, then all meaning would be lost, and life would be unbearable.

It turned out that a training in physics gave me the tools to solve the kinds of problems that required hierarchical analysis and lateral thinking. P_1 continued to have lengthy discussions with P_2, such as:

P_2: "Why am I going to work for the International Atomic Energy Agency in Vienna? We all know that the IAEA was set up to be a support player in the present world order, where the USA has the whip hand. Only the nations that are in possession of nuclear weapons can pursue truly independent geopolitical objectives. Initially, only the permanent members of the UN Security Council were the 'victors' in WWII. Later, the USA plus UK+France could always out-vote USSR/Russia+PRC. Any one of the permanent members has right of veto; thus, the Security Council has become largely dysfunctional and irrelevant. However, the USA could always get its way, especially in the case of the IAEA, such as when the USA needed a fig leaf to justify its invasion of Iraq. The IAEA was pressured into being party to a report saying that the presence of weapons of mass destruction in Iraq could not be ruled out. The IAEA knew full well that there were no such weapons in Iraq but was pressured into remaining silent."

P_1: "You are quite correct in making those observations, and the question is legitimate. I think that I wanted to see the inside of the IAEA. I have discovered that many of the insiders were sincere about what they did and how they acted. Many of them wished that nuclear weapons had never been made or that the properties of some nuclei had turned out to be sufficiently different so as to make fission and fusion impossible."

The very significant event of the arrival of Hasina had the effect of reconciling P_1 and P_2 and made the internal dialogue harmonious and constructive. With her help, the two Ps made peace with the past, and the future was my oyster to be savoured. She taught me to stand outside myself and to objectify what was happening in my mind. A psychiatrist would probably call it externalizing by self-analysis.

* * *

Some readers might suspect that I am trying to explain and

validate my involvement in actions and events that cost the lives of millions and were intended to change human history.

I don't believe I am doing so, but there is the possibility that I am engaging in self-delusion or that I played God in a perverted and misguided game. The reason for me going public is that I am trying to understand myself. How could a reasonably normal person – someone you would pass in the street and not notice – become an object deserving to be hated? Would the thousands of students who have attended my lectures and sought enlightenment about quantum mechanics and such things, over the years, think back and say they always knew I was a bad one? Would the many friends and colleagues that have passed through my life say that they always thought there was something messianic or demonic about me? I doubt it.

Did anyone really know me? For most of my life, I kept quiet about the conversations between P_1 and P_2. The world I knew did not seem to be kindly disposed, and I needed to erect a defensive wall in my mind for protection. Both Hasina and I had demons to deal with. We soon realized that our marriage could work only by a tacit agreement that we would jointly slay the demons and stand shoulder to shoulder, when required, to deal with whatever the world would throw at us.

Soon after we were married, a boy child was born. In a fit of optimism and hope, we named him Eden. Life was then good to us for many years to come.

Almost four years ago, we made the hardest decision of our lives. Hasina and Eden had to leave me – with new identities – so as to be untraceable for a generation or more. From my previous work in the IAEA, I had come to know people who could arrange the paperwork for false identities and who knew about shadowy banks that could make anonymous funds transfers without the transactions being traceable. The IAEA itself was often dependent on obtaining sensitive information from agents whose lives would be at risk if the sources were to become known. New identities and a comfortably safe retirement were usually promised in exchange for credible and important information.

The system was tested out by Hasina. She travelled to Paris by Eurostar with a false passport. There she transmitted by SMS two code words three minutes apart, followed 10 minutes later by the address of the hotel and her room number. Next day, a parcel arrived by courier to the occupier of Room 213. The parcel contained US$5,000 in cash. The system worked.

Some weeks later, Hasina and Eden disappeared from my life. It felt as if a part of me had gone with them. During the following weeks, I tidied up my life as best I could. A flurry of e-mails went out saying I was going to be away for a period of time on urgent business. I cancelled my subscription to *The Economist* and told Royal Mail to hold any mail for a lengthy period of time. All the standing orders were left to pay bills as they came in, and so on. Modern life can be exceedingly tedious. On the last day, I bought a cheap smartphone and sent a code message: "I am on my way." I then threw the phone into the river and caught the X60 bus to Heathrow.

* * *

Close to four years have passed, and I am now back near to where I started, and I have begun writing about what happened during that time of my life. I am trying to write a thousand words a day. The cancer that is gnawing at my innards accounts for the urgency. The nice lady doctor in Innsbruck told me that I am unlikely to have more than six months. She arranged to have a morphine pump implanted. I can press a hidden button when the pain becomes unbearable. I try to leave the button alone because morphine dulls my thinking. I had asked the doctor what would happen if I pressed the button a few times in rapid succession. She said I would go to sleep and not wake up. I like the thought of being in charge at the very end.

Raja

The first few morning rays from the rising sun were creeping in through the bedroom window of the terrace, No. 60, that fronted on to the towpath along the River Thames in the centre of Oxford. One of the sleeping pair reached out an arm and turned on the radio. It clicked into life and began its gentle massaging to arouse the consciousnesses of the awakening couple.

As usual, I focussed on my wish to deny the coming of a new day. Hasina, on the other hand, was a morning person and listened intently to the daily ration of doom, gloom and despair. This morning, the news was going to be different, and it would change their lives.

In the halfway house, between deep sleep and awakening, I felt the hand of Hasina on my back and heard her voice.

"Tropical cyclone Raja has changed course and will make landfall at Chittagong within the next three hours."

The BBC had been revelling in a running commentary and hourly updates during the previous two days on the latest tropical cyclone to threaten the countries on the periphery of the Bay of Bengal. For days, Raja had been hovering offshore while strengthening. It was now a monster with a central pressure below 900 millibar and a maximum wind speed in excess of 280 km per hour. We had been told that Raja was potentially the most destructive cyclone ever to threaten the Bay of Bengal. The BBC kept reminding its viewers and listeners of the previous record breaker that had hit Chittagong in 1991 and killed some 150,000 and devastated the low-lying areas of Bangladesh. At the time, 10% of the land in Chittagong was less than one metre above the normal sea level at high tide. Since then, global warming had raised the level by additional centimetres due to the expansion of the hotter water and the melting of the ice caps in the polar regions.

Hasina looked at me and said, "I'm worried. Can we give them a call if the lines are still functional?"

"Yes, I'd like to hear that Kualeda and Mujibur are OK," I agreed.

The ringing tone kept going for what seemed an eternity, and we were ready to hang up. But then, suddenly, there were scratchy noises and the sound of a metallic and echoing voice. It was definitely Mujibur talking.

Hasina was on the second phone in the study, and in unison we asked what was happening.

Between the intermittency of transmission and the howling of the wind at the other end, we found out that the roof of the bungalow had been torn off and all the windows were broken. They were huddling together in the back room while the front of the house was being pummelled by airborne debris. There was water everywhere, and power had failed several hours earlier.

"Is it possible to get to higher ground and find shelter somewhere else?" we asked.

"It's too late, the wind is too strong," was the answer.

The conversation became intermittent. Their voices faded from time to time and then briefly returned.

"There should be rescue personnel about – can you hear sounds of helicopters?" I asked.

"Nothing!" was the answer.

"Think you can ride it out?" I asked. "Will the house protect you?"

There was silence while the line crackled. Then came a faltering message.

"We think not. The wind's strengthening, and water's rising."

The thin, quavering voice of Kualeda came through. "The sea will take us. I hope it will be quick. I wanted to see Eden grow up, but I know Hasina and you will give him much love and the best of life."

"We will. He'll remember you and be thankful for the times we had."

"There is not much time. The mango trees are gone."

Then from Mujibur: "Remember the gold."

"It will be for Eden when he is 18," I replied.

The sounds from the telephone became increasingly unintelligible. Hasina was gripping the receiver with white knuckles, as if clutching on to life itself. Then the line went dead, and we knew that life was gone, and our family had perished. There would be no more visits after the monsoon to see Mujibur and Kualeda.

We sat in silence and looked at each other. The padding sounds of slippers were from Eden coming down the stairs. "Why are you up so early?" he asked in a manner that made me think he did not want to know the answer. I looked at Hasina, and she nodded.

"A very big tropical storm has hit Chittagong. We talked to Kualeda and Mujibur for a while, but then the line went dead." The word "dead" hung heavily in the air.

* * *

During the next week, aerial and satellite images appeared in the media, together with increasingly sensational descriptions of the extent of death and destruction. Aid and assistance from many sources came on the scene to take the edges off the worst of the suffering and misery of survivors. Estimates of the death toll ranged from 1 to more than 3 million, but the actual number would probably never be known. There was agreement that the greatest contribution to the devastation came from the storm surge, which had reached 12 metres, far in excess of any previous record, with wind speeds of 300 km per hour. We searched the aerial images for the location of where Hasina had grown up, and where her parents had died, but could not find any sign of a structure where the house had stood. In my case, the images were reminiscent of the pictures of the aftermath of the nuclear bombing of Hiroshima and Nagasaki or the result of the fire-bombing of Dresden.

* * *

Three weeks after the onslaught by Raja, communications into and around Bangladesh were gradually being restored. We managed to secure seats on one of the first commercial flights into Chittagong. A local taxi driver was pleased to get the business, although he warned us that there was nothing left standing on the east side of the harbour and that many of the roads had not yet been cleared.

The landscape had changed beyond recognition. The wind had disassembled most of the structures, and then the storm surge had finished the job. Familiar landmarks were gone, heavy trucks were lying overturned in places where there had been no roads. In some areas, we knew there had been bustling communities; there were now just open spaces of rubble and an eerie silence. The outgoing surge of the sea had sucked everything, and everyone, away into a watery grave.

It became apparent that the taxi was not going to get us closer to our destination, so we made arrangements to be picked up at dusk and then set off on foot. Using landmarks across the bay and following a contour roughly 10 metres above sea level, we found what was left of the colonial bungalow that we remembered vividly. All that was left were a few remnants of the foundations and the splintered stumps of the two mango trees. Eden had bravely trudged along in silence, but the sight of the broken trees was too much for him. Hasina sat with him, and their tears joined together. I felt empty and lost.

Mujibur and Kualeda – In Memoriam

Over the years, we had many evenings and long conversations in Chittagong with Kualeda and Mujibur, and we got to know each other and heard about their respective life experiences. This is the story of Mujibur and Kualeda. They had turned into the family to me that I had never had, and I was beginning to relegate my years of loneliness to the past. I had moved on from a past and had found a new present and a future. What more could I have wished for?

Three generations before the birth of Mujibur, during the reign of Queen Victoria, and during the time of the East India Company, the family had lived in Bengal and prospered by trading cotton and jute. There was relative peace on the ethnic and religious fronts. Life had been good for my family. It was not going to last.

During the 1920s, the so-called "Two-Nation Theory" emerged as an ideological construct that was to bedevil politics, culture and inter-ethnic relations on the Indian sub-continent. The tensions have remained to this day. The "theory" held that the population of the sub-continent consisted of two intertwined nations defined by the two dominant religions, Muslim and Hindu. Conversely, ethnicity, language, culture, caste, etc, were held to be relatively less important. Therefore, the populations of the two nations should be unravelled, if necessary, by force. One extreme version of such a theory advocated, in effect, ethnic cleansing based on religious criteria. Other versions were more charitable, allowing coexistence but not necessarily equal status.

Elections in 1946 led to a polarization between the adherents of the Hindu Congress Party and the Muslim League but also fanned the flames of a general popular rejection of continued British rule. Things came to a head during the second half of 1946. Communal violence was escalating, with death tolls in the thousands. Louis Mountbatten was appointed by the Atlee government as the last viceroy of India with a brief to engineer a peaceful transition to independence by 1948. It was too late. Mountbatten was faced with a choice between a relatively peaceful partition versus a violent civil war. He agreed to the former, and independence of India and Pakistan was proclaimed on 15 July 1947. The aftermath was bloody beyond comprehension and may have cost some 2 million lives.

After partition, the predominantly Muslim Pakistan became a country of two discontiguous parts. These consisted principally of the pre-existing Punjab in the West and the predominantly Muslim part of the Bengal in the East. The majority of the territory of the former colonial India was predominantly Hindu and became the new state of India. All the major actors in the drama, Jinnah, Nehru, and Gandhi, favoured secular, modern and outward-looking political structures after independence and partition. As it turned out, the family of Mujibur ended up on the wrong side of a line drawn on the map by a public servant in Whitehall, which became the border between Hindu West and Muslim East Bengal.

* * *

The family had risen to prominence during the colonial years, trading in cotton and jute on behalf of the industries in the Midlands of the UK. The company was called Cotton and Jute Traders of Calcutta and had acquired a well-deserved reputation for honesty and efficiency. Having played a vital role for many years, doing their best to create wealth for the empire, they had become indispensable members of the colonial establishment. So, they set themselves up in Howrah, the British enclave in Calcutta. Soon, they spent the worst of the monsoon season in Darjeeling while boning up on Rudyard Kipling and Henry James.

The partition left the family stranded in West Bengal and at the mercy of the Hindu establishment. The Muslim faith and strong connections to the departing British changed overnight from being a source of power and wealth to being dangerous attributes. Soon thereafter, looting and killing by mobs intent on revenge and religious cleansing became a reality of life in Howrah. The British were melting away, and erstwhile friends were looking the other way. Words came through that they were soon to be targeted. The family met and decided that it was time to join the great migration of 15 million who had ended up being beleaguered and targeted pariahs as a result of being unwanted minorities, as defined by their religion.

Twelve members of the family, carrying seven live chickens in a wicker basket, set off early in the morning in an easterly direction through areas of the city where Muslims were in the majority. Their liquid wealth, 5 kg of gold bullion, was hidden inside six watermelons. Along the way, they joined up with two other groups of Muslims, who were also heading for the safety of the border to East Bengal. For five days, they trudged along, mostly on the dusty main road. Twice they rested during the day and walked through the night when they had to pass through territory that was reputed to be unsafe. On the third day, an elderly woman died during the night. The body was carried along for most of the day until they came to a clump of trees. She was then wrapped in a white cloth, a grave was dug amongst the trees, and she was buried. The grave was covered with large rocks so that stray dogs would not interfere.

On the fifth day, they knew they were close to the border, so they kept walking into the early evening. Finally, they could see a ramshackle border post with the flag of Pakistan beckoning.

The family rested for two days at the border. Most of the jute cultivation was in East Bengal, which had become East Pakistan after the partition. While the head office for trade had been in Calcutta, there was a branch office in Chittagong. Thus, the ultimate destination was Chittagong, where they could pick up the pieces and hopefully rebuild the business. From the border post to Chittagong, they had another 250 km to travel – and walking was not a viable proposition for the older members of the family. Fortunately, a WWII weapons carrier made the journey from Chittagong twice a week to relieve the crew at the border crossing and to bring fresh supplies. For a modest consideration, they were able to catch a ride later that week. So it was that they reached Chittagong and started a new life in a new country.

Within a few days after their departure from Calcutta, they were told that their house and business premises had been looted, vandalized and then torched.

Gradually, some of their old customers migrated to Chittagong, and business recovered. Mujibur was born in 1953, and after a few years of school and tutelage, he showed all the signs of being the next-generation custodian of the business.

Fate had not yet finished with them. From the very beginning, after partition, West Pakistan had claimed the dominant role, while East Pakistan was relegated to a second-class status. There was discrimination on ethnic grounds, in public job opportunities, and Bengali culture and artistic expression were discouraged and suppressed. The East punched above its weight in business, commerce and enterprise, but most of the earnings ended up in the coffers of the West. The elections in 1970 demonstrated that the great majority of Bengalis wanted independence. The Pakistani army invaded in early 1971 with the intention of suppressing the embryonic liberation movement. A popular uprising was the result, and a year-long war of liberation came to cost some 2 million lives. India joined the struggle on the Bengali side. This tilted the war fortunes against the West Pakistani invaders. By the end of the year, the war was won, and Bangladesh was born.

Mujibur had joined the struggle as a fresh-faced 18-year-old youngster. He became a sniper and thought he might have killed upwards of 20 enemy combatants.

In the autumn of 1975, the great and the good of the business community in Chittagong met to celebrate yet another good year and to plan for an even better next year. Mujibur was there for the first time, being inducted into the local world of business. Later in the evening, he was introduced to the daughter of another industrial captain. As it turned out, it was love at first sight between Kualeda and Mujibur. Little did they know that the occasion had been staged in the interest of strengthening the relations between two companies with well-matched synergies.

The wedding took place in February 1976. It became one of the major social events of the season, with more than 500 guests and with industrial quantities of Bengali delicacies. Kualeda became pregnant in 1979, and a daughter was born later that year. Mujibur had been testing the direction of the political winds. The two begums, Zia and Hasina, were the main contenders in the upcoming elections. It seemed to Mujibur that Sheik Hasina would be the better custodian of Bangladesh. It is always wise to go with the winner, he thought, and the newborn daughter was named Hasina. The young toddler was precocious and inquisitive. Mujibur began to describe her as a "why-is-it-so?" child. He took her to work for a few days while Kualeda was in bed with influenza.

At the end of the week, with the young Hasina at his side,

Mujibur pronounced at dinner that she was already an expert in the trading of cotton. It seemed intuitively obvious to her that one would buy at the lowest price the farmer would accept and then resell it to the overseas customer at the highest price acceptable to the buyer. "It is a game," she said, "where Daddy is always the winner."

Kualeda looked with a smile at Mujibur and said, "When are you going to retire so that we can hand the business over to Hasina?"

By the time Hasina was 12, she had exhausted the intellectual offerings of the local schools. In the spring of 1991, her parents decided to enrol her in a boarding school near Abingdon in the UK. Kualeda, Mujibur and Hasina spent a month in the UK helping Hasina to get installed in the environment that was going to be her home for the next five years. Within a few weeks, she felt perfectly at ease and went on to rise up through the hierarchy to be both popular and a star student. During the long summer vacations, she would fly home and temporarily revert to being a member of the Chittagong society. It was beginning to seem that the world was hers for the taking.

In the spring of 1996, Hasina sat for her A-level exams. As expected, she achieved five A* grades in five A-levels. It was all in a day's work. She was strongly advised to go the Oxbridge route.

She was admitted to Christ Church College at the University of Oxford in the autumn and became the first member of her family to be educated beyond high school. She became a voracious consumer of the intellectual resources on offer. She exhibited the rare but much-praised quality of seemingly not being stretched but turning out work of exceptional quality without any apparent effort. At the end of her 3-year degree, supervisors were lining up offers for her to carry on with Part 2 work. Hasina joined a group with a strong reputation in the broad area of Indo-Pakistan relations. She carried out an in-depth analysis of the events and factors that motivated

Pakistan to develop nuclear weapons. The work was subsequently accepted for publication in a high-impact journal. This earned Hasina a first-class degree in international relations. As well, she was awarded a DPhil scholarship. This time, she decided to tackle the history of Pakistan, from partition to the liberation of Bangladesh. Three years later, she was putting the final touches on the definitive review of the period and thereby gained her doctorate. With minor editorial changes, the thesis was published as a monograph by Oxford University Press.

Hasina was now 24 years old. She was ready to take on the world.

Interregnum

Once the PhD was out of the way, my life in the late 80s and most of the 90s was that of a nuclear vagabond. "Have knowledge, will travel" was my motto. After the Three Mile Island fiasco in 1979, the civilian nuclear programmes had ground to a halt. For a while, not a single new power reactor was built, and those that had been ordered were either unordered or never built. But on the military front, nuclear life remained good. The Cold War was at its most intense, with the inventories of nuclear warheads commissioned by the USA and the USSR reaching a peak of just under 70,000 in the mid-80s. Both of the main protagonists were running out of targets to obliterate on the enemy side and were capable of making the rubble bounce. Vast resources were being devoted to the development of weapons systems in order to ensure that any location on the Earth's surface could be targeted and destroyed. By the end of the '90s, there were seven countries that had nuclear weapons, plus another couple that were intending to join the club. There might have been 10 or more that were keeping their options open, just in case.

The period of nuclear overkill allowed me to visit or work at the majority of nuclear establishments located in the West and included some elsewhere.

In 1981, I had a brief secondment to the Urenco facility at Almelo in the Netherlands. During the 1970s, Urenco had been designated as the European facility for enrichment of natural uranium to 3.5% atomic abundance of the 235 fissile isotope by a recently developed centrifuge technology for power reactor fuel. During the development phase of the technology, a Pakistani physicist/engineer, Abdul Qadeer Khan, played a prominent role in bringing the development of the technology to fruition. He had left Urenco before my stint at Almelo, but our paths would cross some years later.

On 18 May 1974, India announced its first successful test of a nuclear device. This fundamentally changed the political dynamics and military balance on the Indian sub-continent. Zulfikar Ali Bhutto, the prime minister of Pakistan, made the following announcement to the Pakistani nation:

"We (Pakistan) will eat grass, even go hungry, but we will get one of our own (Atom bomb). We have no other choice!"

Dr Khan was made an offer he could not refuse; he went back to Pakistan with "borrowed" blueprints in his suitcase and became known as the father of the Pakistani bomb. Later, he was allowed to set up his very own nuclear proliferation business with clients such as Libya, Iran and North Korea. It is likely that substantial sums changed hands in some cases or that nuclear technology was traded for missile technology.

I was at the Almelo plant five years after the departure of Dr Khan from Urenco, but his name used to come up around the lunch table in the canteen at Almelo. Similar conversations were held around other tables at other nuclear establishments where I spent time in the '80s and '90s. The involvements of laboratories, their staff and decision-makers with nuclear programmes became facilitators of the spread of nuclear materials, technologies, knowledge and information. Detailed knowledge was originally closely guarded but became an open secret, and much became common knowledge to most people in the business. I was not the only nuclear gypsy with a head full of information. Conversations in other canteens described how Canada had supplied the CANDU reactor to India – thereby providing the means for nuclear weapons based on the plutonium fuel cycle. It was common knowledge how a triumvirate of nations gave South Africa and Israel nuclear weapons capabilities with help from France and with de facto acquiescence by the USA. Norway delivered heavy water that facilitated proliferation. To an innocent bystander, there seemed to be plenty of guilt to go around in the nuclear proliferation game. It was certainly true that such things were common knowledge to the people in the canteens. It was inconceivable that, at the same time, the proliferation of knowledge was not known to the political decision-makers.

I was beginning to feel increasingly queasy about my choice of career and found it more and more difficult to explain and justify my profession in polite company. The younger generation had seen *Dr. Strangelove* and did not think it was "better to be dead than red". As well, moving house every second year was losing its appeal, and it was bad for my social life. I was in danger of ultimately becoming a lonely and cynical middle-aged man.

After the monsoon in 1998, I took matters in hand. I bailed out for two months and walked in the mountains of Nepal while contemplating the meaning of everything. It was time to get back to basics and decide what I was going to do with the rest of my life. I had realized that my epitaph was not going to make good reading. I needed to close a chapter and start again.

On a couple of earlier occasions, I had worked with people who had either been employed by the IAEA or who had thought of joining. Its reputation was not unlike that of the teaching profession. "Those who can, do; those who can't, teach." It was a time when real men built reactors and bombs; the others joined the IAEA. I decided to have another look at a more benevolent profession.

There was nothing wrong with the constitution of the IAEA, which claimed to be truly independent, although reporting annually to the UN Security Council. It also specified in great detail what were to be its two principal missions. The first was to promote and facilitate the dissemination and use of civilian nuclear science and technology for the benefit of the widest possible community. The constitution was obviously written some years ago when it was claimed that nuclear power was a limitless and cheap source of energy for humankind. We now knew better. The second mission was to regulate and discourage the military exploitation of nuclear science and technology. In principle, there was nothing inherently wrong with the constitution. Later, I came to realize that there were hidden agendas and a mismatch between theory and practice.

In spite of my views about the constitution, I decided to take the IAEA at face value and send my CV to the headquarters in Vienna. Two weeks later, an invitation arrived asking me to appear in Vienna for an interview. I accepted and then spent a few days reading up on the IAEA and what the nuclear community had to say about its work. I also read the literature of anti-nuclear groups. In general, it seemed that the IAEA had kept a low profile and done its best not to offend either side. I read two of the latest annual reports, both of which seemed to have been written by bureaucrats. In the meantime, I assumed that the IAEA had done a thorough job of unearthing any skeletons in my life. I would have been surprised if they had found anything dramatic.

* * *

The interview lasted for the better part of a week. It was thorough, being subtly probing on occasion, and generally civil. On a few occasions, I let my inquisitors get the impression, very gently, that I was reversing the interview and that I needed to be reassured that the IAEA was up to my standard.

The first two days were devoted to meeting people and being shown the facilities. It began with the deputy director speaking on behalf of the Directorate:

"I would like to think that we are the main source of factual and unbiased information and knowledge available to the civilian nuclear industry. Also, that we are the promoters and guardians of safety and best practice in all areas relating to nuclear technology. We are also the custodians of the strongest safeguards against illicit activities in the nuclear sphere, without fear or favour."

It was hard to find any faults with those sentiments. Next on the agenda was the human resource department.

"The scientists and nuclear engineers are our greatest asset. There are few, if any, other institutions around the world that can match the IAEA in its depth and breadth of expertise and commitments in nuclear matters. We believe in looking after that expertise to an extent that will ensure total commitment and loyalty to the tasks entrusted to the IAEA."

Finally, it was time to meet the experts who were most at home in the laboratories and workshops. A couple turned out to be former colleagues.

"Welcome to the zoo. We are a mixed lot, but you will like us."

A few others were known to me by reputation. They had written papers that I had read. The technical facilities were impressive, extensive and complete.

On Tuesday, two of the senior people in charge of the laboratories arranged for a night out. We met at the Restaurant Stephansplatz in the Old Town. It was the kind of place where the maître d' could have come straight out of *Cabaret*. He took us to our table and recommended an aperitif to get us started. It became a memorable evening with much talk about places we had worked at and people we had known. In the back of my mind was the thought that I'd better not blot my copybook and express views that did not resonate with those of the IAEA. The evening was likely to have a hidden agenda, and we might have been actors in an ambiguous play.

The next day was free so that I could have a look around Vienna. I had been there once before as a student attending a conference. There was a vague memory of a female student whose name I struggled to remember. It must have been several lifetimes ago. I walked the streets, had a humble meal, and ended up being entertained by Mozart in a Rococo church. On the way back to the hotel, I decided that this was the kind of place where one could live.

* * *

Then followed two days of serious interrogations. I was pointed to a chair at the focal point in a conference room facing a semi-circle made up of inquisitors who ranged from members of the directorate to engineers from the laboratories. Why did I wish to join the IAEA? Which attributes would I bring to the place? What did I think about the future of nuclear power? Did I think that nuclear power was being misrepresented in the popular press? How would one be able to demonstrate a clear separation between civilian nuclear technology and weapons programmes? It was straightforward stuff. I had asked myself the same questions over the years.

The interrogation got more interesting. For instance, did I think there was a justification for North Korea to acquire a nuclear deterrent? I sought refuge in a brief lecture on the recent history of the Korean Peninsula and how that might have affected the Korean view of the world. As well, the Libyan case might provide an abject lesson in the justification for not relinquishing a nuclear programme.

Gaddafi abandoned his programme in return for a promise to be brought back into the family of "normal" nations. Not long afterwards, Gaddafi was dead, and Libya went on to become a failed state. Giving up one's nukes should come with a health warning. The next question was concerned with finding a way to encourage Iran to curtail its nuclear programme. My response was that the IAEA would have minimal leverage since the answer was to be found in the regional and superpower political domains. However, as in a hypothetical case of the interim solution, brokered by a likely incoming Obama presidency, the IAEA would have a major and essential role in policing any agreement. It went on like this for hours. My reading of the proceedings was that the panel wanted to make sure that my mindset was not that of a Cold War warrior. After two days of being grilled, I was beginning to flag, and the interrogators were running out of steam. The deputy director called a halt and thanked everybody for a job well done. I was allowed to drag my weary body and mind back to the hotel. But before I got away, I was asked to drop briefly into the director's office. There, I was informed that I was likely to receive a contract in the mail that would offer me an appointment as a scientist/analyst in residence. So that was that. Vienna, here I come.

The Vienna Years: The Words of Khan

The promised letter came from Vienna: I was invited to take up the position from the first of the year in 2001. It took two round trips in the trusty old Volvo to bring my earthly belongings to the modest flat I had rented in the Old City and to fill up the spare bedroom. As expected, it was miserably cold for the time of year. The plumbing probably dated from the days of the Habsburg empire and struggled in vain to keep the living room liveable. It was just as well I had never got around to throwing away my old woollen sweaters.

A nice office on the third floor of the scimitar-shaped main building was where I was going to spend my professional life for a few years, as long as I behaved. Most of the first week was occupied with bringing over my library and files that had been collected over the years and then filling the shelves. I was given a new desktop PC. This was followed in short order by being lectured on building security and passwords. All that was left was to be told what I was meant to be doing. I did not have long to wait before getting my marching orders.

Two days later, a memorandum from Mohamed ElBaradei, the director general, landed in my in-tray with a thud. A discussion was arranged the next morning in his office. I needed to do some serious reading overnight.

"I assume that you are familiar, broadly speaking, with recent developments of nuclear weapons in India and Pakistan." He did not waste any time.

My reply was equally concise. "Two years at Urenco, and a stint at Framatome, provided access to a fair bit of hard data and a lot of rumours and guesswork about what was happening."

"This is partly why we made you an offer that you could not refuse. We have many shelf metres of open literature on the topic and at least an equal amount of classified stuff. I have made arrangements that will give you access to everything. I assume that you have been briefed on non-disclosure agreements."

"No problem," I responded. "I have signed official secret acts, or their equivalents, at least once each year for the last 15 years."

The preliminaries were now over, and we understood each other. There was a moment of silence while ElBaradei stroked his moustache as if in thought.

"I will give 15 minutes for you to tell me what you think were the reasons for both India and Pakistan to go nuclear, starting now."

"Once the PRC became a nuclear power and took up its rightful place as a permanent member of the UN Security Council, it was inevitable that India would join the nuclear club. After the involvement of India in the liberation of Bangladesh, it became equally inevitable that Pakistan would go nuclear. The Pakistani programme was a two-pronged affair run by the two Khans, who reputedly hated each other. One, Abdul Qadeer Khan, a physicist/engineer, learned his trade at Urenco and was in charge of the uranium enrichment programme based on centrifuge technology. The other programme was headed by Munir Ahmad Khan, a theoretical physicist, and went the plutonium route. Both programmes were ultimately successful. Qadeer Khan is the more interesting individual. He set up his very own enterprise trading nuclear technology for missile technology and possibly for a great deal of cash. His clients included at least Libya, Iran and the DPRK."

ElBaradei interrupted. "Well done, you are substantially correct. I will now tell you about your job. There is no prospect of rolling back the Pakistani nuclear programme. The best we can do is to encourage it to be capped at, say, 200 warheads and for the delivery systems to be configured as a credible deterrent. At present, there are two concerns that fall within the ambit of the IAEA. The first is concerned with the control of the warheads and with a command structure that precludes accidents or unauthorized use. There is some speculation that command is with the military and has been devolved down to the brigade level. The second issue, as you mentioned, is concerned with the transfer of nuclear technology from Pakistan to other parties. In particular, we would not like to see such technology, or fissile materials, fall into the hands of sub-national groups, such as Al Qaeda. Put bluntly, we need to know what is going on and who is in charge."

"Where do I fit in?" It seemed like an obvious question. By now, I was beginning to realize that ElBaradei delivered his responses in a convoluted manner.

"The IAEA prefers to work through back channels. Indeed, some of our successes have been the result of two people sitting down together, away from the public glare, and talking things through to a logical conclusion. I have met Qadeer Khan on two previous occasions, once some years ago at Urenco, and once recently, when we agreed to meet in a secret location. I feel that we have established rapport and mutual respect, even though we are very different people and have different objectives. The IAEA has trawled through your life in great detail. I think I know what makes you tick. You and Qadeer are two of a kind. It seems to me that both of you are loners who thrive on solving problems. Once the problem has been solved, boredom sets in, with you and Qadeer moving on to the next challenge. I can set up a clandestine meeting in Pakistan, where you and Qadeer will get to know each other and then talk off the record about the issues of greatest interest to the IAEA. I want you to go away and give some thought to our conversation. Let me know if you agree to take this on. Arrangements will then be made."

The meeting was over. I went away to read everything that had ever been written about Qadeer Khan and the Pakistani nuclear programme. It was an interesting problem. Did I want to tackle it?

* * *

The approach to Jinnah International airport in Karachi was announced over the intercom. Please fasten seatbelts, etc, and so on. It had taken the IAEA just over two weeks to set everything up. I had a visa for Pakistan and a letter from Qadeer Khan inviting me to visit the Khan Research Laboratories near Rawalpindi to discuss matters relating to the disposal of nuclear waste. It was as legitimate as one could make anything in this world. I had actually co-authored several learned papers on the subject matter. My passport was my own, and my nationality was one of the most innocuous known to suspicious immigration agents. An executive jet with the markings of the Pakistani Air Force was waiting to fly me to Rawalpindi.

On arrival in Rawalpindi, a car and driver took me to the officers' quarters. My papers were checked one more time before I was told to have a quiet evening to myself. The next morning, I was accompanied by yet another uniformed officer to the laboratory. I signed in at the entrance gate and was handed over to a new minder. It was time to meet the great man himself.

Khan, being in his late 60s, had aged well. The full head of hair and the well-cropped moustache were beginning to go grey, but the handshake was firm, and the smile was friendly. He was wearing casual clothes and gave me the impression of being in total control.

"Mohamed told me that you were on your way. He and I go back a long way. He says that you and I have many things in common.

You seem to have come out of nowhere but have become well known in nuclear circles. I am curious to find out the rest. I look forward to your visit and hope that our conversations will be fruitful."

I was surprised by his words. Many had described him variously as difficult, vindictive and thin-skinned. My first impression was very different. He might have mellowed with age.

We were interrupted by a young woman who seemingly floated on air while bringing a silver service tea set.

"This is the best tea that money cannot buy. There are some things we in the East do better than you in the West."

I responded in kind. "I have never doubted that. Neither did Urenco when you left Almelo some years ago." We were beginning to bond.

We agreed to meet again for dinner. In the meantime, I would be treated to a guided tour of the laboratories while Khan had to chair a meeting.

* * *

Dinner commenced at seven in a small casual dining room attached to the office where we had met earlier in the day. A selection of dishes from the Punjabi cuisine was brought in by the same girl who had seemed to be able to float on air. From my days in the UK, I recognized lamb biryani, chicken tikka, khichdi, and saag dhal, all emitting a delicate and exotic aroma of local spices. I offered my compliments to the chef, and the meal could begin. A few mouthfuls later, Khan asked about the state of affairs at Urenco.

"It seems to be a well-run and successful operation. In addition to the main plant in Almelo, there are now enrichment plants in the UK and Germany. The plants produce and deliver low-enriched –

usually 3.5 atomic % U-235 – reactor fuel to the civilian power industry. It is a cost-plus operation."

Khan said, "This is all in the public domain. Does my name still come up at Almelo – and what is the prevailing view of the manner in which I left?"

"There are two schools of thought. One is that Urenco would have been a failure without the pioneering work that you carried out there. The other says that you were given full access to facilities and support at Almelo but paid it back by deserting and taking the blueprints with you."

There was a brief silence while Khan thought about what I had said. It was followed by his reply.

"In a way, they are both right. I did some of my best work at Almelo. But when it came to the crunch, my country was more important to me. Pakistan had just been humiliated by India and had lost its Eastern provinces in a short war. India then tested its first nuclear device, and Pakistan was at the mercy of its bigger neighbour. The words of Zulfikar Ali Bhutto counted for more than any allegiance I might have had to Urenco. I took the blueprints and defected. It was a necessary and honourable act."

"I understand your reasons, and I accept the validity of your actions."

"Thank you, my friend."

"How did you avoid being extradited to the US?"

"It was a bit tense for a few years. I had taken some precautions. Part of the deal was that I was given an official document, signed in blood by the Chief Justice of Pakistan, that under no circumstance would Pakistan agree to extradition. The downside was that I effectively became a prisoner in the laboratory, with 24-hour armed protection in case the US should decide to send in the special forces. Once Pakistan became a declared nuclear power, Uncle Sam dropped my name from the most wanted list and lost interest in me. I became a national hero, the father of the nuclear bomb."

"It is a good story, and it had a happy ending," was my comment.

There was a brief lull in the conversation while we returned to the delicacies on offer. The comfortable silence was broken by Khan.

"When Mohamed set up the meeting between the two of us, he was particularly interested in two issues. One was the command, control and security of the nuclear deterrent of Pakistan. I will open up the dialogue by describing my view of the utility of nuclear weapons."

I nodded in agreement, and Khan continued.

"It is an indisputable fact that nuclear weapons have been used once in anger, some 55 years ago, and then to obliterate Hiroshima and Nagasaki. Since then, vast resources have been expended on military nuclear science and technology. At one stage, there were more nuclear warheads and delivery systems than there were targets. Nuclear war was high up on the list of events that could possibly end all life on planet Earth. I am sure you have read the literature, as I have, on nuclear strategy. You probably came to the same conclusion that the only utility of such weapons was, and is, as instruments of deterrence. In the lingo of game theory, a rational actor would not initiate a nuclear exchange. The downside of a nuclear war would always be greater than any possible gain. You might ask, what about an irrational actor? The answer is that command and control of the weapons must be configured in such a manner that a mad person could not ever be in charge of the 'button'. That goes for Pakistan, as for all other countries with nuclear weapons."

I nodded. "We are singing from the same hymn sheet. How has Pakistan dealt with the problem of madness?"

"I will make one more point and then explain. There is a widespread view in some quarters that leaders in some countries, such as Pakistan, tend to be irrational and therefore are not to be trusted with nuclear weapons. I can think of quite a few past and present leaders of the so-called 'advanced' countries that would not rate highly on the rationality scale. As J will explain, our command and control systems are far superior to the one that entrusts a president with the nuclear 'button'. We recognize that an individual can be irrational or foolish, some of the time or all of the time. On the other hand, a committee is far less likely to be irrational, especially if its members are selected on the basis of intellectual and rational criteria. Our committee consists of one member of the government of the day, selected by secret ballot by all ministers; one member from the senior ranks of the public service, again elected by a secret ballot of senior public servants; two members from the senior military ranks, elected by secret ballot of officers of rank from and above general. Finally, there are three scientists/technical members selected by secret ballot from the members of the academies of science and engineering. Each member will have two unique passwords, each of which signifies either permission or denial of the launching of nuclear weapons when requested by the government of the day. Each member of the committee downloads a password to a secure communications channel. From there, the majority vote for permission, or denial, is entirely computer-driven. If five or more permissive passwords are received, then Pakistan will launch nuclear weapons. There are some contingencies built into the system to ensure that unauthorized tampering has not occurred or that two or more members are no longer available to vote. It sounds byzantine, but we have run exhaustive checks and have engaged people and agencies to attempt to circumvent the system. The government of the day has the power to order a state of emergency and can request a state of alert and readiness of nuclear forces, but that is where its powers end. What do you think?"

"We have people back in Vienna who have spent their lives thinking about these issues. Do I have your permission to check your system with the computer geeks on the fourth floor? Alternatively, I could try to send one of them to you for a few days. I would see this as a confidence-building measure for both friends and foes."

Khan said in response, "Let me think about that."

It was time for me to offer a commentary on the scheme.

"It is an interesting way of dealing with what is arguably one of the most important problems of our age. The Pakistani scheme has the very real merit of forcing seven people in isolation to search their souls and possibly be the first group since the time of Hiroshima and Nagasaki to give the order to start a nuclear war that will kill millions. There is a de facto requirement that a decision to use nuclear weapons as a first or retaliatory strike cannot be delegated to political or military leaders. This ensures that the principal value of the nuclear arsenal is as a deterrent. The reason for having such an arsenal is to avoid having to fight a war against a nuclear-armed enemy. The one possible weakness is that that the arrangement leads to a Yes/No situation, with no clear route to a limited war, such as a demonstration strike."

We looked at each other, as if to decide what to say next. Khan broke the silence.

"That was a good session. It is so delightfully different to the kind of verbal warfare of a formal negotiation where both sides know that the only outcome is a negative sum. I think we will now call it a day, a good one at that. We will have dinner again tomorrow and talk about the physical security of the weapons and the delivery vehicles."

"I look forward to that. Please give my compliments to the chef for the exquisite dinner."

"Tomorrow, I will introduce you to my daughter. She is the one that brought us the dinner and the one I treasure above all else. How could I ever send off a permissive code word?"

* * *

In the morning, I discovered a tray outside the bedroom door with a Thermos of rich and sweet coffee, four pieces of toast with marmalade and honey, and a cubed mango. It was just what I needed to get me going. During the rest of the day, I reviewed the activities of the previous day and prepared a file for a memory stick. Nothing would go on the laptop, just in case. Then I organized my thoughts for the evening. Physical security of nuclear warheads and fissile materials were not my areas of expertise and not my favourite topic. I would have to wing it.

We convened in the early evening and confined ourselves to small talk about people we had known and worked with.

A different variation on the Punjabi culinary theme was brought by the lady I now knew was the daughter of Khan.

"I should have known. You have your father's bones and eyes. Are you his muse?" She blushed and made a hasty retreat.

Then it was down to business.

"I will begin with an overview. Then we can get down to specifics. Some details I am not at liberty to reveal in case they should fall into the wrong hands. Is that agreed?"

I nodded. "You must use your judgement when it comes to sensitive information."

"At this moment, Pakistan has just under 100 nuclear warheads in service. There is roughly a 50:50 split between those based on highly enriched uranium and those based on separated plutonium. A small number are enhanced with a greater yield due to a boost from fusion reactions. Less than 10 of the available warheads are attached to delivery vehicles – either a missile or a fighter-bomber. The remainder of the warheads are stored separately from the delivery vehicles. Most of the warheads are located at two of the main air force bases. These locations are protected by two concentric perimeters separated by minefields. Several types of sensors monitor various kinds of possible ground activities. The air space is under continuous radar surveillance, and there are at least two batteries of surface-to-air missiles in case of airborne intrusion. Warheads in storage are located in deep bunkers that can withstand any direct attack based on conventional explosives. There are gas sensors located at numerous locations in the case of an attack by poison gas. Missiles and aircraft armed with nuclear warheads are on constant alert and can be airborne in less than 10 minutes from the arrival of a valid launch code. Every warhead in service is fitted with an anti-tamper device. If triggered, it will set off a small conventional explosive that will disassemble vital parts of the device and render the warhead permanently dysfunctional. Finally, there are safeguards in place that preclude unauthorized diversion of amounts greater than 5 grams of fissile materials. All relevant areas involving the presence of such materials are under constant CCTV tamper-proof surveillance."

"So far, I have not been trained up by the IAEA safeguards division, but it sounds as if your security systems are comprehensive and impressive. If I was going to be concerned, then it is because I have been to a number of institutions. Some of the facilities date back to the early post-war years. Some of them have a rich heritage of hosting spies who, for ideological or financial reasons, collected sensitive information and passed it on to third parties. The other problem is that the systems tend to degrade with time for a variety of reasons, such as cost savings, lack of commitment, boredom, or lack of proper oversight. Passes are no longer scrutinized, bags are no longer routinely inspected, petty pilfering is being condoned, low-level bribery becomes an issue, and so on. The vigilance becomes slack, corners are being cut, and some people look the other way. These effects can potentially occur in all institutions and bureaucracies and are tolerated when their cost is less than that of rooting them out. When one is dealing with nuclear weapons and materials, then the level of tolerance must be low. I have no reason to think that that there are any significant problems with your systems."

Khan took this calmly, but I could sense that he was anxious to respond.

"Pakistan has a reputation for grift and corruption, it is an unfortunate reputation, but it is deserved. I agree wholeheartedly that, when dealing with nuclear weapons, this kind of behaviour is intolerable. I have insisted on having a number of enforcers on the staff. They have been recruited on the basis of having a proven record of being incorruptible. Their sole function is to maintain oversight of the systems and to identify individual and collective deviations from the highest standards we expect and require. So far, we have not had any serious problems. A small number of staff have been dismissed, but for relatively trivial matters."

"I will take this back to ElBaradei. He is my enforcer."

During the discussion, we made good use of the dinner. It had been a conversation that could have gone astray. As it turned out, I felt we had handled the difficult issues quite well. But we should not push our luck. There was yet some rocky territory to deal with, but that would be for another day.

* * *

Breakfast sat waiting outside my bedroom door. I made a mental note to revisit this excellent establishment. This was going to be the day for the make-or-break conversation. Before the meeting, I rehearsed in my mind how the upcoming dialogue might unfold.

We began earlier than usual and started with a cup of coffee. I thought I might as well open the discussion.

"I realize we will be talking about the most painful years of your life when you were effectively a wanted criminal and were fighting for your reputation and possibly for your life. During the morning, before meeting you here, I went over in my mind what I have heard and read of the events. Then I discounted the headlines, the demonization, and the rhetoric at the time. I thought I could see a rationale that was consistent with what I now know about Qadeer Khan."

My words hung in the air while I waited for a response. Khan was ready to explain himself.

"It was the nadir of Pakistan's belief in its nationhood and its reason for being. We had just lost a third of our country and 40% of our population and been humiliated by the Indian army. We were standing naked and alone on the world stage, without even a fig leaf to hide our lack of nationhood. China had taken its rightful place at the UN as one of the five great powers, India was cementing its place as the nuclear-armed leader of the non-aligned nations, and Pakistan was a pitiful basket case. I responded to the call of my country, and within a few years, we had shown that a poverty-stricken Third World, largely illiterate, country could join the ranks of the great powers. I was proud of my contribution to the rebirth of Pakistan. I was prepared and willing to be demonized and declared to be a criminal."

Khan stopped talking, and both of us waited to break the silence.

He continued.

"There was an unintended consequence of the Pakistani nuclear programme. It turned out to be an object demonstration that, given the right political and popular will, any country could aspire to, and be successful in, becoming a nuclear power. It had long been clear that any country without such weapons could not aspire to true independence in an anarchic bipolar world. A refusal to align oneself with one of the two superpowers would have the consequence of being deemed to be a 'rogue' state and could therefore suffer the consequences through devastating sanctions, or worse. Only by having a nuclear deterrent was it possible to avoid such a fate. Israel had shown the way and got away with it. Pakistan was next, and there were other national actors thinking along the same lines. I am sure that you are aware of the number of countries that were keeping their nuclear options open well into the 70s."

I had to agree with the latter assertion, having seen facilities and hardware in several laboratories that were either dual-capable or did not seem to be required for civilian nuclear applications. But I wanted to focus on more contentious matters. Both of us knew the question I was about to ask, but Khan stopped me with a shake of his head.

"It is better that I tell the story in my own words and in my own way. Why did I supply nuclear know-how to so-called 'rogue' states? There were two main reasons. Let me now deal with the one that I think is most important. Being a Pakistani, I was acutely aware that the world order did not work for us, and neither did it for many other states. In many cases, the recently 'liberated' former colonies were left to fend for themselves after the former masters had packed their bags and left. In other cases, they became mere pawns in the Cold War and were caught up in bloody power games that cost millions of lives and set any national development back by generations.

"A few states rebelled. Libya exiled a king, who was a mere figurehead for de facto Italian neo-colonialist rule. Gaddafi came to power and introduced a regime and political system as set out in three Green Books. The regime was supporting groups that were prepared and able to resist policies and actions set in place principally by the USA. In Iran, there was a regime headed by a Shah chosen by a former colonial power. The Shah was overthrown and was replaced by a Shia theocracy. A Ba'athist regime in Iraq was encouraged and abetted by Western powers to invade Iran shortly thereafter. A bloody war lasted for eight years and cost a million lives. In both cases, our sympathies were with our Muslim brothers and with those that were seeking to curtail the dominance of Western powers in geopolitical affairs. My involvement had the tacit approval of the military-security complex in Pakistan, which de facto was in charge of foreign policy, but did not want to have its fingerprints attached. The provision of nuclear assistance to Libya and Iran was therefore deniable by all, except by Qadeer Khan, and all was well. If I was to be demonized for rocking the boat that ought to be rocked, so be it, I thought at the time.

"There was a second motivation for engaging in clandestine nuclear dealings. The cost of developing a functional nuclear device is relatively modest and was well within the means of Pakistan. The real cost comes when the device is turned into a functional warhead and then mated to a delivery system, such as a fighter-bomber or a missile. As well, there are very considerable ongoing costs of control, command and security systems. Pakistan was not a rich country. I was reminded that Zulfikar Ali Bhutto had promised the people of Pakistan a nuclear bomb even if the people had to eat grass. I wanted to save them from that.

"Libya and Iran were blessed with vast resources of oil and gas and had very significant dollar incomes. They were happy to trade hard currency for nuclear know-how. The proceeds could be used to import fighter-bombers from France, and missiles from the USSR, via North Korea. Sure, the activities were clandestine and borderline illegal – but no worse than many things done in the name of democracy and freedom. When you are among wolves, you have to act like one. I rest my case."

After a pause during which I was digesting what I had just been told by Khan, I decided to probe a bit deeper.

"The relationship with North Korea is somewhat surprising. It is true that the DPRK has been labelled as a rogue state, as in the cases of Iran and Libya. But there are few cultural or social commonalities that would make it an appealing partner for Pakistan. I am sure that you have an explanation."

"Yes, I have. There were reciprocal needs. The DPRK wished to acquire a nuclear bomb and a credible delivery system. Pakistan had no direct access to missile technology, but we had a well-developed programme for producing highly enriched uranium with ultra-centrifuge technology. The DPRK had been the recipient for several decades of mature, but redundant, missile technology from the USSR, but they were entirely dependent on the plutonium route from a reactor for their source of fissile material. It was an obvious relationship of convenience. Also, unlike the Libyans, the Koreans knew what they were doing, and why they were doing it, and they had a very good technical infrastructure – again, unlike the Libyans, who at times struggled to read a blueprint."

"I have another question. Are you still involved in the trade of nuclear technology?"

"No, I have retired from the fray and become a 'Grand Old Man'." He smiled as he was saying it. "In any case, my previous sponsors in the 'Deep State' are now preoccupied with the running sore of Kashmir, and with managing the Taliban as the means to retain our interests in Afghanistan, and to annoy the USA. In such matters, I have nothing to offer, and nothing is asked of me."

In part to satisfy my own curiosity, I wanted to ask one final question.

"When I was given the guided tour of the facilities the other day, I noticed machinery that could be of use only for fairly exotic instrumentation, such as ultra-stable accelerometers for inertial guidance of missiles. Are the warheads fabricated in your laboratories – or are components – being manufactured here for assembly elsewhere?"

"The answer is yes, and no. At any one time, we are producing two new warheads from scratch. We also fabricate bits for non-nuclear missiles – principally guidance mechanisms. We also do maintenance work on pre-existing warheads. A convoy of armoured vehicles arrives once a week on a randomly chosen day bringing warheads for refurbishment and checking, and then returning with new, or refurbished, ones. Another convoy brings fresh supplies of enriched uranium for the production of the cores for new warheads. You might have guessed that the centrifuge facility is well hidden elsewhere in a deep bunker that can survive a direct hit from an enemy nuclear-tipped missile."

We had agreed to save the dinner until after the conclusion of our business. The daughter of Khan brought a very special meal this time, which included both local delicacies and some appetizers more familiar to me. I thanked her profusely, and she blushed again.

Khan had the final word. "In another place, I would now have asked for a bottle of fine French wine. As it is, I will propose a toast to friendship and happiness with a glass of mango lassi!"

"When I have returned to Vienna, I will convey those sentiments to ElBaradei," I reciprocated.

There was a period of silence. Neither of us knew what to say or what was left to say. Khan was the first to break the spell.

"ElBaradei knew what he was doing when he sent you. He told me that he thought we were very much alike, and he was right. Like you, I was once an outsider and a single-minded person. Being able to work for my country and its people probably saved me. I got married. I had a daughter, who you have met, but my wife died some years ago. I am happy now. I am no longer driven."

He paused and then continued. "I hope to see you again, Inshallah. I am getting old now. I want to see my daughter grow up and have a family so that I have immortality. You must do the same. You must ask ElBaradei to send you back."

"I will not see you in the morning. A plane will take you back to Karachi, and then you will go back to Vienna. Give my regards to ElBaradei."

"Thank you, Abdul, for the hospitality, and for sharing your wisdom. I promise to see you again, Inshallah."

His daughter had just appeared. I bowed my head to her, and this time she did not blush. Then, I left.

* * *

Back in Vienna, I left the memory stick in the office for ElBaradei and spent a couple of days at home. I needed the days to walk the streets and to wind down. The processing of the events in Pakistan needed some thinking time. When I returned to my office, there was a message from ElBaradei asking me to please come and see him.

"It seems that you were a great success with Qadeer Khan. I think he has mellowed over the years. At home he is a legend, and he has nothing more to prove to himself or to anyone else. He is mid-

60s now and must be thinking about his epitaph. It also seems that he is de facto in control of at least a portion of the warheads. The collegial system of control ensures that the weapons have the sole function of being a deterrent. I wish some other countries would adopt the same system. Getting that spelled out and confirmed was very useful and comforting to me. I'll use your notes and will write a report to the board of governors. By the way, what did you think of Khan?"

"I actually enjoyed the assignment in Pakistan. Qadeer Khan was my kind of person. We come from the same background, and we were speaking the same language. What is next on the agenda for me?"

ElBaradei stroked his chin while thinking and then said, "I think we need to broaden your horizons. Most of the work of the IAEA is relatively tedious, in the manner of book-keeping, but very necessary. I'll let you know by the end of the week. In the meantime, you could read one of our annual reports to the UN Security Council in order to get the flavour of what it is like to be an inspector."

* * *

Thus, it came to be that I, and a few helpers, were sent on a guided tour of some of the least scenic places in Europe. It began with the inspection of a selection of the aging Magnox reactors in the UK. These were getting on for 40 years in operation and were due to be decommissioned. The inspection amounted to walking around with a clipboard and ticking boxes. Have the CCTV cameras covering all angles of the control room been tampered with? A box was ticked: No. Then, there was verification of fuel being loaded, the hours and power of operation, and spent fuel being removed, and then being loaded into heavy shielded casks for interim storage in deep swimming pools, all done by remote control while being watched by CCTV cameras. And so on, and so on. Everything was done in duplicate and then reconciled. If the numbers and the ticks did not add up, or agree, it had to be done once more by different scrutineers. The same was done at three PWR reactors in France and at another three in Germany that were shut down for refuelling. The complexity of the system was such that anomalies were to be expected. We found one camera had stopped working, and three radiation monitors gave low – and presumably faulty – readings. But we trusted our European brethren and did not make a fuss.

The inspection of the Chernobyl complex was arguably the low point. The IAEA team was driven in through the deserted area on a Soviet vintage bus each morning after a fairly ordinary breakfast outside the exclusion zone. Of the four units, only two remained functional after the disaster in 1986. The two working units were the principal objectives for the inspection. As usual, we checked the records obtained from fixed CCTV cameras and other monitors and from radiation monitoring instrumentation. Particular attention was devoted to the modifications introduced in the aftermath of the core meltdown and the steam explosion which obliterated Unit 3. The released radiation came back as fallout over most of Northern Europe. We were especially interested in the number and nature of anomalies logged since last time. Inherent problems with the design of the Chernobyl-type of reactor were identified after the disaster by a subsequent inquiry and rectified. The damaged unit was encased in a concrete "sarcophagus" in order to limit the extent of the ongoing release of radiation and stood there as a monstrous monument to bad technology and sloppy operational procedures. It would be standing there as an ever-present reminder of why the IAEA was in the business of making civilian nuclear technology safer and better. It was a depressing place, and we were glad to leave.

Urenco was the last stop on the journey. It felt strange to come back as an inspector, as opposed to being inspected and worrying about what the IAEA might find. As it turned out, I enjoyed meeting up with former colleagues. There was an outing to a local watering hole, for yet again enjoying the local beer and talking about the old days rather than acting as an annoying inspector.

Then it was back to the fleshpots of Vienna.

* * *

One of the many missions of the IAEA was to offer training courses for aspiring nuclear technologists. To my great surprise, I was asked to get involved. Why was ElBaradei doing this to me? I knew that my contract essentially specified that I would do whatever the director asked me to do. Consequently, the latest task meant a period of burning the midnight oil, writing lecture notes and preparing PowerPoint slides. Once the preparations were under control, I would give lectures in the morning and have the rest of the day to myself.

I decided to find out what else Vienna had to offer. There was a lot to see and do. There were walks along the Donau or joining a short cruise while thinking of Strauss. In the city centre, there were stunning palaces from the late Middle Ages and innumerable Rococo churches. Then there were the white Lipizzaner horses being put through their paces. There was a café on every street, and Mozart's genius could be enjoyed in half a dozen places every night. I tried it all.

One fateful evening I was listening to a Mozart Requiem while thinking of the meaning of perfection. I happened to sit next to a young woman who seemed to be in the same state of enrapture as I was. When the applause had died down, and we slowly worked our way out, she turned to me and asked if I had enjoyed the performance. I said I had. She spoke proper German rather than my Viennese version. My German had reached the functional stage but not up to her standard, so we settled on English while making our way out and into the night.

"There is a nice café around the corner; I have tried it before. Do you fancy a snack after Mozart?" she said invitingly. We were standing wondering what to do next.

"That would be nice," I responded.

Her name was Walheide. She was in the midst of her doctorate studies at the Free University in Berlin. Her topic was History of Art During the Habsburgs. She had been given a stipend for six months in Vienna to collect data. She had three months left. I had to reciprocate and explain myself. My experience had been that this was often the end of a potential relationship. I confessed to working for the IAEA. Fortunately, this did not seem to be information that disqualified me from the human race. I made it sound slightly more interesting by saying it was just another multinational organization answerable to the UN. I felt that I had successfully navigated through treacherous waters. Walheide was easy to talk to. She had travelled to some of the places I had been, so we could compare notes. Her politics seemed to be left of centre, so we agreed that the EU was a uniquely admirable attempt to bury nationalism once and for all. We both thought that the nation state had a lot to answer for, and the sooner it withered away, the better.

When we parted, there was a mutual sense that it had not been a wasted encounter. She led the way.

"It was nice talking to you. Should we meet again for dinner? How about on Friday, at the same place?"

"OK, see you next Friday."

And then she wandered off into the night, turned around, waved, and continued walking.

Two days later, I had left work and was crossing the square in front of the building. The day had been tedious, devoted to editing a report. I heard someone call out. It was Walheide, sitting on a bench.

"I couldn't wait for Friday, and I worked out where the IAEA building was. I thought I might find you here. Can I take you to dinner?"

"Certainly. Lead the way."

There was a humble restaurant that advertised traditional Viennese home cooking. We had Wiener schnitzel, vegetables and mashed potatoes, just "like Mum used to make". For dessert, we lashed out on Sachertorte and ordered a bottle of Eiswein. There is nothing like a good dinner, and good company, to make one feel at peace with the world. The joy of relating to a woman, sitting in a café in Vienna after a good meal, suggested that life was worth living. I looked at Walheide, saw that her eyes were fixed on me; her hand reached across and clasped mine. We paid the bill and left.

"Where do you live?" she asked.

"It is a 20-minute walk from here."

"Can I walk you home?"

"I think I am supposed to say that."

She laughed and put her arms around me.

"This is the new world in which Walheide is the assertive one. I command you to submit!"

"I submit." Then we walked home to my flat on the third floor. This was the beginning of the affair. It was to last for three months.

* * *

There was a new routine in my household. Walheide had filled a taxi with her belongings, most of which shared the spare bedroom with my books, paperwork and assorted junk. She went off each morning to one of the art museums and rummaged through the second-best works of the Habsburgian masters in the basement. She would then write a précis of each painting on her laptop. I went for my morning run and then spent the rest of the day giving a lecture or two on such topics as the four-factor formula and neutron kinetics. Occasionally, I was allowed to give a lecture on 'Nuclear weapons – to have or not to have'. I had been told to chair the weekly meeting of the publication committee. Its role was to vet everything written by the IAEA to ensure that it was fit for seeing the light of day.

We took turns making dinner. I favoured Mediterranean cuisine, while Walheide preferred more substantial Germanic meals. In the evenings, Walheide told me all about the history of art, which turned out to be quite interesting. I tried to reciprocate with the theory and practice of nuclear power reactors, but that was a failure. Instead, I related my favourite anecdotes of spies who had passed nuclear secrets to their masters.

There was one memorable long weekend in late summer. We walked for four days in the Austrian Tyrol from one hotel to the next in spectacular scenery fuelled by burgeoning breakfasts and solid dinners. For one blessed long weekend, we were together 24 hours a day. This was probably as good as it was going to get for us. We returned to Vienna footsore and sunburned, and with a sense of foreboding.

The days before Walheide was due to return to Berlin got increasingly tense. I could sense that she was brooding over a permanent end or the beginning of a more transient relationship. I went for walks along the Donau so that I could talk to myself in private. This had been my way of dealing with life at its most traumatic. Did I want Walheide to leave, or did I want her to stay? What was my life going to be like if she stayed? Could Walheide manage to live with what was inside the hard shell within me, and with the core of my existence, and with that which made me tick?

When I came home after the walk, I found Walheide sitting on the sofa in the Lotus position. This was what she did in her free association mode. She recognized my presence and said in a flat mechanical voice, "What you see is what you get. I am not a complicated person to be dissected and understood. I have lived with you, and loved you, during these weeks. I have been happier here with you than ever before. But I feel that I don't really understand you. There is a door to your soul that is closed and locked. I don't know if there is a key that will let me in. Would I love you, whatever I found inside, if I was to keep searching and should find the key? If I go away, will I miss you for the rest of my life? Will you miss me for the rest of your life?"

It was my turn to explain myself.

"Walheide, you are the best thing that has happened to me for years. I am painfully aware of what you are saying. I cannot promise that I will change. Things happened to me a long time ago that made me what I am. What you cannot see of me is what you might not get, it seems. I wish it could be otherwise. For now, I think we need to part and lick our wounds. If our paths should cross, then maybe I will be a better mate."

There was a long silence.

"I want to have one more night with you. I will leave in the morning."

Then Came Hasina

During the next two years, I became increasingly engrossed and buried in the workings of the IAEA. It seemed that the remedy for my failing to offer Walheide my soul on a plate was to bury myself in work. More committees came my way, and I was increasingly being seen as a safe pair of hands when delicate matters came our way.

At the end of 2002, I went along as an aide to ElBaradei for his annual presentation to the UN Security Council. The session confirmed my suspicion that the Security Council had degenerated into an arena for point scoring and mutual acrimony and denigration. Once upon a time, according to its constitution, it was meant to be a forum for mutual cooperation where the main powers were to agree on ways to foster peace and harmony in the post-WWII world. The USA had long since taken to berate the IAEA, in general, and ElBaradei, in particular, for not being sufficiently in tune with policies favouring the Western powers, in general, and the USA, in particular. Russia and P. R. China thought that the IAEA was doing a good job, while France and the UK sat on their hands. It seemed thoroughly ritualistic and dysfunctional. As it turned out, the world did not blow up on that day, although the five permanent members should not be credited with that outcome.

* * *

On the way back from New York, I sat next to ElBaradei in

business class. We talked about our respective impressions of the UN Security Council. Our views did not differ a great deal. The present term of office for ElBaradei was coming to an end. I asked him if he thought he should stand again. He responded, with a wry smile, that he sensed the knives were being sharpened in Washington to ensure that he could not get sufficient support for yet another term.

Then he said, "Let us make the most out of what is left of my tenure. Would you like to have another excursion to Rawalpindi and meet up with Qadeer Khan?"

My instant response was, "Yes, I would."

* * *

Two weeks later, I was shaking hands with Qadeer Khan in his quarters inside the laboratory compound. He looked tired and anxious.

"My friend, I am pleased to see you. We have much to discuss."

The silver tea set appeared, as on command. His daughter brought it, as before, but along came a boy toddler.

"Meet my grandson. I can now happily go to my grave."

"I think he has inherited good genes and will grow up to be a fine man, like his grandfather," I said. Then we got down to business.

"Not much has happened on the nuclear front since you were here last time. We have added 100 centrifuges so that we can take some out of service for maintenance purposes without losing, to any significant extent, the rate of production of HEU. Also, we have added 15 warheads to the arsenal. This has been done in order to match the arsenal held by India. As you know, we have a formal arrangement with India by which we keep each other informed about the respective nuclear arsenals. Currently, we are discussing an agreement to cap the arsenals at 200 warheads for each country. Also, we are in the process of deciding whether or not we should phase out the Pu-based warheads. If there is agreement to do so, then we can open up the reactor area to the full IAEA inspection regime."

I was beginning to think that I would be going back to Vienna with good news. There was more to come from Khan.

"There is another issue that is far more important than talking about a nuclear deterrent. I would like to ask you to be a backchannel for information that I believe is highly significant. Let me explain. Then you can decide if you are prepared to act in that capacity. As you are aware, Pakistan has got vital interests in Afghanistan. In order to protect those interests, we have a working relationship with the Taliban. At the present time, the Taliban is the de facto ruling faction. Al Qaeda has been given sanctuary on Afghan territory, but otherwise, the Taliban offers no material or political support to Al Qaeda. Information has been obtained by the Taliban that Al Qaeda is planning a major operation in the near future, on US soil, against US interests and assets. If the information is correct, then there are major security implications for Afghanistan and possibly for Pakistan. I would like this information to be given to ElBaradei. He will know what to do next."

I could not think of a good reason to decline the request, so I nodded my agreement. I had suddenly become a shady operative involved in high politics.

Khan seemed to be relieved – and I was relieved that he was relieved. We agreed to save the rest for the next day and declared dinner to be the final item on the agenda for the day.

The discussion the next day was quite unexpected. As usual, Khan was the one that decided the topic of the day.

"I have begun to think about global warming, in general, and the likely effects on Pakistan, in particular. It might be that now, when I have a daughter, and she has a son, I need to think about the world we are handing down to the next generations. The climate that makes Pakistan tolerably liveable is intimately dependent on what happens in the Himalayan mountains to the north and on the rivers that bring the water south from the glaciers. The meltwater makes the lowlands sufficiently fertile to feed 200 million people. The glaciers store the water in the rainy season and prevent the worst of the floods. During the hot dry season, the meltwaters from the glaciers provide a steady supply that prevents the droughts. Even now, it is obvious that the receding glaciers, due to global warming, are the cause of both the worsening floods and the more severe droughts. In another 20 years, it is on the cards that crop yields in the lowlands will be less than half of what we have now. Pakistan may then suffer from large-scale starvation. I am beginning to think that global warming is a greater threat to humanity than a nuclear war. The great difference is that global warming is a near-certainty due to the inability of the world community to act in a concerted and constructive manner. On the other hand, a nuclear war has a near-certainty of being avoidable forever. In my declining years, I will be more concerned with preventing global warming than with making more nuclear warheads. You are younger than I. If you can think of what to do, please come back, and I will try to help you in whatever ways that are available to me."

Our discussions had taken a totally unexpected turn. Here we were, two people who had spent their entire adult lives being concerned with nuclear matters and with avoiding a nuclear war. We were beginning to think that there was a worse fate. I could see his point. What good is a nuclear arsenal if you have no water and your people are starving? However, nuclear war was similar to global warming in the sense that a mutual suicide pact was involved. If I nuked you, then you would nuke me, and both of us would die. If I don't stop pumping greenhouse gases into the atmosphere, then you will also continue to pump greenhouse gases into the atmosphere, and both of us will die.

"Abdul, I agree with you. The problem, as I see it, is that the immediacy of the horrors of a nuclear war is readily visualized by nations, politicians and the people in the streets. So, there is a tacit agreement that we do not want to go there. Global warming is much more difficult to visualize, and its horrors are not as immediate and as comprehensible. Another problem is that avoidance involves an immediate sacrifice of many aspects of modern life, and that is not readily acceptable. The downsides of avoiding global warming are felt immediately, while the upsides will be apparent only decades later. The downside of avoiding a nuclear war is minimal, on the other hand. I'll go away and think more about what you have said about global warming. Maybe we can meet again with some thoughts and ideas."

"Please do come back. I am an old man. I am asking not for my sake but for the sake of my people and also for your people."

The next morning was devoted to pumping CO_2 into the upper atmosphere as the plane took me back to Vienna.

* * *

When I reported back to ElBaradei, he was pleased to hear about the confidence-building measures being introduced between India and Pakistan.

"I never thought that either country viewed nuclear weapons as anything but these being instruments for deterrence. One could argue that the weapons solve the problem of the disparity in military, economic and political strength of India versus Pakistan. It certainly saves Pakistan from beggaring itself by trying to match conventional military power with that of India. The 200 nuclear warheads seem to be a credible number for those who seek to project a nuclear deterrent. As far as the IAEA is concerned, all is as well as can be expected on the sub-continent." This was ElBaradei's summary.

Then I told him about the rumours of an attack by Al Qaeda coming out of Pakistan. He said he would take them on board and pass the warnings on to the appropriate agencies. He thought that without any concrete information about the nature of the operation being planned by Al Qaeda, all that could be done was to raise the threat level.

I wanted to explore some ideas with ElBaradei while we were dealing with wider issues.

"It seems to me that the existence of nuclear weapons cannot be wished away. They are here to stay and will not be a significant threat as long as they are not used in anger. The important issue is that of control and command. There are essentially two models. In the cases of the USA and UK, the decision-making is entirely in civilian hands. That is, in the hands of a president or a prime minister and their advisers. The other model vests some, or all, of the decision-making in military hands. For most of my life, I have been a fervent believer in civilian control, and I have thought that the military should play no part whatsoever in the decision-making. Now, I am not so sure. There are cases where a democratic system of government brings forth leaders who are intelligent, rational, informed and thoughtful. There are states that are notionally democratic but tend to bring forth leaders who fail one or more of the tests for intelligence, rationality, and so on. Then, there are examples where there is not even a pretence of adherence to democratic norms. In the two latter cases, control and command could be in safer hands if it was partially, or wholly, in the hands of military leaders. It could be that military leaders and institutions are more likely to be intelligent, rational, and so on, than political leaders and institutions. What do you think?"

ElBaradei was a patient man and was prepared to let me make my case.

"Your argument has merit. There is an unfounded view that leaders of some countries are less intelligent, more irrational, and so on, than the leaders of some other countries, and therefore nuclear weapons in their hands are inherently more dangerous. In general, my view is that decisions about the use of nuclear weapons should never be in the hands of a single person. Decisions made by a collegial panel is inherently safer. One day, when we have the time, we might write a joint paper on this."

I had been thinking about the conversation concerning global warming that took place in Rawalpindi before I left Khan. Should I report this to ElBaradei? He sensed that I was not quite finished and made an inviting gesture.

So I told him about the daughter and the grandson and how Khan had come to view global warming as a greater danger to future generations than nuclear weapons.

ElBaradei nodded and said, "Abdul is an interesting and thoughtful man. He is almost always right. It is unfortunate that global warming is not part of the brief of the IAEA."

I trotted back to my office, feeling somewhat deflated.

* * *

Then followed a period of business as usual for me. There were reports to be written, lectures to be given, and meetings to be chaired. If bureaucracy and paperwork were going to save the world, then we were doing a splendid job, and we were good value for money.

There are very few events happening during a lifetime that are of such significance that one remembers thereafter precisely what one was doing and where one was when it happened.

The attack by Al Qaeda on the World Trade Centre in New York on 11 September 2001 was one such event. I was sitting in my office while laboriously editing a report when suddenly there was furious banging on the door.

"You must come to the canteen and watch CNN. There is a live report of two airplanes bringing down the twin towers of the World Trade Centre!"

For the next two hours, we watched with morbid fascination two jetliners slice through the towers, then smoke rising from the towers, before they both collapsed in a huge cloud of smoke with dust rolling down the cavernous streets of Manhattan. Could this be the end of world order as we knew it? The uncomprehending face of a president, when told the news, suggested that it had been a seminal event.

Two more events were going to play out in my personal life during the next two years. One was to change my life. The other was to change my relationship with the IAEA.

* * *

As it turned out, the unipolar world order remained intact but with a new admixture of anarchy and violence. The foreign policies of the Bush administration had two principal enforcers, Vice President Dick Cheney and Secretary of Defence Donald Rumsfeld, who were the dominant characters in the aftermath of the 9/11 tragedy. Both felt it was intolerable that the 90-pound weakling should be allowed to kick sand in the face of the muscle-bound hero and not suffer serious retribution.

* * *

The first Monday in February 2002 was to be the day when my life changed. I did not know that as I was heading for the canteen to get my plate of spaghetti carbonara and a bottle of mineral water. I was carrying my loaded tray and looking for a place to sit when ElBaradei caught my eye and waved me over to his table. Next to him, a young woman was sitting.

He said, "Please join us so that I can introduce you to Hasina. She has signed on with the IAEA as our resident authority on modern history and international relations. We managed to steal her from Oxford University. After completing the DPhil, she stayed on as a research fellow while writing a highly praised monograph on the history of Bangladesh from partition to liberation. I believe both of you have been to Oxford at various times – either as a student and scholar or as a researcher with the UK Atomic Energy Authority at Harwell."

Hasina seemed slightly embarrassed by the praise but was able to take it in her stride while nibbling at her salad. ElBaradei went on to point out that we might have common interests in the politics of the Indian sub-continent and that I had recently been to Pakistan and been concerned with its nuclear weapons programme. Hearing this, Hasina rested her eyes on me. It felt as if, in that brief moment, I had been comprehensively assessed and analysed. I hoped it had been a friendly diagnosis.

She finished her lunch, stood up and said, in my direction, "It will take me a few days to settle into Vienna and the IAEA. I may need to consult you. I gather we have offices on the same floor." Then she wandered away.

It suddenly occurred to me that she reminded me of a china doll and that she moved with the same languid manner as the daughter of Qadeer Khan.

"I think you will enjoy working with her. She came with glowing references from people who do not suffer fools gladly," said ElBaradei.

"I'll do my best."

* * *

Later that week, there was a soft knock on my office door. I responded with a "come in". It was Hasina. I pointed to the visitor's chair in the corner, and she sat down after having made a quick survey of the office. I hoped she was impressed by the metres of books on shelves and the piles of reprints leaning against the wall.

"Can I have a half-hour of your time?" she said.

"Certainly," was my answer.

"Why am I here? What is my role in an organization such as the IAEA?"

"I'll try to tell you the answers if, in return, you tell me what made you apply and then accept the offer?"

"That is fair. You go first."

"There are several reasons. You will soon discover that there is only a handful of women working in the IAEA; it is an anomaly in this day and age. I would like to think that the IAEA would be a better organization with more input from women. There is a much more important reason. Nations that have acquired nuclear weapons do so for various reasons. A very significant but greatly unappreciated factor in such decisions is the recent historical context. The USA was the first nuclear power, partly because it preferred and valued technology and science as the drivers of progress and as the key to winning. The UK needed nuclear weapons as compensation for no longer running the world. France needed such weapons to match the UK. The USSR needed the weapons to avoid being invaded and yet again having its population decimated. And so on. If we look closer to your area of interest, then we can see that India needed nuclear weapons in order to match the rise of P. R. China. The consequence of India becoming a nuclear power, and of winning encounters with Pakistan in Kashmir and elsewhere, and being involved in the loss of Bangladesh, forced Pakistan to go nuclear. You can look at the recent history of the Korean Peninsula and that of Iran and can then construct rationales for the DPRK to go nuclear and for Iran to do the same. I may be boring you, but in my own way, I am explaining why you are here. These are just thumbnail sketches, but there are many shelf metres of scholarly volumes that support a historical context to nuclear programmes. The majority of people working in the IAEA might appreciate history lessons up to high school level but most likely hated the topic at the time. This is the main reason why you are here. I will now draw a breath and let you explain yourself. Why are you here?"

"I have lived a sheltered life at boarding school and at university, both in the UK. I am the perfect student: clever, hard-working, motivated and industrious. As you know, Oxford University is a parallel universe. Once you enter the gate of the college, or go to the Bodleian Library, you depart the real world. The question is: can I deal with the everyday 'real' reality? After the DPhil and having authored a published monograph, something happened to me during a vacation with my family in Chittagong. I suddenly realized how far I had travelled from my childhood, and from a life in Bangladesh, and how impossible it would be for me to go back. I have to apologise for giving you my life story before I can deal with your question."

"That is OK. I know how you feel. Just take your time."

I was beginning to sense the vulnerability that can live under the surface of someone who is uniquely gifted.

She continued. "It is as if I suddenly woke up and knew I should do something that mattered. My family and my nation were borne out of violence. My father was a sniper in 1971 before I was born. My parents never talked about those times or about the time when their parents fled for their lives in 1947. This may have been the reason why I was sent to boarding school in England. They did not want me to inherit such memories, I think. If I did not know any better, I would think that such memories can become encoded in the genes and then ripple down through the generations. So, I came to Vienna wanting to work for a better world."

She had looked at me and sensed something that made her stop. I knew what it was: memories encoded in the genes. It was as if two tortured souls had recognized each other.

"Maybe that is why both of us are here."

* * *

A week passed before she knocked on my door again. This time she asked if it was time for lunch.

"How are you settling in?" I asked.

Hasina told me that the climate in Vienna in February was distinctly colder than Oxford, but she had invested in an ankle-long padded coat and some warm underwear, plus a knitted bobble hat.

I suggested that we bypass the canteen and have lunch in a nearby café. Hasina agreed to that. I had worked out that the average distance between cafés in Vienna was no more than 200 metres, and that made walking around town bearable during the winter. I guided her to the nearest one.

"I have discovered that the central heating in my flat leaves a lot to be desired. It reminds me of a winter's day in a college in Oxford. The radiators seem to gurgle a lot while struggling in vain to keep the temperature liveable."

"You are repeating my experience. There are ways to solve the problem. You might wish to invest in an electric radiator and spend the winter sitting in front of it. The alternative is to have a couple of blankets placed in strategic locations so that you can wrap yourself up if it gets too bad. More importantly, tell me how you are settling in at the IAEA?"

"I was taken in hand by the nice human resource lady. She has fixed me up with a plastic ID card and a magnetic key. She has also organized an e-mail for me, and I have been given a brand-new desktop computer. I spent half a day with the security folks, and I was told what I am allowed to say to the outside world. I was warned against journalists and CIA agents and other spies. At the moment, I can access hard copies and online files that are in the public domain. If I need anything classified, I must get written permission from my line manager."

"Well, the security people have been here since the Cold War, and they believe that Vienna is still swarming with spooks," I said and she laughed.

"There is one question I forgot to ask. Is there really only a women's toilet on the even-numbered floors? I am on the third floor. It seems that I must go up, or down, one floor."

"That's all there is. It used to be worse, I've been told. When they designed this building, they assumed that only males would work for the IAEA. At that time, there was a male toilet on each floor, but just one for women next to the canteen. There is a good story from those days. Madeleine Albright, the former US Secretary of State, was visiting. When she discovered that there was only one female toilet, you could hear her outrage throughout the building. 'What f***ing kind of place is this?'"

Hasina seemed to like the story. "I promise I won't make that kind of fuss – at least not before I have been here for a few weeks."

When we were walking back from lunch, she said, "What I know about nuclear science and technology could fit on the back of a small envelope. I have a feeling I should do some reading about these things. Any suggestions?"

"The literature is vast, ranging from the trivial to the incomprehensible. Starting next month, I will be giving six double lectures on the basics of civilian nuclear technology and on some of the main applications in the small lecture theatre on the first floor. I specialize in making what is incomprehensible blindingly obvious. We prefer not to tell anyone about nuclear weapons technology, but we do give some lectures on the pros and cons of having nuclear weapons and then a couple of lectures on what is the use of having them. I give some of those lectures."

"I should probably talk to my line manager about this – if only I knew who it is."

"I am sure you will be told soon enough," was my answer. Then we went back to our respective offices.

There was a knock on the door. I thought I recognized it and said "yes". It was Hasina, and there was thunder and lightning in her eyes.

"Did you know who is to be my line manager?"

"No," I replied, but there was something that made me fear the worst.

"Are you absolutely sure you don't know and haven't been involved?"

"Yes, this is ElBaradei territory, and I don't want to be involved, but please sit down and tell me. What has happened?"

"You are my line manager!"

"God acts in mysterious ways. I think ElBaradei is playing a game with us. He is a wonderful man, but he can also be a bastard on occasion. You can, of course, go back to ElBaradei and say that under no circumstances could I be your de facto boss. But let me say that it would never occur to me to tell him what to do. I don't believe in giving orders. I believe in talking things through before arriving at an agreed position and then deciding collectively who is in charge of taking action. In my own ham-fisted way, I think I am trying to say that I don't believe in master-servant relationships."

"It is just that I don't want to be a pawn in a silly game."

"Then we are on the same wavelength. I don't believe in being a pawn or playing silly games either. Let us agree that you are fully entitled to complain about being manipulated. I suggest we proceed for a trial period of a couple of weeks, then we can go to ElBaradei and tell him jointly, or separately, what we are happy to do, and what we are not happy about. How is that?"

"OK, agreed. I'll be back."

In the end, it all turned out well. Hasina came back and asked me to convey her agreement to ElBaradei and to find the best way to say that she was not pleased with the way things were being handled. I put on my best manners and had a constructive session in the director's office. Peace and harmony were restored within the IAEA, if not in the rest of the world.

Hasina and I spent one long day deciding which areas of the IAEA should be within her ambit and discussed how she could contribute most effectively to a better understanding of the historical contexts that affected why some states decided to go nuclear or refrained from doing so. Initially it seemed obvious to both of us that she should begin with the Indian sub-continent. She would deal with the history from colonial days to the present time, while I could handle the necessary technicalities of the nuclear issues. The outcome of the day's work was a 10-page proposal that would be submitted to the requisite committee for approval.

It was late in the day, so we decided to stop at the local café for a meal before heading to our respective homes. While we walked, it went through my mind that I had been there before with Walheide, but that had been yet another short chapter in my life. The page had been turned, and that chapter was closed.

We were waiting to be served, and she looked at me.

"You probably know a lot about me, assuming that you have seen my CV. I know nothing about you, aside from what I could find on the Web. You have worked in lots of places, published an impressive number of papers in reputable journals, and given talks here and there. I think there is more to you than that. Tell me who you really are."

"There is a saying, 'What you see is what you get'. I have been cursed with seemingly being ordinary while not allowing the world to enter into that which cannot be seen from the outside."

She gave that some thought.

"I have the impression that you are not married. I sense that you have never been married. Someone who has never been in one place for more than three years is not the marrying kind. You seem like the type of person who ought to be married. Please explain this to me. I have no hidden agenda for asking."

"I have thought about that question. I think it has to do with that which cannot be seen. At times like these, I wish that I could explain myself. Maybe another day."

"One final question before dinner," she said. "Am I allowed to try to hack my way in?"

The dinner was on the table. I felt that a brief comment was in order. "You have my permission to try, but not now. I am too hungry."

After dinner, we stood in the square and said our goodbyes.

"It has been a really good day. A long session of straining the intellect, then a nice dinner with meaningful conversation involving a mysterious stranger. Please let us do it again."

"We will. Now go home."

* * *

The worst of the winter was over, and the days were getting longer and brighter. Hasina was engrossed in working on her analyses of history and politics which would ultimately lead into decisions about nuclear programmes in India and Pakistan. She had begun with the colonial times, when Britain controlled the sub-continent by a process of divide and rule, thus setting the stage for a subsequent fragmentation of the tapestry of ethnicities, religions and cultural diversities held together by the thin glue of wanting to get rid of the colonial master. Every couple of days, she handed me drafts which I did my best to read through and then handed back with comments. She became a hard taskmaster, while I was running as fast as I could to keep up. I was hoping that I might be able to hold my own until we got closer to the time of the first testing in India of nuclear devices. Once a week, we went out for dinner, partly to talk about work and partly to wind down. We seemed to grow closer during those weeks and were beginning to need each other's company. A strange kind of intimacy was growing. What had begun as mutual respectful companionship was gradually transforming into something else, as yet unspoken, but hanging in the air. I think we were both wondering how and when it would reach a kind of destination. We knew what we had but were not certain that rocking the boat was the way to go.

It had been an increasingly busy period, and I had missed most of the opera season and was beginning to feel deprived. I was sitting in my office with the open daily newspaper, to see what I was missing, when Hasina appeared with yet another chapter for me to read.

"Am I allowed to interrupt your reading of the paper?" she said jokingly.

"I was hoping to find the time for an evening of opera before the season is over. Do you want to come along?"

"I'd love to. What is on offer?" was the instant reply.

"At the State Opera on Friday, *Madame Butterfly* is on the programme, and on Saturday, they do *Tosca*, both by Puccini. Tosca has the better music, but *Madame Butterfly* the better story. It has a heart-rending finale."

After some thought, she said, "I think my emotions need a bit of work. *Madame Butterfly* it is."

"Let us leave work early for a change. Then we can have a light dinner before the opera. I'll get the tickets. You can bring the tissues."

* * *

We met outside the familiar café. Once inside, Hasina disrobed from her scarf and padded coat and revealed a china doll inside a small black dress above stiletto heels. Eyes were definitely turning. I had done the best I could, but with inferior starting material.

The light dinner and a carafe of house red was definitely what we needed. The State Opera was just a short walk away. Hasina held on to my arm, possibly in part because of the high heels and the cobblestones. The outdoor clothes were disposed of in the wardrobe, and we found our seats on the balcony in the middle of the second row.

"I tried for the first row, but they were sold out," I said.

"These are perfect. I read up on the plot on the Web, just in case it was being sung in Italian. I see what you meant by it being emotionally challenging." She was whispering into my ear.

"It is not uncommon that it will be sung in Italian, but then there are German subtitles. But the story is sufficiently universal, and any language will do," was my comment.

The curtain went up, and the overture began. The dashing American naval officer arrived in Japan and became besotted with the beautiful Madame Butterfly. She resisted at length but ultimately surrendered. Then, there was a period of bliss. Duty called for the dashing naval officer. He had to leave his Madame Butterfly. In the last act, we saw Butterfly with a baby child, now living in desperate poverty. The dashing officer returned with his American wife. The wife said that she would look after the child and give it the best of life in America, but Madame Butterfly must then relinquish her child. Her anguish was boundless. She handed over the child. In the last scene, she killed herself in the midst of a heart-rending aria.

I had seen the opera several times before and was prepared. Even so, the music, with its promise of impending doom and the mother's grief at the end, had remained equally powerful for me each time. Hasina was unprepared, and I could sense the impact on her. The grip on my arm was steadily tightening. In the middle of the last aria, she buried her face on my shoulder, and I felt her sobbing.

During the applause, the tissues came out, and she was discreetly trying to salvage her make-up. She went to the ladies afterwards to regain composure and to fix up the damage.

Afterwards, we went to the bar and had a soothing drink in order to recover.

"You did warn me," she said, "but if you had not, I still would have come if for no other reason than to understand you better. Maybe I am now inside the first shell of the Russian doll."

"You being with me tonight is the best thing that has happened to me for a long time." I heard myself say it, but I did not know where my words came from.

"I would like us to stay together this weekend." Again, it seemed as if another person was saying my words.

She looked at me and nodded, reached over, and held my hands.

We agreed that my flat was closer, and had an extra room, and marginally better central heating. When we got there, Hasina made an inspection of its content and its state of systematic disorder.

"There is a lot to learn and understand about a person from the state of the surroundings where the person lives. I have learned that you are doing too many different things but that there is order in your chaos, and your kitchen is tidy. I like that."

"Well done. You are reading me like a badly written, but open, book."

She came over to the sofa and snuggled up. If Hasina had been a cat, her purring would have been loud and clear. We agreed it was time to inspect the bedroom. There, she stepped out of the little black dress and became the perfect unclothed china doll. I disposed of my clothes, and we could have been auditioning for *Beauty and the Beast*. It was a long and gentle coming together while we explored each other's needs and wishes. We slept entangled, safe in the knowledge that we were doing what we had wished for. In the morning, I found a track suit that was undersized for me, but Hasina thought it would do for now. After coffee, marmalade on toast and yoghurt, she put on the padded coat and high heels, tottered over to her place, and collected the bare necessities of life.

Afterwards, we held hands while going for a stroll along the admixture, joining love-struck couples, single mums with baby buggies, and elderly couples looking after their constitutions. We were at peace with the world and felt for once that the world had been nice to us. After an early dinner, we walked randomly through the cobbled streets of the Old City. We were enticed into an extremely baroque former church to listen to the best of Mozart, specially selected for tourists and lovers.

On Sunday, it was time to get serious. Were we ready to live together and start the process of becoming an established couple and dealing with our respective rough edges? We compromised by deciding to live apart for a couple of weeks but have the weekends together. Then, we would decide. We were pretending to be sensible and mature about these things, but instead, we acted like teenagers in the midst of our first serious romance.

Two weeks later, we realized that we spent each week wishing that the weekend would come sooner rather than later. We decided to look for a bigger place and then move in together.

It was time to gird our loins, so we booked a meeting with ElBaradei; we needed to confess to our sins. Much to our surprise, he claimed he had known all along that this would happen.

"Just make sure that it does not end in tears because if it does, at least one of you will have to leave. And both of you will be mortally wounded. Now go away, and continue the good work," was his message and a kind of blessing.

War

The spring and early summer were good for us. Our relationship moved from being novel to being special. We moved to a bigger apartment so that both of us could have a sacred corner with a desk and computer surrounded by bookshelves and folders with useful and useless papers, reprints and notes. Our dinner routine settled down to Hasina making Bangladeshi delicacies containing secret ingredients during half the week, while I cobbled together pasta dishes and salads during the other half. On the seventh day, we went out. Hasina joined me in the morning run ritual doing laps in the nearest park so that we could return home and have our guilt-free croissants. Then, we went off to work.

The projects were coming along nicely. Hasina was close to putting the final touches on the definitive analysis of the modern history of the Indian sub-continent based on historical trends and recent events. The project was intended to be both explanatory and predictive of the likelihood that some countries would go nuclear and others would not. My specialty was to be the devil's advocate and try to find faults in her chain of reasoning. In a few instances, I suggested that she might wish to insert clarifications or qualifying statements. In general, she would point out that I had not understood what she was saying. My repost would then be that if I did not understand the story, then most other readers would give up in despair. It was a good intellectual sparring game that kept us on our toes. We submitted a paper to one of the reputable journals. It got accepted, but only after the predictable haggling with the referees and a few minor changes.

In the May of that year, we went off to a conference in Boston dealing with the dangers of nuclear proliferation and the adequacy of measures for preventing the spread of nuclear weapons. Once we were there, it became obvious that we were in the midst of a group of neo-conservatives and Cold War warriors. The party line seemed to be that nuclear weapons in the hands of the USA and its allies were good, but nuclear weapons in the hands of anyone else were bad. We decided that it was best that Hasina, rather than I, should deliver a seriously discordant message. The rationale being that the wolves would treat her with some respect, seeing that she was the one and only female non-Anglo-Saxon in the room.

The delivery went perfectly well. It became clear during the questions from the audience that the message delivered by Hasina was not going to be unchallenged.

"What does history have to do with North Korea thumbing its nose at world opinion – given that it is a brutal dictatorship run by a madman?" was the first question.

Hasina took it all in her stride and responded with a thumbnail sketch of the past 100 years of Korean history, then finished with a rhetorical flurry. "If you place yourself in Korean shoes, would you not conclude that you live in a dangerous world? Would you need to be a madman to decide that a nuclear deterrent was the one and only route to security?"

The next question was, "How do we know that nuclear weapons in the hands of a ruthless dictator do not pose a threat to South Korea and, indeed, the rest of the world?"

Hasina was relishing that one. "At one time, the USA stationed 1,000 nuclear warheads on South Korean soil. Even a madman would not wish to commit suicide, much less want to see his country turned into a radioactive wasteland unfit for human habitation."

There were a couple of additional questions, but Hasina was now in total control.

During the afternoon break for coffee, I was cornered by one of the warriors, who wanted to know where she came from. My response, with a straight face, was that she was a secret weapon capable of making people look stupid. He just walked away. I was asked by another warrior if her talk represented official IAEA policy. I pointed out that the constitution of the IAEA says explicitly that it is a non-partisan organization. The gentleman mumbled that it was time for ElBaradei to step down. I was surprised when a grey-haired man from MIT came and said quietly, "We needed that talk."

That evening we agreed that it had gone well and that all was not lost. A few weeks later, we attended a so-called workshop in Tokyo. This time I did most of the talking but referred a couple of tricky questions to Hasina. We probably could have continued on the talking circuit and become known as the "one-two team": if one did not get you, the other one would. There were more important things to worry about.

* * *

The backdrop to our current lives was the increasingly louder beats of the drums of war.

Within a few days after the 9/11 attack on the World Trade Towers, it was established that Al Qaeda was responsible and that Bin Laden had been the mastermind. Al Qaeda had set up training camps in Afghanistan, and the Taliban had de facto given Bin Laden sanctuary of a kind. The Taliban was the dominant faction at the time, even though it did not control large parts of the Afghan countryside. The USA launched an overwhelming air and ground assault on the bases of Al Qaeda and proceeded to round up guilty and innocents alike in order to root out the evil that was deemed to be responsible for the attack on the US homeland. Adopting a policy of guilt by association, the Taliban was considered to have been an accessory enemy of the USA and got caught up in the same process of punishment. It was somewhat ironic, in the sense that most of the Taliban, not so many years earlier, during the intervention by the USSR, had been the mujahedin and then been labelled as brave freedom fighters, much beloved and supported by the USA. The USA exacted its revenge but ultimately came to pay a heavy price. It did not seem to occur to the USA and its allies that the price paid by the Afghans was far greater.

The American national psyche demanded additional retribution, and Iraq seemed a likely second target. There was one problem, however. There was a serious lack of evidence that Iraq had played any role whatsoever in the 9/11 attack or had indeed been a known promoter of, or participant in, state-sponsored terrorism. After the revolution that deposed the Shah of Iran, the USA became a friend of Iraq. The motto was "an enemy of my enemy is my friend". Encouragement and tacit support were given to the Saddam Hussein regime for Iraq to invade Iran in 1980. The war lasted for eight years and cost more than 1 million lives. It was a thoroughly brutal war where Iraq deployed poison gas while the USA and its allies looked the other way.

The Iraq–USA friendship came to an end when Iraq invaded Kuwait. The Iraqi pretext was that Kuwait had once been an integral part of Iraq but was excised by the then colonial masters due to its very considerable oil reserves. The invasion was reversed by the brief Gulf War when the USA and its allies demonstrated the overwhelming fire power that could be marshalled in short order. The comprehensive decimation and defeat of Iraqi forces, followed by unconditional surrender, led to a complete removal of all weapons of mass destruction and ancillary facilities from Iraq.

Personnel from the IAEA were then involved in the aftermath.

The one remaining pretext for extending 9/11 retribution to Iraq was the claim by the USA that the Hussein regime possessed undeclared weapons of mass destruction (WMD). After an acrimonious debate in the Security Council, it was resolved to set up a body of inspectors headed by Hans Blix, a former secretary general of the IAEA, to undertake a comprehensive investigation of Iraqi capabilities. This would then determine if there were any WMDs in existence or any programmes underway to develop such weapons. A number of experts from the IAEA were co-opted, and a lengthy programme of inspections was undertaken. Predictably, nothing was found, with the exception of some rusting shells that might once have contained poison gas, and a few defunct facilities.

When the report was finally published, it claimed that even though no smoking gun was found, there were unspecified reasons to think that Iraq could have, or could develop, a WMD capacity. It was claimed, falsely, that Iraq was in breach of its treaty obligations and should be punished. The Security Council refused to authorize military action, the UK Prime Minister, Tony Blair, joined the Bush administration and provided the fig leaf of "the coalition of the willing" that allowed an invasion to take place in March 2003.

* * *

My computer pinged to draw my attention to a news flash. Iraq was being invaded by coalition forces. Within seconds, my office door was flung open by Hasina. Her facial expression was a mixture of anger and consternation.

"This is the end of the post-WWII consensus that might is not right and that the rights of the weak should not be trampled on with impunity by the high and mighty. The hypocrisy of claiming to be a force for peace and stability and then basing a flagrant violation of sovereignty on blatant lies!" Hasina stopped to draw breath.

We closed up shop and went for a walk. We found a bench in a park and sat down.

"I think we knew, even after the carnage of WWII, that we would soon return to business as usual. Pax Americana was not going to be any different to Pax Romana, or the aftermath of the 30-year war in Europe," I said to break the silence.

"I get your point," replied Hasina. "At the height of the Roman Empire, all roads, and most of the wealth, went to Rome. If you were protected by the Romans, life was pretty good. But if you were rocking the boat, then the legions would deal with you swiftly, ruthlessly and efficiently. There are many similarities with the present-day Pax Americana. Economic, military and cultural powers reside in, and are controlled by, the USA. If you enjoy the protection of the USA, then life generally is not too bad. If you choose to rock the boat, then you are dealt with swiftly and ruthlessly."

"The claimed merits of Pax Americana depend on where you are and what you do. Since WWII, roughly 20 million lives have been lost, with the USA as a main combatant or as a puppet master in the background. The hand of the USSR has played a somewhat lesser role, usually as a supporter of proxies that are doing most of the killing and dying. Some people think it has been worth it," I added. Then I continued.

"There is a glimmer of light in the current gloom that seems to be settling over the world. Thanks to the EU, there has not been a major war in Europe since 1945. I cannot think of another 60 years in European history when there was not a war. Moreover, the major nations of Europe have ceded great slabs of sovereignty to a central authority, without a shot being fired, and nationalism has been neutered by a technocratic priesthood, and by the rule of law. Regrettably, the UK has been an outlier and still seems to be wedded to 'punching above its weight'."

"You have cheered me up marginally, but it has been a bad day for humankind, in general, and for the Iraqis in the street, in particular. I am enough of a historian to know that invading Iraq is a game for losers. History will prove me right."

"I know better than to argue with that," signalling my agreement.

The "war" was over in a month; the destruction from the air, the firepower on the ground and superior technology overwhelmed the defending Iraqi forces. The Saddam Hussein regime collapsed like a house of cards, and chaos ensued. The interim US administration disbanded the armed forces and the entire Ba'athist state apparatus. Iraq became ungoverned and ungovernable. The glue that had held the disparate ethnic, tribal and religious factions together, after a fashion, had vanished overnight. Violence between Shias and Sunnis flared up, and the Kurdish Peshmerga saw an opportunity to further its objectives. In the aftermath of the invasion, conditions deteriorated and took on the character of a civil war, with the allied forces ending up being the meat in the sandwich. The result was an outcome that had no relationship to the naive view that the removal of Saddam and his regime would usher in democracy, peace and harmony in Iraq and throughout the Middle East. In contrast, it did set the stage for ISIS to emerge from the shadows and wreak chaos, death and destruction throughout the Middle East.

Each evening we watched the daily bulletin covering the latest news from the Middle East. There was a grim satisfaction in noticing that we, or someone we knew, had predicted most of the events before they had unfolded. In hindsight, we were thankful that the IAEA had not been involved institutionally in the lead-up to the war. The ones that had been involved, or had allowed themselves to be used, ended up on the wrong side of the debate and ultimately became damaged goods.

Life Does Go On

The five years of 2004–9 were partly about mid-life routine, but mainly about what we ultimately were going to do with our lives, and in my case, the manner in which my life was going to progress beyond middle age.

One weekend morning in the spring of 2004 became important to us. Hasina had been quiet, almost absent, for a few days, and I had a feeling she was in the midst of a decision that had to be made. Finally, I asked what was on her mind.

"Remember after the first night we spent together, I said I wanted to hack my way into your mind to see what was there. Even then, I thought that if we never saw each other again, I would miss you for the rest of my life. Now when you look at me, and touch me, it seems to me that you feel the same way. Am I right?"

There was only one answer. "Yes."

At that moment, I was overcome by the urge to bare my soul to Hasina. I began by telling her about the two voices in my mind that were trying to make some sense of my life and of the world around me. Most of the time, it was the obsessively rational voice that informed my public persona. There had once been talk of autism from time to time at an age when I had no idea what the word meant. The other voice was largely hidden from view but did the talking in private. At times of real or imagined danger, or at times of uncertainty, or when the world was working in mysterious ways, the hidden voices were in charge. The two Ps learned over time to live together and to have long, and mainly constructive, conversations.

Being outwardly obsessively rational, I had been deemed to be a difficult child. I knew that I was objectively different, mainly because I did not seem to have any parents or close family. The parents were reputed to exist in some unspecified location. Once it was said, possibly as a joke, that I was found in a supermarket where I was walking in the aisles. I thought the voices would stay with me for the rest of my life, and the discordant internalized dialogue was there to stay. But then, my life changed. I met Hasina. The voices remained, but the nature of the dialogue changed. The obsessive borderline autistic voice became less obsessive and increasingly comfortable living with human emotions. The other voice, which always expected to be mugged by black swans, even when there were none in sight, became more relaxed and more trusting of the world as it was. Over time, and being with Hasina, the voices began to merge together. Now they seemed to have joined forces in seeing my life as being as good as one could reasonably expect. This was how I tried to explain myself to Hasina.

"Now you know everything."

She had sat silently while listening to what I had to say.

"I am so glad you told me. I will never forget the words. I have never felt as close to another human being as I do now."

There was nothing more to be said, and no other words were needed.

* * *

Later that evening, she said, "Should we get married?"

"In the past, such an idea would not have occurred to me, but I think the time has come. I propose a civil wedding here in Vienna. Then you should take me to Chittagong so that your parents can meet me. Later on, we can come back to Chittagong and have a proper wedding with two hundred guests. How does that sound?"

"Perfect," said Hasina.

* * *

Two weeks later, we were duly turned into husband and wife so that we could have a better-than-average dinner afterwards. Later we spent the night together in perfect conjugal bliss.

* * *

A month after the civil ceremony, we were landing in Chittagong. Kualeda and Mujibur were at the airport to greet their prodigal daughter and the prospective son-in-law. I had been slightly apprehensive, although Hasina had been reassuring me that she had prepared the ground via a number of lengthy phone conversations. It all went very well. We were welcomed with open arms and driven to the family home, which turned out to be a sprawling reproduction colonial bungalow overlooking the harbour. We were taken to our bedroom, which turned out to be an airy room with fans whirring above us. There was time to sort ourselves out, and then a very special dinner was ready. After dinner, Kualeda and Hasina disappeared to deal with women's business. Mujibur and I repaired to the balcony with a large jug of lemon tea; it was time to get to know each other. I began by describing how Hasina and I had come to meet and how we then got to know each other. That gave me a chance to explain to him how special she was. He agreed with that and told me that even as a toddler in Chittagong, she was miles ahead of all the other children of her age. Mujibur and Kualeda decided to send her off to boarding school in the UK.

I launched into a long explanation of how I had come to work at the IAEA and the reason why Hasina was a unique person within the organization. It was luck, or fate, that had brought us together, but then fate works in mysterious ways. It soon became obvious that we were meant for each other.

Mujibur told me about a life of highs and lows and of struggles and successes. Life was now good, the business was flourishing, and politics in Bangladesh was stable and predictable. He and Kualeda were pleased that Hasina had found a good husband, and they hoped to see us as often as possible. He thought that Kualeda was wishing for good news about a child. I said I would do my best.

"That is a good plan," he said.

Hasina and I reviewed the events of the day after we had retired.

"It has been a perfect day. Kualeda thinks you are a perfect man and tells me I have to look after you. Like all men, you need a good woman. There was a thinly disguised hint about offspring. I think that Kualeda has been missing me. She is hoping that they will see more of us in the years to come. I have promised her a visit each year. I am getting the feeling that my parents are beginning to feel their age."

During the next few days, we were shown off to friends, business partners and some distant relatives. One night we had dinner with their circle of friends. Yet again, we had to explain ourselves as best we could. Our lives must have seemed alien, possibly exciting, to most people in Chittagong. How does one explain the IAEA and describe Mozart's operas in Vienna?

One evening was set aside for planning our second wedding, this time in Chittagong. We decided it would be best to wait until after the monsoon. The rest would have to be in the hands of Mujibur and Kualeda. We offered to come a few days before the wedding so that we could help out. So that was that.

It was time to say farewell. Hasina and Kualeda shed a few tears,

Mujibur and I embraced, and all of us said that we were going to miss each other. My feelings and promises were entirely earnest. Finally, I felt that I had a family that loved me.

* * *

It was nice to get back to Vienna and to resume what had become normal life. It was mid-summer, and Vienna was heading for the hottest summer on record. It was even hotter in France. The TV news headlines were reporting that elderly and frail people were dying and that tourists were sitting in the fountains.

I began thinking about the last conversation with Qadeer Khan. Maybe it was time to start taking global warming seriously rather than spending the rest of my life doing book-keeping of fissile materials. I decided to have another outing to Rawalpindi.

One Sunday evening, after dinner, I told Hasina about Qadeer Khan and about my meetings and conversations with him. She had heard of his reputation as the father of the Pakistani nuclear bomb. She was taken aback when I proposed that she should come along for the next visit. I pointed out that there was an obvious historical context that ultimately would lead to the bomb, and there was no better person than Qadeer Khan to explain how and why it happened.

"This is your bread and butter. I will warn him that you are coming to pose some serious questions. In any case, he is a most interesting person. Last time I talked with him, he claimed that he and I were very much alike. My guess is that he will find you to be a kindred soul, as well." The latter sold Hasina on the plan. Now we just had to get ElBaradei to give us the go-ahead.

Permission was granted. ElBaradei said he was particularly intrigued by the last conversation in Rawalpindi about global warming. I had told him about the grandson of Khan, and he thought the conversation might have had something to do with his worrying about the fate of future generations. Hasina, in the meantime, was scouring the library for the latest on what was known about the Pakistani nuclear programme. Then, we went off to Rawalpindi.

* * *

I had briefed Khan by e-mail before we arrived to make sure that he knew that Hasina was coming with me and that she was there both as the tame historian at the IAEA and as my wife.

As usual, we convened before dinner in the small meeting room attached to his living quarters. Khan surprised us by having read the monograph dealing with the history of Bangladesh from partition to liberation, authored by Hasina. He praised it as an accurate, even-handed and sensitive account of one of the darkest periods in the life of Pakistan.

Hasina responded to Khan's praise. "If I had been working with the IAEA at the time, I would have liked to have consulted you as a unique source of information about the period."

She also described her role in the IAEA and that she was hoping to give full justice to the historical context of the nuclear programmes on the sub-continent.

Khan explained that he and I had met before and had established a strong professional relationship, as well as a personal bond. He was pleased that I had brought Hasina this time, both in her professional capacity and as my wife.

It was time for dinner. Once again, it was brought by his daughter and by the young son, who was no longer a toddler.

The conversation turned to the political situation in Pakistan. Pervez Musharraf was then the current president after leading a successful military coup in 2001. Khan expressed his feelings, possibly for the benefit of Hasina.

"Musharraf had been a vital player in the decisions leading up to Pakistan becoming a nuclear-armed state. I am no great friend or admirer of Musharraf, and I predict that his reign will end in grief. Pakistan has had an ambiguous, and at times unhappy, relationship with the democratic system of government."

Khan and Hasina agreed that many of Pakistan's problems went back to colonial times when the British chose to take advantage of ethnic tensions and encouraged the fragmentation of power structures based on ruling families in order to strengthen colonial control. Partition became a bloody affair that, in hindsight, was a disaster for Pakistan. The armed forces had emerged as the only institution, with its internal discipline and cohesion, that was capable of maintaining some semblance of order.

"I think it will take two or three generations to develop institutions that can support a proper modern democracy." This was Khan expressing his views.

Hasina joined his thinking aloud. "The recent history of Bangladesh is similar to that of Pakistan. The colonial masters have a lot to answer for. The result is that both countries are captives of ruling families."

They agreed that the origins of present-day woes could be found in past history. Present solutions would be counter-productive unless due regard was given to past history.

I enjoyed having the luxury of being a silent partner while Khan and Hasina sorted out current problems by referring to recent history. I realized it had been a masterstroke to involve Hasina.

The next day was devoted to doing the ritual inspection with a clipboard and a laptop. Hasina came along to get her first insight into a live nuclear programme where we checked on tamper-proofed CCTV cameras and radiation monitors and accounted for sub-gram quantities of fissile materials. We also inspected the workshops where nuclear warheads were being constructed, repaired or refurbished. For Hasina, it was a chance to change her thinking about nuclear weapons from abstract concepts to concrete realities.

We had dinner to ourselves that night, while Khan was away for an important meeting concerned with the budget for the next year. His daughter brought the food, which gave Hasina the opportunity to establish rapport. She discovered that the daughter had been sent away to boarding school in the UK. They compared notes on their respective times of loneliness in an alien environment.

After dinner, Hasina asked me about how one could, or should, relate to nuclear weapons.

"It is an interesting question. Most people, including myself, who have been involved in that business, have asked that question of themselves. Over the years, I have met and talked to several people who spent time at Los Alamos during WWII. All were scientists who either had, or should have had, the Nobel Prize for their contributions to the basic science. For them, it was the heady days of modern physics, and this was their chance in a lifetime to push the frontiers into uncharted and truly exciting territory. Developing the atomic bomb was, for them, a manner of vindication of how they thought the world worked in accord with physical laws. For some, it was also the firmly held view that Nazism had to be defeated by all available means."

Hasina was not going to let me get away with that.

"What about the people, such as Qadeer Khan, and the ones we have met while walking through the laboratories here in Rawalpindi?"

"Most of us, myself included, were, in the beginning, besotted by the elegance and inherent beauty of the natural laws and their consequences for the societies we live in. Such feelings are similar to those that some people have for the music composed by Mozart or the plays written by Shakespeare. It is about perfection of things, and about ideas, that are beyond the comprehension of most other humans. Most of the people that we have met today are technicians who have the same reverence for a nuclear warhead as they would have for a finely crafted Swiss watch or a Ferrari racing car. Most of us, myself included, are perfectly aware of the devastation that a nuclear warhead can wreak, but this is pushed to the back of our collective consciousness. We have convinced ourselves that the warheads will never be used in anger. We believe that their sole functions are to be known to exist because they have certain potentially devastating properties and, therefore, can only serve to deter. Thus, the argument goes, they are means that make at least one type of war unthinkable. This is a long answer to a short question. Books have been written on the topic."

Hasina smiled at me and said, "I like it when you go into lecturing mode. That is enough for today. Time for bed."

The last day in Rawalpindi with Khan was going to be devoted to talking about global warming. We convened earlier in the day than usual for a light lunch so that we would have more time for the discussion. We began by reminding ourselves about the conversation that took place the last time Khan and I had met.

I had briefed Hasina on the essence of our earlier talk. Then, Hasina took the floor, so to speak, to give an overview of the likely impacts on Bangladesh of the predictions for global warming.

"My country, Bangladesh, is uniquely vulnerable for three main reasons. Bangladesh is a country with a relatively small land area, roughly 150,000 square km, a large population of 15 million, and a correspondingly high population density. Some 80% of the land area is fertile, but most of it is just a few metres above the present sea level. The lowlands are dominated and irrigated by three great rivers: the Ganges, Brahmaputra, Meghna, and their tributaries.

Bangladesh is exceptionally vulnerable to devastating floods, and in the longer term, it may be permanently submerged as the oceans rise due to the melting of ice caps in the polar regions. The fertility of the low-lying areas is critically dependent on the rivers being fed by water from the Himalayan glaciers, which store rainfall during the wet season, and this is then released during the dry season, thus preventing floods and droughts, as in the case of Pakistan. Global warming will result in a major deterioration of the ability of Bangladesh to feed its population. Finally, Bangladesh has been visited by tropical storms with monotonous regularity, some of which have resulted in death tolls in excess of 100,000. The prediction is that global warming will give rise to a greater frequency of ever more powerful storms."

She stopped talking and invited me to take over.

"Let me make some initial observations. The average rise in global temperature in 2003, above that of pre-industrial times, is roughly 0.5 degrees. Even so, the average global temperature this year is going to be one of the 10 highest recorded. There is increasing evidence of climate-related events that are more extreme than expected by insurance companies. Ten years from now, the global temperature rise will be greater than one degree, and there will be increasing rates of diminishing glaciation and greater rates of melting of the polar ice caps. The rise in sea levels will be measurable. Possibly the most significant change is that the rate of temperature rise in the polar regions will be twice as high as that of the global average rate. Modelling shows that climatic zones will be moving from the equator toward the poles. The significance of this trend is that desertification will be the norm in places such as Southern Europe, the Mid-West of the USA and the savannas of Africa. The zones that are currently temperate will get hotter, with summers having 40-degree spells being more common. Parts of the

Arctic will become temperate. Such changes will have major impacts on agriculture, native fauna and flora, fisheries, etc. Similar changes have taken place in the distant past, but with transitions that have taken some millions of years, which therefore allow the ecosystems to adapt. The timescale we are concerned with today may be 100 years, and adaptation will be difficult or impossible. Modelling suggests that a 3-degree temperature rise could be a point of no return. At that point, the permafrost will begin to thaw with the release of vast quantities of greenhouse gases, methane in particular. This will create a positive feedback mechanism that may ultimately lead to large parts of the globe being unfit for life. This is the bad news. I rest my case."

There was silence in the room while the message was being digested.

"What timescale are we looking at before we hit 3 degrees?"

This was the question from Khan.

"I am guessing 30 to 50 years," I said.

"Will current plans for reducing emission of greenhouse gases save us from disaster?"

The question came from Hasina.

"The answer is emphatically negative. Current trends will, within two to three decades, get us to a point where even a complete cessation of the generation of greenhouse gases will not suffice. We would then have to plan for rapid deployment of technologies for the removal of gases from the atmosphere. Such action seems impossible unless there is a comprehensive rethinking and reconstruction of our civilization before it is too late."

Khan said, "It seems that we are forced to think about the abandonment of many activities of the existing civilization so that we can build something new and different from scratch that has survival value."

Hasina looked thoughtful, and then she said,

"One would have to deliver the kind of jolt to the worldwide system that would effectively demolish current institutions and ways of thinking. In one sense, the fear of the known would have to be greater than the fear of the unknown. There would have to be a global understanding that business as usual will lead to certain doom and that a new paradigm for the species would be the one remaining hope of survival."

After the heavy session, we needed a break, and dinner was being served. We decided to banish the gloom and doom until later in the evening.

When we were ready to carry on, Khan proposed that we should meet again. "Since I cannot come to you, given that I am still a wanted person in some quarters, you have to come to me. Any more visits would undoubtedly be noticed, and we do not want that. However, I have friends in the security services. They can set up secure encrypted communications links in the dark Web, as well as provide false identities, passports and documents that will get you in and out of every country in the world. These things came in handy when sanctions had to be circumvented in order to obtain sensitive supplies for a nuclear programme. I am confident that such procedures can be reactivated."

"As long as Hasina and I remain with the IAEA, we have a legitimate reason to appear in your laboratory once each year for the ritual inspection," I said.

For the moment, there did not seem to be much more to be done. We promised each other to keep thinking of how one might engineer a solution to the problem. We thought we might have 10 years to think before urgency would set in. Also, we agreed that a solution was more likely to come from a sub-national actor than from one or more state actors.

Next morning, Hasina and I travelled back to Vienna.

* * *

Organizations have a way of making history repeat itself. A report was prepared based on what was on the clipboard and the laptop. Then, we had a cursory debriefing with ElBaradei. He wanted to know if Khan was still obsessed with global warming. I confirmed that this was still the case but left it at that. The discussions of the last day in Rawalpindi were no business of the IAEA and were best left unreported. Then, it was back to life as usual for us for a while.

* * *

Our marriage in Chittagong was next on the agenda. My level of fear and apprehension was rising as the date came closer. I had done some reading about the traditional weddings in Bangladesh, and that provided little comfort. Families were terribly important and played major roles during the various phases, it seemed. The wedding would usually go on for three days and seemingly involved an endless sequence of rituals. For instance, I found it difficult to see myself suited up as a Bengal prince. I had no family to call on, so that complicated the carrying out of roughly half of the rituals. Hasina did her best to calm me down. She assured me that the wedding was going to be semi-modern, with the emphasis on the formal act of getting legally married, followed by serious festivities. She told me in jest that I could always pass myself off as "the man from Mars" with no provenance, family or history. I was not convinced that she was joking. I checked my wardrobe left over from the outing to the UN some time ago and decided that the dark suit and tie would have to do.

We arrived a few days before the fateful day in order to be told about the plans, the arrangements and proceedings. Some hundred guests were expected, and it was going to happen in the City Hall Convention Centre. Kualeda wanted Hasina to be the perfect fairy-tale princess, being married off to a fine foreign prince. They disappeared for most of one day to find the requisite fineries and to book Hasina in at the beauty salon for the morning of the wedding. Mujibur tried his best to keep a low profile while arranging a Rolls for the day and making sure that there was going to be food and drink for the 100 or so guests. Live music, an angel choir and a dancing troupe were also booked. Everything was double-checked, and nothing was left to chance. It was going to be the kind of event where local dignitaries wanted to be present and be seen. Mujibur kindly found the time to take me through what, and when, everything was going to happen and what my role was going to be.

The morning of the wedding was devoted to getting dressed. Hasina appeared in an ornate red sari and did indeed look as if she was a Bengali princess. I got into my Western dark suit and silk tie and looked like a moderately successful businessman. Just before lunch, the Rolls appeared and drove us to the ceremonial venue. Mujibur was going to act as my family representative, and Kualeda was to be in charge of Hasina. Given my total lack of family, this was the best we could do. Hasina and I were seated apart while questions were asked of each family to ensure that the marriage was agreed. The official contract was drawn up and signed. Once that was done, Hasina and I were allowed to sit next to each other on an embroidered and brocaded sofa, whereupon singing and dancing could commence, and sweet pastries were passed around. Kualeda shed a few tears, and Mujibur shook my hand. For a person who had been a loner for most of his life, it was overwhelming.

The next day was the time for feasting, enjoyment and circulating among the many guests. From lunch onwards, the festivities went on until the early evening. Hasina looked after me and steered me toward families that were known to her from her childhood. We became good at repetitive explanations of our lives and what we had been doing, and where we lived. It was all very friendly. We promised to come back frequently and to spend time with Mujibur and Kualeda.

We stayed with Mujibur and Kualeda for a week afterwards in order to wind down and to properly cement the family ties. Mujibur introduced me to the mysteries and art of trading cotton and jute, while Kualeda and Hasina went to town to check out the shops and to be ladies who do lunch in all the best places.

Then, it was time for farewells before returning to Vienna, this time as a twice-married couple.

* * *

The next three years were a time for consolidation, professionally and personally, for the two of us. As it turned out, it ended with a termination followed by renewal.

Hasina worked her way through all the nations who were declared, or de facto, to be in possession of nuclear weapons and then set the decision-making in the respective historical contexts that affected the "yes" or "no" outcome. The work had been published in a series of scholarly papers and presented at conferences. A synthesis of her work was then used to construct a model with explanatory and predictive powers. This was finally presented to the world in a monograph. It did not make the best-seller lists, but it did ruffle feathers in neo-conservative circles. As an afterthought, she applied her theory to the EU and was able to demonstrate that its success in keeping the peace in Europe for some 70 years was entirely consistent with the visions of the founding fathers and with their historical heritage of two world wars in thirty years. The work pleased the EU but was studiously ignored by the USA and the UK.

My own life with the IAEA went on as usual but was beginning to seem increasingly trivial. The brief of the IAEA to prevent nuclear proliferation was largely irrelevant, having been effectively subsumed into the state department and the executive branch of the US government. This left the nuclear safeguards and the safety of the civilian nuclear industry to be monitored, inspected and promoted by the IAEA. In my view, I was beginning to think that the civilian nuclear age had come and gone. The only justification for building nuclear reactors seemed to be the argument that greenhouse gases were not emitted by nuclear fission. Electricity generated in reactors was neither cheap nor convenient, and the disposal of nuclear waste had not showed signs of being dealt with to the satisfaction of the wider community.

* * *

There was another outing to Rawalpindi to meet up with Khan under the disguise of carrying out the annual inspection. In between this visit and the earlier one, we had established that encrypted communications through the dark Web worked according to plan. We had bought an anonymous laptop in the UK, installed encryption software given to us on the last visit to Rawalpindi, and sent a trial message from a public Wi-Fi location during a weekend visit to Prague, as per instructions. We got an all-clear response from Khan in Rawalpindi.

On the final day with Khan, after having finished the book-keeping and checking of all things nuclear, we settled down to talk about global warming. I pointed out the generic approach to the problem by reminding Khan and Hasina of one of the many statements attributed to Archimedes: "Give me a fixed point in space, and I will move the Earth."

His point was that given a sufficiently long lever, and a fixed point, an object of arbitrary mass could be moved.

In our case, we were dealing with a civilization in a state that could be described as having certain economic, social and political structures and attributes, most of which now were inconsistent with the maintenance of the ecosystem of the earth which was expected to support life into the indefinite future.

"We must recognize that the inertia of the current system is enormous; no event in recent times has been able to shift its centre of gravity. There have been perturbations and temporary excursions, but the world has always returned to a state of business as usual. A latter-day Archimedes would now give some thought to the length of the lever and the force that would need to be applied to its end."

Hasina chimed in, "In recent times, I can only think of the inter-war events, such as hyperinflation and a deep depression that set the stage for WWII. The outcomes were changes of governments, nationalism, fascism, communism, and so on. There was a lot of thinking along the lines of a better world and how one would engineer a 'never again' state for the world. As we know, it did not last. Maybe we need an encounter with an asteroid of suitable size, or a visitation of beings from space, or a series of truly horrible climatic events in quick succession?"

Then Khan had his say. "Being the kind of person I am, what about a nuclear war – one that is not too big or too small?"

I tried to think about the unthinkable.

"The time would have to be ripe, when a fuse had been lit by other events, such as a near-total financial meltdown. Then, maybe one could engineer a limited nuclear exchange. This might lead to a new trajectory to a sustainable future for human civilization."

We tacitly agreed that at the moment we did not wish to think about options that were patently unlikely or demonstrably unpalatable. The decision was to go away and to think about the unthinkable.

As expected, ElBaradei told us that he had read the tea leaves and come to the conclusion that he would not have the votes for the next term of office. The US State Department had exerted its influence and wanted a more pliable voice in the IAEA. In any case, ElBaradei had been watching political trends in Egypt, his country of origin. It was his assessment that the Mubarak regime was coming to an end. ElBaradei was hoping that genuinely free and fair elections would be held in due course and that he might have a role to play. Hasina and I went away from his office with the feeling that it was time to move on to new pastures.

Oxford – The Turtles Return

Turtles are reputed to return to the beach where they once were hatched in order to bury their eggs in the warm sand above the water line.

Oxford was where Hasina was reborn as a scholar and where she realized that there was a world for the taking. I had been there before and had mixed feelings about returning. Until I met Hasina, my life had been governed by the wish to find out what was on the other side of yet another hill. Once I had got to the other side, and looked around for a while, I would move on to climb the next hill. I had not been able to decide whether I was doomed to run away from something or run towards something. I had changed and decided that nirvana was not to be found on any side of a hill. This had happened mainly because Hasina had affected my life at its most fundamental level, but also because I was tired of climbing hills and being disappointed. There was something sad about someone who was approaching middle age but was in denial of the aging process. It was a bit like seeing someone with long greying hair carrying a skateboard. I decided I did not want to go there. Oxford was not a bad place to stop running.

* * *

We were lucky to find an affordable terrace on the banks of the Thames with three bedrooms, and a conservatory, within easy walking distance of the town centre. It took a few weeks to sort out legal and financial affairs. It was fortunate that the IAEA believed in competitive salaries and that the financial crash had done terrible things to house prices. We invested in a truckload of furniture from IKEA to make the house liveable. The place soon felt like home.

Hasina had, in the meantime, sorted out her relationship with the Department of Modern History and with her old college. She had brought along two half-finished projects from Vienna to get her installed and had started working in a slightly threadbare office in a Victorian annexe. It took the university a couple of months to offer her a permanent appointment funded jointly by the college and the department.

I did the rounds of places and people that I knew from last time I worked in the Oxford area; I settled on the Department of Engineering Science as a suitable base. A colleague from the past was working on a project funded by the Ministry of Defence and was looking for another pair of hands. I joined the group. A few weeks later, the head of department knocked on my door and asked if I would be interested in writing lecture notes for a course on nanotechnology. *Why not?* I thought. The outcome was that I got my foot in the door. It was good to be at a loose end and to be intellectually omnivorous.

The morning run had become a necessary routine during the years in Vienna. Instead of running along the Donau, we took advantage of the towpaths along the Thames and the Oxford Canal to get the mornings off to a good start so that we had earned the croissants before going off to work.

One morning Hasina said she felt unusually tired. For once, I had a lonely run. The next morning, she continued to feel off-colour and decided that maybe she should consult the GP around the corner, just in case. I went off to work. At lunch, Hasina called and said, "Guess what the doctor said?"

"No, tell me."

"I am pregnant!"

We took the day off to have a minor celebration and had a discussion of the ins and outs of parenthood. The GP thought that Hasina was six weeks on the way to becoming a mum, so counting forward, the birth would happen in the early spring of 2010. We realized we were moving into unknown intellectual and practical territory and decided that we needed to invest in a couple of handbooks for expectant parents.

Progress seemed to go according to what the book was telling us. The bump became visible, and then it gradually expanded. During the final trimester, Hasina worked from home.

When we were certain that all was going to plan, we called Kualeda and Mujibur one evening with the news, and there was no mistaking the joy at the other end of the line. Kualeda insisted that when the birth was expected, she would come to Oxford to help out. I got the impression that men were pretty useless when it came to childbirth, and Kualeda was probably right. The many tests and scans said that it was a boy doing all the right things. Hasina said she preferred a midwife at home, and she would be delighted if I remained present at the time. Kualeda announced her arrival a week before the expected day of delivery, and I went to Heathrow to meet her. Nature did its things in accord with what the book was telling us. Contractions began, Hasina gritted her teeth, the midwife came … a healthy baby boy arrived and had a lot to say about the light of day. Kualeda thought he was the most beautiful baby boy she had ever seen, and Hasina looked suitably exhausted but satisfied with her day's work. We had become a proper nuclear family.

Later that evening, Hasina had been fortified by a cup of special tea from Bangladesh, and she was ready to doze off. I kissed her forehead and whispered, "Well done, my love." The One, as yet unnamed, was peacefully asleep in his crib, blissfully unaware of what the world had to offer him. Kualeda had gone to sleep in the guestroom, and the house was silent. It was time for me to work out what it all meant.

One thing was clear in my mind. The start in life for the one yet to be named was going to be very different to my own start in life. He would have parents who were present and who would do their very best to make him feel wanted, secure and loved. He would always know that there was a family unit within which there was protection from whatever the world had in store in the years to come. For once, I was confronted with the need to think about a personal world containing three souls rather than two. I had come a long way from the time when it was just me against the world. As well, the idea of handing the world on to the next generation had suddenly got a whole new meaning.

A few days later, we were sitting on the sofa in between the feeding sessions. Hasina looked at me and said, "We need to think of a name. I would like a universal one that is easy to spell, to pronounce, and to remember. Not too ethnic and not too strange. Any ideas?"

I had been thinking about it.

"I would like the name to remind us of the private life we as a family unit will try to create for him, as well as what we wish for the world that he will inherit. What do you think about Eden?"

"I like that. Let's hope that we and the world will live up to expectations. Would you be happy with Mujibur as a middle name?"

"Done!" Yet again, our minds had been working in synch: Eden had a name.

* * *

Life returned to a new normal with a bit of help from Kualeda. Hasina returned to her job part-time, although the nature of her work did not require a presence in her office. She decided to provide her breast in the morning, then Kualeda delivered the bottle in the afternoon, and Eden seemed to be happy with the arrangement. I was trained up by Kualeda to do my share of the diaper changes and managed to be marginally useful and involved. I would go into the laboratory for a few hours three days a week and did some writing at home between dinner and bedtime. At two months, Eden was baptised and became formally known by his name. He did not seem all that fussed. Two months later, he was crawling, so we had to move all the books from the bottom shelves to stop him from rearranging the library. He was getting to the stage of enjoying being taken in the baby-buggy on outings to Christ Church Gardens and the university parks. Not long after, he took his first unsteady steps and knew the difference between Mum, Dad and 'Leda. Soon there would be no stopping him.

* * *

The worst of the financial crash had played itself out by the end of 2010. For most of us, austerity became the new normal, while the top 0.1% somehow managed to keep on increasing their wealth, according to the annual *Times* supplement known as the *'Rich List'* of the 1,000 richest people in the UK. It did not seem right that the billionaires had a combined net worth of roughly £150,000,000,000, equal to approximately 10% of the annual UK GDP, while the food banks were stretched beyond their limits. For a while, there was a vigorous debate in the communities dealing with finance and economics as to whether or not the post-war consensus about the best of all economic worlds was terminally broken or just needed a bit of tinkering around the edges. As time went by after the collapse of Lehman Brothers, followed by the central banks injecting eye-watering sums into the banking system, the old model of business, as usual, gradually gained the upper hand.

* * *

From time to time, we had been continuing the dialogue with Qadeer Khan via the dark Web. He was not surprised to hear that we had left the IAEA and had found greener pastures in Oxford. We were still looking for an event that would destabilize the status quo and hopefully lead to fresh thinking about the viability of the prevailing economic, financial and political models. For a while, we thought that the 2008 financial crash might be such an event, but the financiers closed ranks and patched the old system together. We would need to wait for the next Black Swan.

* * *

During the next few years, we were devoted to becoming reputable academics in an environment where scholarship was valued above all else. The trick seemed to be that one should never be seen to be trying but then occasionally produce a stunning piece of work. There were certainly some members, of what I had come to think of as the sheltered workshop, that were legends in their own minds. Then, there were also some that did not need to tell the world that they were genuinely scholars of note. Hasina and I liked to do what we did, and on occasion, we did a good job while keeping our heads down.

Hasina was a product of Oxford University and continued to exceed any reasonable expectations held by the system. She produced another monograph dealing with the history of Bangladesh from liberation to the present. Then she published a popular account with the title 'Britain's Bomb: The Illusion of Greatness'. The volume made for good reading and actually paid a few bills, and earned Hasina an invitation to present a documentary on BBC 2. As a consequence of having made her mark at the IAEA, and then at Oxford, she continued to be asked to chair sessions at international conferences and to give plenary, or keynote, presentations. In due course, she was headhunted by the Centre for International Relations and was offered a personal professorial chair.

I was not as upwardly mobile as Hasina. My work on preparing the course on nanotechnology was finished. Not surprisingly, it then turned out that I was the obvious person to do the teaching. I quite enjoyed dealing with the 20-year-old Oxford students who seemed to be members of a different species and never got any older. Three years later, I was getting bored and handed the teaching over to a younger person.

Global warming had finally begun to rate a mention on the political agenda. Coal-fired power stations were being phased out, and some of the first-generation nuclear reactors were reaching their use-by dates. A major advantage of nuclear power was that fission does not produce CO_2. As a consequence, reactors were once again being planned, and contracts were being negotiated, generally with foreign companies. The 1960s generation of nuclear scientists and engineers had retired or fallen off their perches by now, or their knowledge was out of date. Suddenly I was of some use as a consultant or advisor. A nuclear power station was a very expensive object and would not leave much change from £20 billion. Those with current expertise tended to be sought as consultants and to be very well paid. I was not going to starve in my old age or end up being kept by Hasina.

A by-product of the years at the IAEA was that Hasina and I had established cordial relations with a number of past and present members of the The International Institute for Strategic Studies (IISS) in London. Several exchanges of information and useful discussions had taken place on numerous occasions. Not long after we arrived in Oxford, the relationships were resurrected. We went down to London and explored various possibilities for collaborative work. Hasina agreed to give a series of seminars once she had established herself at Oxford. In my case, we settled on a part-time visiting fellowship. I would be in residence in London one to two days a week while being involved in the updating of the monthly report on nuclear weapons and delivery systems around the world. These activities were sufficiently flexible to allow for childminding and to maintain a reasonably civilized home life. Its main merit was to keep boredom at bay.

Toward the end of the monsoon season in Chittagong, we would often spend a couple of weeks with Kualeda and Mujibur. When Eden merited having his very own passport, and was ready to make the journey, he came along and occupied the centre stage in the household. Eden quickly got the hang of grandparents, while Mujibur proclaimed that he had inherited the brain of Hasina, and Kualeda was sure that he had my nose and blue eyes. I thought that we had become a multi-cultural family made in heaven.

One night at dusk, we were sitting outside contemplating life under the two mango trees. Mujibur decided it was time to talk about the future. He said that he and Kualeda wished to see Eden grow up and have a happy life. But, he said, one can never know what might happen. The experience of the family said that life can be tenuous and fragile. Since independence, life had fortunately been good in Bangladesh.

"We have lived in peace and comfort and accumulated wealth.

In our culture, we value gold as the only safe form of wealth. We carried gold when our family fled for their lives in 1947. At the end of each year, I work out the profit we have made and buy a quantity of gold. This is then deposited in a vault in a special institution. The gold can only be accessed by a series of code words and numbers. I can ask for the gold, or any part of it, to be liquidated in any currency; the proceeds are then transferred anonymously to any account, or as cash, to any place in the world. We will give you the information in a sealed envelope for your safe-keeping. When Eden is 18 years of age, we want you to tell him about the gold so that he can decide how and when he needs it, to get a good start in life. If anything happens to both of you, or to both of us, it would be best for the envelope to be in a safe place with a trusted executor with instructions to open it in the presence of Eden."

It was a sombre conversation. We promised that Eden would be here on his eighteenth birthday, and we would all celebrate his coming of age, Inshallah. It could have been that Mujibur had a premonition. The conversation stayed with us.

The Black Swans Are Coming

We were in touch with Qadeer Khan at least once a year through the dark Web. It was agreed that we should not meet in person except in a dire emergency. Now that we were no longer connected to the IAEA, we had no legitimate reason to visit Rawalpindi. ElBaradei had departed, as predicted. The IAEA had become largely irrelevant and was now acting as a tame appendage to the US State Department.

During the years, we had been discussing global warming with Khan, and we had always ended up concluding that the only hope was to deal with a system that was in a metastable state so that a relatively small perturbation would nudge it from one state into another. In 2008, we thought the financial meltdown was what we wanted, but we were disappointed. The world relaxed back to a state of business as usual. The period after the crash was financially stable, but the politics became increasingly volatile, where polarization and inequality were driving a wedge between the traditional politics of right and left, with the middle ground losing its appeal. On some days, I thought I could discern a rerun of the inter-war years of the 1930s.

* * *

The southern summer of 2019 was the beginning of a series of extreme climatic events. The south-eastern states of Australia were ravaged by forest fires of unprecedented ferocity and extent. It began with a drought; this was followed by a heat wave that set records and culminated in what can best be described as firestorms. While thousands of homes were lost, and dozens perished, the major damage was environmental. Forest fires of even greater extent did enormous damage in the Amazon region during the dry season by burning out some 10,000 square km of area, devastating local biodiversity and being a major annual contributor to CO_2 emissions. In the northern summer, unprecedented temperatures were recorded in Europe, followed by fires ravaging great areas of the Siberian forests and adding yet more CO_2 to the atmosphere.

Then, tropical storm Raja struck Chittagong, and in one terrible night, our family was reduced to three members. While the rest of the world soon went on its merry way, for us, the storm remained an unforgettable personal tragedy. The grief stayed with us for weeks and months. We had each other, but the loss of Kualeda and Mujibur remained an open wound, and the scar tissue would take a long time to heal and dull the pain. The one important message from Raja was that this was just the beginning of what global warming had in store for us unless the world should come to its senses.

* * *

Shortly thereafter, the coronavirus, Covid-19, struck. Its outbreak appeared to be relatively innocuous at first. In the beginning, early in the new year, it was confined to Wuhan in China. The assessment was that it was another version of the SARS virus, which had also been confined to Asia. The experts thought it was only moderately deadly and not especially infective. Authorities in the affected regions dealt rapidly and efficiently with the outbreak. The assessment was that it could be contained in Asia, as in the case of the SARS epidemic. Covid-19 turned out to be different. It was not particularly deadly for young and healthy people. Its lethality appeared to favour the elderly and the ones with underlying health issues. It seemed to have a mild preference for men over women. It also seemed to prefer certain ethnic groups and was more lethal for people with over-active immune systems. In a highly connected world, the virus swiftly invaded Europe and North America. The most ill-prepared countries found themselves in the grips of a major epidemic; their health systems were soon struggling to keep pace with exponentially increasing numbers of affected patients. It became apparent that this was the real thing: it was the killer virus that had been predicted for years and had been making epidemiologists wake up in the night in a cold sweat. The WHO declared it to be a pandemic. It was also the kind of event feared by politicians. They soon realized that inevitably the decisions and actions made by them would, in hindsight, be seen to be inadequate, irrelevant or misguided. When the bodies then piled up, someone would need to be blamed, and politicians would be first in line.

Many Asian countries managed the outbreak of the epidemic better than others. The combination of previous and recent experience with epidemics, such as SARS, with an authoritarian single-party regime, and a collectivist culture, had distinct advantages. The Western industrialized countries fared less well due to their dependence on decision-making in a multi-party context and with an individualistic culture. The fear of alienating even a small segment of the electorate tended to mitigate against early and decisive collective actions. The action was then deferred until the exponential growth of the epidemic was well underway.

In the end, the majority of countries adopted a lock-down strategy in order to limit person-to-person interactions, while praying for an early development of a vaccine. The well-documented overall excess mortality in the developed industrialized countries was in the hundreds of thousands during the height of the peak rates of infections. The loss of life in other parts of the world was probably greater but tended to be a relatively modest perturbation in comparison with the lethality of other communicable diseases, such as malaria, and deaths from other causes, including organized violence. Such observations were a rather sad consequence of the current state of the world.

The consequences of the lock-down strategies turned out to be that a majority of the working population no longer went to work or they worked from home. In some countries, they received financial support until life returned to a more normal condition. In other countries, the support was through the unemployment benefit system. However, because of the lockdown, factories no longer produced, shops no longer traded, and consumers no longer consumed. The hospitality industry was closed down, as were the tourist and travel industries. At best, economies suffered a deep, but hopefully short, depression. At worst, parts of the pre-existing economy would not survive, and there was an expectation of years of frugality and significantly lower standards of living. As they say, we lived in interesting times. Most developed countries found themselves living on the overdrafts, where the public purse was going increasingly and deeper into the red. The UK was racking up deficits unheard of since WWII. Estimates suggested that the developed nations would incur a collected debt of 20 trillion dollars in order to salvage national economies and, on average, end up with national cumulative sovereign debts of up to 150% of GDP. Was this going to be the shock to the system we had been waiting for?

* * *

The practicalities of life in Oxford during the pandemic for Hasina and me were relatively uncomplicated. The nature of our commitments allowed us to work from home. We gave our lectures online and kept in contact with colleagues and students by e-mail and Skype or Zoom. Once in a while, one student at a time would consult with one of us at a distance of two metres in the front garden while being treated to coffee and slices of Black Forest cake. Three hours per day, one of us would sit down with Eden and deal with online educational material, or with home-spun maths and science, or with arts subjects, from me or Hasina, respectively. Educationally he did not suffer, but he missed his friends. Occasionally Eden would complain that the workload and expectations were far higher at home than at school. "Why must I do differential calculus? I am only ten years old."

Three times each week, we went to the university parks and kicked a football hither and yonder. The spring was warm and dry for once. There were some drawbacks. Our annual outings to Chittagong had come to an end. The two weeks of exploring antiquities and cultures around Europe had to wait for another year.

There was a silver lining to Covid-19. The streets were almost completely devoid of cars during lockdown. Some days in Oxford, one could have filmed the aftermath of a nuclear war. People seemed to have vanished. In the evenings, children could go outside and see stars. I did a back-of-the-envelope calculation which showed that the cleaner air in mega-cities in China and elsewhere most likely saved more lives from fewer respiratory ailments than were lost to the virus. Indeed, satellite imaging, courtesy of NASA, provided irrefutable data for the change in air quality. And there were reliable data showing that 2020 was going to be the first year since pre-industrial times when the concentration of atmospheric CO_2 had not increased. Some people claimed that the bees were back and that wildlife, in general, was doing better.

Was this the event that was going to change the way we lived so that we would once more co-exist with the environment and maybe even with each other? Could Covid-19 be the Archimedean lever?

* * *

Not so long ago, we would have had our annual outing to Chittagong. Mujibur and Kualeda would have been pleased to see us. Eden would then have shot up another 10 cm since last year, and that would duly have been commented on. There would have been sessions under the mango trees with conversations about the past, present and future and about the meaning of life. This was not a normal year. We did not go to Chittagong. We tried in vain to find a new normal, but without success.

* * *

There was a message from Qadeer Khan. "Can we talk?"
Our response was, "Yes, but give us a few days to think."
For those with a masochistic streak, there was a lot of interesting news to keep up with. A few weeks in Chittagong would normally have left us seriously out of touch with events in the rest of the world. This year, we could remain glued full-time to the internet and other news media.

The state of the dollar-denominated financial system seemed to be heading for trouble. The Federal Reserve and other central banks were printing money by churning out huge quantities of government bonds, thereby using the new money to buy assets and injecting liquidity into the financial system. This had worked during the financial collapse in 2008. This time, however, the markets might ultimately lose faith in the dollar as a safe haven. The Trump presidency was in terminal meltdown, and all the signs were that a second term was a non-starter. The likelihood of a quick recovery was fading. A second spike of the virus was underway, and the availability of a vaccine was not expected until the beginning of 2021. The world economy was definitely wobbling.

The economists had long since given up on the V-shaped recovery and were not optimistic about the U-shaped one; the current betting tended to favour a deep recession followed by an L-shaped recovery with a generation of serious financial misery. There were signs that nationalism would rear its ugly head, as happened in the 1930s after the Great Depression. Unemployment rates could reach 15% in some of the "rich" countries, tariffs and trade disputes were already on the rise before the pandemic as countries sought to protect themselves against real or perceived predatory policies elsewhere. It seemed likely that borders could be closed against an influx of desperate migrants, and governments might be seeking to create enemies within, as well as from outside, in order to legitimize their hold on power and to deflect any blame for misery at home. Globalism, pluralism, liberal and social democracy might become endangered ideologies.

The people who were in the business of dissecting and identifying the fatal flaws that caused the pandemic did not seem to agree on why it had happened, much less on what was to be done. Like many others, we tried to make sense of what was happening. We could only come to the conclusion that there had to be change.

After the financial crash in 2008, there was a great deal of agonizing over the perceived failures of the theories and practices of economics and finance. Some attempts were made to rein in the excesses of the financial machinery, but these did not amount to much, and the system relaxed back to business as usual. Would the same happen again?

We thought it was too early to tell the political outcome of the pandemic. Once the post-mortem inquiries got underway in earnest, it was highly likely that the governments of the day would not fare well. This could work both ways. Right-of-centre governments would be shown to have handled the pandemic badly and be committed to the political wilderness. Likewise, a left-of-centre government having done badly would suffer the same fate. The only certain outcomes would be political mayhem and chaos. An optimist might hope for a greenish incoming government with a strong mandate to undertake a root-and-branch financial and economic restructuring for the benefit of those that had not partaken in the growth of wealth during the post-WWII period. The dystopian pessimists might fear that revolutions, coups and extreme authoritarian regimes might be back in vogue, even in countries with long traditions of liberal or social democracy. One possible scenario was that regions of wealth, such as China, the EU and North America, would retreat into isolation inside a cordon sanitaire and become self-sufficient entities and would let the rest of the world fight to the death for the remaining spoils. This might be a temporary "solution" of a kind. Ultimately, global warming would impose its own solution. This might be a far uglier outcome than all the other possibilities.

It was time for another session with Khan.

Assignment in Karachi – The Beginnings of a Plan

Life was a struggle after Raja. The loss of Mujibur and Kualeda had remained an open wound. Hasina was listless. Most nights, she would wake up after a dream about two people fighting enormous waves and then disappearing, not to be seen again. Then she would cling on to me and weep. I knew how she felt. The image of broken and splintered mango trees haunted me. Each time it flashed up in my mind, I felt empty and abandoned. Eden was old enough to understand that his grandparents were not coming back and that the family was in mourning. In his own way, he was trying to comfort us and remind us that we had each other.

The wound was gradually healing, and the scar tissue was dulling the pain. We were picking up the pieces, putting them together, and getting on with life.

* * *

The message from Khan was a signal that we had to banish personal grief and melancholy to a special place in our lives. We could allow ourselves to return to the feelings of loss, from time to time, and to pay homage to a past life that had been precious. On the other hand, it was time to deal with another reality where we would talk to Khan to see if, and how, we had roles to play.

The second message from Khan began with his appreciation and understanding of our need to grieve. It then went on to explain that he had just celebrated his 84th birthday with his daughter's family and his grandson. He was not certain how much time he had left before it was his turn to depart this world.

Then the message went on to agree with our assessment of the current state of the world and that few of the options for change being discussed in the public domain were likely to have sufficient impact on global warming. Finally, he essentially pleaded with us to join him in an attempt to force an outcome that would ensure that a return to status quo was not an option. Reading between the lines, we were beginning to see what he had in mind. We agreed to meet and talk.

* * *

It became clear that we had to enter the murky world where the dark arts of spies and terrorists were plying their crafts in order to achieve their objectives. For obvious reasons, Khan could not come to us, so we had to go to him. He pointed out that Hasina and I were well-known to many at the laboratory from our days at the IAEA. He then proposed we should meet in Karachi.

"I can arrange for us to stay in a safe house, where we can meet and have discussions. Also, I can send you three passports to each of you so that we can choose different identities. The passports, and other paperwork, will be produced by the Pakistani security service in their unit for clandestine activities. The assumption is that we might need to arrange further meetings." Khan vouched for the arrangements by pointing out that they were similar to the ones he had employed on numerous occasions during his wheeling and dealing in nuclear materials and components. Indeed, individuals from countries that were subject to sanctions had made use of the system for person-to-person technology transfers. We agreed to the arrangements. Our previous meetings with Qadeer Khan had built up the kind of reciprocal trust that had allowed him to reveal information that was strictly in confidence and for us to take him at his word.

We explained to Eden that we were going away for a few days. This had happened before, when we were off to conferences and workshops. Eden had wisely acquired a good friend in a family not too far away; the family was also attached to the university. They had the same problem of what to do with their young son during short periods of absence. Eden would, from time to time, take his pyjamas, toothbrush and tablet in a small backpack and stay with our friends. Now and again, we would reciprocate. It was an important part of the socialization process for Eden and made our lives easier.

A thick envelope was delivered two weeks later to us in Oxford by a pimply youth on a scooter. As promised, it contained six passports that looked used but not too used. I was now a national of Ireland and represented a small high-tech firm, now in administration, selling pre-fabricated stainless steel profiles. I had been invited by a similar firm in Karachi to negotiate a takeover. Hasina had also become an Irish national, in between jobs, on a study visit to Karachi, to look at sex education in primary schools. Enclosed were two business class return tickets from Heathrow to Karachi with Pakistan International Airlines.

A driver with a peaked cap holding a piece of cardboard with our new names was waiting at the arrival gate. A Mercedes with tinted windows was idling outside. What seemed to be a gated compound with a miniature manor house was our destination. It was probably Victorian and had been intended to be the antidote against home sickness for a British owner, who might have retired in 1947 to the Cotswolds to tend his roses.

We were shown to our room and given an hour to settle in. Later, we were greeted by Khan in a room that might once have been a library or possibly intended for a billiards table. I thought that it would be hard to fault the standard of safe houses in Pakistan.

"It is good to see you again, my friends. I have been missing your annual visits to count our warheads." Khan's greeting came with a smile. Hasina responded by saying that he was keeping well and had not aged a day since last time.

"That is very kind of you. My grandson is helping me to stay young."

Then, on a more sombre note. "My heartfelt condolences and sympathies on the loss of your family in Chittagong. Let us pray that we can help to prevent a repeat of Raja." We nodded in unison.

Khan continued. "I have taken the liberty of preparing a brief bullet-point summary of where we are with global warming and of the present state of play in mitigation. I am also summarizing where current policies may take us, and the likely consequences if those policies are actually implemented, and the outcome if the world fails to meet future targets. If you are happy with that, we can then move on to discuss how one might be able to achieve the necessary changes in the thinking of decision-makers."

We agreed, and a series of dense slides went up on the screen.

The current average global increase in temperature since pre-industrial times is now just under 1.3 degrees centigrade. Scientific papers predicted this from computer modelling more than 10 years ago, and it happened. Other studies have suggested that the warming would be greater in the polar regions, possibly by a factor of 2. This has also happened. There is a causal relationship between the greenhouse gases in the atmosphere, principally carbon dioxide and methane, and global warming. The concentration of CO_2 has risen from 270 to 440 ppm over that time period, and the rate of increase has been steadily greater with time. The consequences are getting increasingly obvious and ever more difficult to deny. Nine of the 10 previous years during the last decade have been the warmest on record. Glaciers worldwide are receding or disappearing. Extreme climatic events are getting more common, and insurance companies are revising their risk tables. During the northern summers, the polar sea ice in the Arctic is retreating and breaking up. During the southern summers in the Antarctic, more ice is lost each year than is restored during the winter. These are hard data obtained by multiple reliable observations.

Projections based on current trends for generation of greenhouse gases suggest that average global warming may reach 2.5 degrees within 20 to 30 years. The polar regions will then reach 5 degrees above pre-industrial temperatures. At that point, the Arctic Ocean will be ice-free most of the year, the ice shield on Greenland will be in the process of melting. The most important consequence will be the melting of the tundra giving rise to a release of greenhouse gases which have been locked up in the permafrost layer. That contribution will exceed any contributions from human activities. Moreover, it will give rise to a positive feedback process. The release of gases from the permafrost will trigger additional warming, which releases more gases from faster rises in the temperature in the polar regions, and so on. A contributing factor is the change in reflectivity, when reflecting ice and snow surfaces are replaced by heat-absorbing soil and rock surfaces. As the polar regions warm up, the southern and northern ice shields will melt at a faster rate, and the sea level will rise at a greater rate than expected. There is persuasive evidence that an average 3-degree rise will take the world to a "tipping point", beyond which there can be no return.

Global warming represents the first time that human activities can genuinely be shown to affect all countries of the world. A failure to solve the problem will be to the detriment of the totality of the world's population and to the entirety of Earth's biosphere.

Accordingly, it was thought that the UN was the most appropriate forum for policy formulation, which became known as the United Nations Framework Convention on Climate Change (UNFCCC). Its first proper meeting was in Kyoto in 1997, at which time most nations committed themselves to legally binding targets for mitigation. The binding framework has since been abandoned and was replaced in the Paris meeting by a commitment to keep the temperature rise well below 2 degrees. Since then, some countries have adopted their own aspirational targets for a transition to carbon neutrality by dates that range from 2030 to 2050. On current trends, such targets are unlikely to be met. Even if they are met, the average global warming will still exceed 2 degrees. Modelling shows that in order to stabilize the world at a rise of fewer than 2 degrees, there has to be a net removal by 2050 of greenhouse gases from the atmosphere.

Global warming is one of those problems that societies cannot easily deal with. It falls into the same category as how to deal with the care and needs of an aging population, how to solve the problem of inequality, and how to eliminate the gender gap. Aspirational solutions can be proposed, but actual and practical processes are best left until after the next election. In the case of global warming, the industrialized rich countries are in charge of the global economic and financial agendas. They are also historically the greatest cumulative contributors to the generation of greenhouse gases. The remaining countries have little, if any, practical influence over the global economic and financial structures, and their historical contributions to the emission of greenhouse gases are trivial. They are also the most vulnerable societies to the effects of global warming. The financial crash in 2008 principally affected the wealth of the rich countries, but within a few years, the wealth was restored, and there was a return to business as usual. The concentration of greenhouse gases in the atmosphere kept rising at roughly the same rates. The more recent coronavirus pandemic was somewhat different. It affected the mortality rates in most countries and had a disproportionate effect on the segments of the populations that had no wealth to fall back on when the jobs disappeared. The one silver lining was that emission of greenhouse gases took a brief pause in its rise. But there are signs that the financial system is fighting back in order to restore the pre-pandemic status quo. The more recent COP-26 meeting in Glasgow made some headway. The majority of countries committed themselves to carbon neutrality by 2050. The two very significant emitters, China and India, broke rank, while Australia as the largest exporter of coal, negotiated its own exception to the consensus. The most noteworthy positive outcome was concerned with an aspirational commitment to curb deforestation.

How does one bring global warming to the top of the agenda? Some opinion makers have tried and failed. We can just about recall Al Gore and his *An Inconvenient Truth*. More recently, we marvel at David Attenborough's Blue Planet or are impressed by the teenage Greta Thunberg. But their impact has been transient and incomplete. They may be effective influencers but are not decision-makers. As long as the present system can be patched together until the next Black Swan event comes along, the current state of civilization will limp along. Even the coronavirus is unlikely to change that.

"Abdul, you have done your homework. We are impressed. There is not much Hasina and I can add to your summary and overview."

Hasina had been following intently. "I have an unspoken question. Are the three of us sufficiently un-ordinary to find a very long lever and then use it to shift the earth? So far, it has been demonstrated that neither a financial crash nor a pandemic has had a noticeable effect on the prevailing models that are based on an ever-increasing need for consumption and exploitation of the earth's resources. That is leading indirectly to an unsustainable degradation of the global environment. Is there anything that will change the manner in which humanity is managing its affairs?"

In a previous meeting, we had thought about this question. At that time, we had come up with two unlikely, and one unthinkable, possibility. The two unlikely ones included a visitation from space by a civilization further advanced than ours, and with more sense, or the earth being struck by an asteroid of a suitable size. The damage from a large asteroid could return the earth to a pre-life state. A small asteroid would do serious damage, but no worse than that of a pandemic. Neither event is even remotely likely to happen on a timescale of some tens of years. The dinosaurs went extinct some 63 million years ago after an asteroid struck the earth in the region of the Yucatan Peninsula, and it took some millions of years for new forms of life to emerge and flourish.

"Once the impossible has been eliminated, the merely unthinkable remains. We are forced to think about a nuclear war," I said.

"Let me do some thinking aloud," I continued. "My entire professional life has been devoted to nuclear science and technology. I can fool myself by arguing that I have mainly worked on the civilian side. But deep down, I know that the energy released when a U-235 nucleus undergoes fission in a power reactor is precisely the same as the energy released when a U-235 nucleus undergoes fission in a detonating nuclear warhead. So how can I live with myself? There are two components to a saving grace. Number one is that nuclear power stations do not emit greenhouse gases. It is true that there is radioactive waste to be disposed of. However, that problem is solvable and is minor in comparison with a very large number of other problems that also ought to be solved. Number two is the important one that I will invoke in order to save my unworthy soul. It is an empirical fact that nuclear weapons have been used in anger once, in 1945, to obliterate Hiroshima and Nagasaki, and so far, never again. Those who control nuclear weapons, and those who might be threatened by them, are perfectly aware that one nuclear warhead aimed at one metropolitan area would cause death and destruction on an incomparable scale. Thus, the argument goes, nuclear weapons cannot be used for fighting wars. Their only rational purpose is to deter. We are in the process of considering the proposition that the use of nuclear weapons can be permissible if the purpose is to avoid a far greater disaster, namely global warming beyond the tipping point."

It was the turn of Hasina to explain the value of a shock.

"It has been nearly two generations since the world worried about a nuclear war, and three generations have passed since Hiroshima and Nagasaki. Financial crashes come and go and have been essentially a part of life for every generation. Likewise, epidemics come and go. The great majority of people alive today in Western countries have not experienced a proper war on their homelands. The 9/11 attack was hardly a war, but it was a profound shock to the USA because it was completely unexpected and because, unlike a financial crash, it was a unique event. Imagine nuclear bolts from the blue obliterating whole cities. The shock would be several orders of magnitude off the scale of known events. The merit of shocks is to change the emotional and political climate, and thus be the trigger for change."

"Both of you have made your points clear," said Khan, "in the same way as the Catholic Church accepted the moral case for nuclear weapons. In our case, there is a moral rationale for a unique shock if it can prevent human extinction or even unprecedented death and suffering from global warming. Likewise, I accept the argument for the value of a shock. I think there has to be an unprecedented event that will truly change the present status quo. There is at least one worry. The present worldwide inventory of deployed nuclear weapons is about 4,000 warheads that can be delivered on short notice by a variety of systems. There are an additional 14,000 nuclear warheads in reserve. The explosive yields per warhead range from a few kilotons, for tactical use, and up to more than 100 kilotons, for strategic purposes. The great majority of the warheads are held by the USA and Russia, roughly 8,000 each. The remainder is held by the other seven known nuclear powers, each of which has arsenals in the low hundreds. During the Cold War, the total inventory peaked at just under 80,000 warheads, principally held by the USA and the USSR. At that time, the fear was that deterrence could break down, and any first use of nuclear weapons would lead to loss of escalation control and then result in an all-out exchange. Modelling of a hypothetical nuclear war on such a scale showed that an all-out nuclear exchange could render the earth an uninhabitable radioactive wasteland and possibly lead to a nuclear winter. An all-out exchange of the present arsenal would certainly be an incomparable disaster for the majority of the world's population, but the human species would survive, and the earth would recover. But there must be a better way."

This was Khan speaking. Since he was one of those who had his thumb on the "button", he must have thought long and hard about why, and what, could be unleashed.

I thought it was time to focus on some of the possible ways that a nuclear war could be limited.

"We do not wish to trigger an all-out nuclear war. As well, we do not wish for any nuclear use to be traceable back to Pakistan. We are aiming for shock value, not for maximum death and destruction. The USA is, and has been, the principal architect and protector of the present economic, financial and political system. The shock value has to be focussed on the USA. Whatever damage is inflicted on the US economy will then ripple out to the rest of the world, as in the case when toxic financial products in the US brought the financial system of the world to its knees in 2008. The collapse of Lehman Brothers, a moderate-sized investment bank, caused the entire system to seize up. Heroic and coordinated intervention by the major central banks around the world saved the day. Our possible analogue is the destruction of a large metropolitan area in the US, with a near-instantaneous loss of life in the millions. I cannot think of any remedy for dealing with that kind of event, such as the equivalence of the injection of liquidity into the financial system in 2008. The other analogue is that of the 9/11 attack in 2001 on the World Trade Centre. This was not a financial calamity as much as a major blow to the national psyche of the USA. In the case of 9/11, the response was retribution and punishment inflicted on countries deemed to be hostile. A similar response to a nuclear attack on a city in the US could take the form of a reply in kind, namely nuclear retribution on a perceived enemy. Such retribution would be self-defeating in the sense that a nuclear exchange would result in incomparable destruction of at least two nations. An outcome far worse than that of the original attack would be the result. The USA would know that the perpetrator had to be one of the countries known to possess nuclear weapons. The USA could retaliate in kind but would then trigger a tit-for-tat exchange leading to a far worse loss of life.

"One way to lessen the chance of triggering a major nuclear war is to have two identical, and synchronized, attacks on the USA and Russia. Then, clearly, neither of the two could be the perpetrator.

Why would anyone respond in a way that would inflict further death and destruction on one's own country and people? If possible, the actual perpetrator should ideally be untraceable. This would avoid an all-out exchange between the two countries that account for 80% of the deployed warheads and well over 90% of the total number of warheads in existence. The worst-case outcome would involve the USA with, or without, involvement by Russia taking action against a third party that was known, or suspected, of being the perpetrator."

I could feel that Hasina needed to express her apprehensions about the turn of the discussion.

"I am sensing that the minimal death and destruction we are inflicting on innocents could be, say, two large cities and 5 million victims. If our assessments are wrong, and we trigger an all-out nuclear exchange, we could end up with thousands of cities destroyed and a death toll in the billions. Is that a price worth paying? Is there a way to limit the damage? For instance, could one associate the initial attack with a message to the world explaining that the twin attacks are meant to sound a warning about a far greater disaster unless global warming is curbed?"

"That is a relatively straightforward technical issue, as well as a good idea," Khan said. I nodded in agreement.

Having launched into technical issues, we decided to discuss some in-principle problems that could present impossible obstacles.

"We have two main assets that are only available to a small number of people. These include the possible access to nuclear warheads and the detailed knowledge of how to handle them," I said, thereby pre-empting what Khan might say.

He nodded and then continued. "At any one time, there are 10 to 15 nuclear warheads in the laboratory at Rawalpindi, either being built as upgraded versions, or repaired, or checked for functionality. There is also a large inventory of spare parts and a stock of fissile bomb-grade U-235. The inventory is sufficient for four to six cores. There is an additional stock that has never been declared but was used some years ago for illicit bartering purposes. It is possible to recall a few of my most trusted technical staff, now retired, to assemble two nuclear 'devices' that would never need to appear in our paperwork, and would be out of sight from any CCTV cameras. The problem is then to deliver the warheads to suitable locations. We need to think about this since it cannot be done by regular means and systems. Space-based and land-based early warning systems will detect and track enemy planes and missiles more or less from the point of take-off or launch. Submarine-launched missiles is probably the only reasonably secure retaliatory launch system at this time. Planes can be intercepted and shot down. Land-based missiles can be targeted and destroyed by a first strike or by land-based anti-missile systems. In any case, there will rarely be any doubt about the identity of the enemy. Our problem is that we do not have access to any of the known methods of clandestine delivery. The means of delivery is critically important for the sake of Pakistan. The identity of the perpetrator must be unknown and preferably unknowable."

I thought that I could contribute to the discussion of the delivery of the warheads to their targets.

"During the early years of the nuclear age, there were discussions about delivery by what now seems primitive technologies. The IAEA thought about this, as did many others. For instance, there was talk about putting a warhead in a crate labelled 'machinery parts' and then shipping it by commercial means to its destination, at which point it was detonated. It was taken sufficiently seriously for radiation detectors and X-ray imaging equipment to be installed at ports of entry. There was even talk about suitcase bombs. Another hypothetical method would be to bring a nuclear device into a port on board a cargo ship. As far as anyone knows, none of these were actually attempted. Bringing fissile materials through customs at some airports has been attempted in a few instances. Radiation detectors are now installed at most airports and probably at many land border crossing points. Our best bet is to think about ocean travel with a port city as the destination."

We needed a devil's advocate, and Hasina was the best we could have.

"How certain are we that the USA and Russia will respond in the way we think they might? For instance, will one of them deliberately or accidentally trigger an all-out exchange? Could it be that either country is on a hair-trigger alert?"

Khan and I looked at each other to see who wanted to go first. I volunteered.

"Nuclear deterrence is arguably the most firmly embedded strategy of all time. A fully-fledged nuclear war is intellectually and emotionally hardwired to be disastrous for all concerned. Paradoxically, deterrence is reliant on being believed to be fragile. Therefore, both sides pretend that there is a leader carrying a box with a red button, which is the only thing between normal life and Armageddon. Also, it helps that the leader pretends to be irrational. Both of these pretences encourage extreme caution on all sides. There are lurid and terrifying accounts of how a flock of high-flying Canadian geese came close to being identified by radar as a swarm of Soviet missiles heading for the USA or a B-52 bomber accidentally dropping several nuclear bombs over Greenland. These and many other incidents are real, but there was never actually any danger of starting a nuclear war by accident. But the stories are valuable in the sense that they strengthen deterrence by the fear of 'What If?'

"If a metropolitan area on the East Coast of the USA is obliterated without any lead-up in international tensions, and no sign of any warning signals, there would certainly be a shock to the system, in addition to chaos and confusion. Within minutes, the hot-lines in the White House and in the Kremlin would be ringing. There would be near-instantaneous messages to the effect that: It was not us. Hold your missiles! The collective outrage would be palpable. In parallel with the emergency services being galvanized into action, there would be frantic activity in the action control centres with the activity being focussed on 'Who did it?' and 'Why did they do it?' For once, the USA and Russia will agree to demand total and unfettered access to all facilities in the current nuclear nations and to any facility in any other country that could conceivably and clandestinely construct a nuclear device. Also, the ground zero would be pinpointed in order to trace any unusual activity in the area. The one advantage of a nuclear explosion is that any incriminating evidence would have been vaporized. It is possible that analysis of the fallout might identify trace elements that could be matched to a particular batch of fissile material."

The reaction of Hasina to my monologue was to say that she never realized that we lived in such a peculiar world. We decided to wind things up for the day so that we could think about the issues and make some decisions the next day.

* * *

We had gone to bed and were reviewing the proceedings of the day.

Hasina said, "How certain are you that we would not trigger an all-out exchange?"

"There are at least three good reasons, it seems to me. Firstly, the people who matter are strong adherents of deterrence being the only utility of nuclear weapons, and we are all terrified of an all-out exchange. Then, the second reason. It is possible to utterly destroy the UK as a viable state, and as a liveable country, with six or seven nuclear warheads targeted strategically. Does this mean that someone has won? The UK will no longer be of any value to the 'winner', especially if, in its death throes, the nuclear-armed British submarines manage to launch one or more nuclear-tipped Trident SLBMs (Submarine Launched Ballistic Missiles). There is a third reason. Two metropolitan areas have been targeted. One in the USA and one in Russia. An all-out exchange can only make any sense for the two dominant powers, with most of the nuclear weapons, seeking to degrade the nuclear capability of the other. Thus, we have a situation of mutually assured destruction, known as MAD. When the dust settles, there will be one remaining and substantially intact superpower: the People's Republic of China. That outcome is worse than death to the politicians and warriors in Washington DC and in the Kremlin. I could probably think of some other reasons, but that will do."

"You are so right, my dear," was the response of Hasina. She was deep in thought for a while before deciding to explore further what could happen after the shock to the system was administered.

"Let us assume that the current geopolitical and financial world order disintegrates. I agree with you that a nuclear world war is unlikely. I also tend to go along with the argument that there will be financial and economic chaos. What happens then? Can we learn anything from recent history? Can we learn anything from the period before, during, and after WWI? The initial conditions consisted of empires, heredity of absolute rule, rampant colonialism, industrialism at its peak, and a transition from an agrarian society with a lord of the manor being supported by an underclass of sharecroppers to an industrial society headed by factory owners, supported by a proletariat. The war and the Spanish flu put an end to most of the pre-existing world order. Some of the empires bit the dust, and most of the absolute monarchies vacated the thrones in favour of some kind of democracy. Soon women were given the vote. Communism won power in what became known as the USSR, with the expectation that workers of the world would unite and usher in a new era. Social democracy became the halfway house of a mixed economy and a welfare society. Colonialism did not go away, and the aftermath of WWI led to an economy built on shaky foundations. The question of who was going to be the hegemon in Europe, and therefore run the world, was not resolved and had to wait for another war. The USA was rapidly outpacing the rest of the world economically but wisely kept its head down geopolitically. Many things had changed, but there was plenty of scope for status quo to unravel. In the '30s, it did unravel, and the stage was set for WWII.

"A few years after the war, and after the Spanish flu pandemic, hyperinflation struck. This was followed by the worst depression in 200 years. The fragility of democracy ended up being blamed by the purveyors of nationalism, populism and fascism. Demagogues such as the Führer in Germany, Il Duce in Italy, the Caudillo in Spain, and others wiped democracies off the map. This set the stage for WWII. Thus, by any standard, the shocks of WWI, and of a pandemic, did not lead to a happy outcome. In terms of lives lost and material devastation, WWII beat all previous records. Unlike WWI, the outcome of WWII was decisive, and the victors had a free hand to construct a new world order. There were two competing visions of the future. One was based on liberal democracy, individualism and a market economy, while the other was based on a Marxist ideology, collectivism and a centrally planned command economy. Both models were pursued with great fervour. The contradictions between the two were never reconciled, and a Cold War ensued, which was going to last for more than 40 years. There was agreement about the winding up of colonialism, but at great cost in lives and lost opportunities. The Cold War turned hot in the Third World as the USA and USSR competed by proxies. The one silver lining was that Western Europe was relegated to a bit role in the post-WWII drama. The EU was formed in order to retain some semblance of control over its own affairs, and this kept the peace in Europe for a period of 75 years and counting. The defining trend in the post-WWII era was the emergence of P. R. China as an industrial and economic superpower. There are now indications that the rise of China is being seen as a threat to the world order set in place by the USA after WWII. The signs are that the USA will not relinquish its pre-eminent role with grace and that a new cold war is brewing. The silver lining is that a hot war between two nuclear-armed superpowers is unthinkable. We may have seen the end of shocks arising from total hot war. Currently, a shock is being administered by a pandemic leading to major economic and financial disruption. The outcome of that is uncertain. On the horizon is a disruption, global warming, that can potentially be the mother of all disruptions. Thus, endeth the lecture."

"Very impressive and very interesting," I said and continued. "I think you are telling me that wars, whether of the hot or the cold variety, are a favourite human pastime. In accord with what historians tell us, we are doomed to repeat our mistakes. I think we agree that nuclear weapons, in a perverse way, have forbidden a repetition of world wars of the hot variety. Also, I think you are telling me that one cannot easily predict what comes after the war, or after the shock, in our case. Who would have predicted in 1935 that something like the EU was a possible outcome of a war? And who could have predicted nuclear weapons in 1935? Finally, who can predict today how the world will respond to a nuclear strike if the strike is intended to have the effect of making global warming less likely? There is now solid evidence that the coronavirus pandemic has had the effect of interrupting the seemingly inexorable rise in the emission of greenhouse gases. Some decades ago, there were papers written by some of the most reputable scientists of the day showing that a nuclear war could produce a nuclear winter for the same reasons that very large volcanic eruptions in the past have been the causes of climate change."

The last word was had by Hasina before we nodded off.

"I am struggling to resolve our roles in what is fundamentally an argument about commission versus omission. We are effectively proposing to commit an act that may cost the lives of millions, as well as change our own lives for the worse. Our justification is that acts of omission are the alternatives and are likely to be inevitable and will cost many more lives. Morally, I think we are doing the right thing. At the personal level, it boils down to the impact on our own lives. I am fond of the life we have made together. Can I bear to throw that away?"

I did not think I had a satisfactory answer, and I closed my eyes and went to sleep. We needed to talk this one through at another time.

* * *

We met again the next morning. Khan opened the proceedings.

"I wish to explain my rationale for contemplating the use of nuclear weapons in order to avoid global warming. For the sake of my country, I have laboured long and hard to ensure its security from external threats. It is now clear that my country will suffer misery and death from a far worse enemy. My only available weapon has to be used so that we can avoid a catastrophic future. Unlike many others, who are working on nuclear weapons, I am not an evil genius. I am doing it because I think it is best for my country and my people."

He stopped to collect his thoughts.

"It seems that we find ourselves in the aftermath of a pandemic and at the beginning of a process to recover from a deep worldwide depression. Vast quantities of economic stimulus, roughly 10 to 20% of pre-pandemic global GDP, have been pumped into the world economies. As well, sufficient liquidity is being made available to avoid a financial crash along the lines of what saved the day in 2008. The global death toll directly attributable to the pandemic has passed 5 million, and we are still counting, and the excess mortality may be more than twice that. For comparison, the global annual death toll of malaria is roughly similar, but seemingly does not shock anyone, and has no perceptible impact on the GDP of the world. The reason is that the people that die would have generated a contribution to the world's GDP at the noise level. In the developed world, the economic impact of the pandemic is far greater due to the annual contribution per capita being greater than $20,000. As well, citizens in a developed country can choose, or be told, to be economically inactive, in order to avoid being infected. This option is not available to the majority of potential victims of malaria and the virus pandemic. I am belabouring these issues because in my country, Pakistan, malaria and other contagious diseases are a matter of life and death for a majority of the population. Global warming will tilt the balance further towards death in my country."

He stopped again and continued,

"There is no doubt that the pandemic has been the cause of death and misery and that the associated economic depression will drive millions back into extreme poverty. For those people, that will be a new and unwanted 'normal'. There are talks about other kinds of 'normals' that may emerge from the pandemic. For instance, working at home in a digital age may become more common. The centres of cities may be more friendly for those who choose to walk or cycle, the transition from the internal combustion engine to emission-free personal travel might be hastened, short-haul flights may be banned in favour of ground-based public travel, and so on. In general, there is talk about alternative industries and units of production and of different types of employment. Resistance by the traditional industries will no doubt delay those kinds of 'normals'. It is possible that consumers will vote with their choices of consumption, or governments might become more interventionist in the marketplace. It is too early to tell, but the signs are not promising. So far, governments have intervened to support existing industries, many of which depend on producing outputs that are disproportionately high contributors to global warming."

I felt that Khan was trying to present a pros and cons overview of what might happen once the dust settled over the coronavirus pandemic and what might be its aftermath. There was a lot of wishful thinking suggesting that somehow the world would come to its senses and find a way to prevent being overwhelmed by global warming.

Hasina joined the chorus.

"I wish that the world would surprise us, and possibly even surprise itself, and find its way to a new 'normal'. If so, there would have to be a transition to negative carbon emissions within the next decade. If that was remotely likely to be the case, we could forget about our plans to administer a lethal shock. We could go out and have a good dinner, travel home to Oxford, and sleep well at night. Until I joined the IAEA, I had lived in a bubble where rationality prevailed, and problems were discussed dispassionately by intelligent people until workable solutions were identified and agreed. In the world outside the bubble, the games played and decisions made by states, political parties and those that lust for power inevitably result in negative-sum outcomes. The winner is the one that loses the least. The success of ideas that we are all in it together and that there is a need to share the pain, as well as the spoils, cannot be taken for granted. History has shown that a painless change for the better is not to be expected. If I put my rational hat on, I think we must continue to hope for the best but plan for the worst."

Khan and Hasina were looking at me, and I realized that I was meant to contribute my views. With a group of three, there will always be a majority decision – either unanimity or two against one.

"Observations and experiences during my lifetime make me think that actions and decisions by individuals and groups are predicated on what is perceived to be advantageous for the individual or the group. Possibly this is hardwired into our genes, in the sense of the selfish gene, and is the best we can do. The problem with the gene argument is that the gene has backward memory but no capacity to plan for the future. That is not the whole story. We are sentient beings. I have been able to do what I think would give meaning to my existence. I have met Hasina, we have had a son, we are asking ourselves about how to live our lives. I want the musings of sentient beings to continue after we, as particular individuals, have ceased to exist. The crude genetic selfishness will lead to annihilation and to the irretrievable loss of everything that makes us human. I will join the two of you with a hope for the best and a fear of the worst. In my case, the hope is outweighed by the fear. Once the decision to act has been made, we must focus on practicalities."

In the words of Julius Caesar: "We had crossed the Rubicon."

* * *

After a heavy morning of metaphysics and soul-searching, we needed a break and went for a silent walk in the walled garden.

Afterwards, a whiteboard had appeared in the meeting room. We could get down to business.

Item 1 on the list was concerned with the warheads. Khan was confident that they could be completed within six months. He was also certain that the construction could be done clandestinely. A small team had worked with him during the time when the Pakistani programme was in its infancy. At that time, secrecy had been essential. Some members of the team were now retired, but Khan knew where to find them. There were a couple of minor variations that had to be included in the design. For instance, the trigger mechanism had to be timed and pre-set so that synchronization of the two detonations would be assured to within a minute. Otherwise, the entire package would be sealed, shielded, and protected from any environmental variables.

Item 2 dealt with the means of delivery. This required a lengthy discussion. An airborne delivery was ruled out. Even private airplanes were tracked by radar, and if in doubt as to identity and purpose, they would be intercepted or brought down. Likewise, a ground-based method seemed impossible. For instance, one could, in principle, envisage a panel van, carrying a warhead, somehow being driven across a border from Mexico or Canada, through the USA, and to its destination by two drivers who could not easily pass as locals. Likewise, the complications of transporting a warhead to Europe or the Far East, then bringing it overland to its target location seemed equally fraught. This left us with a seaborne method of delivery. A commercial transport, as in the case of a container ship, was out of the question. A great deal of paper documentation would be required. Even though a minority of containers are actually opened and the content inspected, they were generally x-rayed and monitored for radiation. Private ocean-going sailing vessels were more promising. These are left alone in international waters and can generally come and go from designated small-vessel moorings. Moreover, such vessels can be crewed by no more than two people. A nuclear warhead could be disguised as part of a freshwater tank or as a fuel tank for an auxiliary engine. We decided to explore this option further and then report back within a month.

Item 3 consisted of a preliminary estimate of the number and types of people needed for the operation. Khan would, of necessity, be responsible for personnel in the laboratory and for fitting the warhead inside a containment compatible with the vessels. We decided that the vessels should be acquired in Pakistan, or possibly India or Bangladesh, and that they would be bought on behalf of a shell company. They would then be collected by crews engaged by the shell company and sailed to an anchorage in Pakistan. In the meantime, four special service soldiers from the elite detachment, charged with security for the laboratory in Rawalpindi, would be seconded to the operation. After selection, they would be given training in the Maldives in the handling of ocean-going sailing yachts. A necessary cover story would have them employed by a company that intended to offer charter tours in the area of the Maldives archipelago. In parallel, Hasina and I would do the scouting for suitable anchorages close to St Petersburg and at a location on Long Island.

Item 4 was devoted to security. Activities within Pakistan would take advantage of procedures that were used in the early days of the clandestine Pakistani nuclear programme. Khan was confident that he could tap into the security systems set up to fund and arm sections of the Taliban and opposition groups in the disputed parts of the Kashmir. The art of producing fake passports and identity papers has a long tradition within the security apparatus in Pakistan. Hasina and

I had been the beneficiaries of that system. Likewise, the four individuals who would crew the delivery vessels would be supplied with false identities and relevant documentation. The assessment was that the main need for security measures would be in the aftermath when every intelligence agency in the world would focus their attention on finding the perpetrators.

Item 5 was a brief rundown on the funding of the operation. The budget turned out to be remarkably modest, considering what we were intending to achieve. It is reputed that funding by Al Qaeda of the 9/11 attack was in the tens of thousands of dollars. Allowing for inflation, our budget would be in the same ball park, in the hundreds of thousands of dollars. We had the great advantage of the warheads being essentially free. The rest was principally the cost of two ocean-going yachts, and their modifications, some airfares, and not much else. We decided on a timeframe of more than one year but less than two years.

* * *

There was just enough time left to wind things up and to get us to the airport. None of us felt like celebrating. In the back of our minds was the thought that, maybe, this time, the world would come to its senses. We agreed to stay in touch through the dark Web.

Planning, Watching and Waiting

Some 18 hours later, we were back in Oxford. The first port of call was to retrieve Eden. He seemed pleased to see us. We had bought him a new pair of running shoes. Then there was a need for some quality time together. The summer holidays had another week to go, so we decided to take the tent and walk for a few days upstream along the Thames. Eden could try out his new shoes, and we could wind down. At night, we pitched the tent and became sardines on sleeping mats. There was a chance to sit outside before bedtime and to look at the stars. Hasina and I decided to temporarily forget about the days in Karachi and to act as if life was back to normal.

The students were returning to the university, and we reverted back to our old routines. But the decisions made in Karachi were never far away from our thoughts. The pandemic was under control aside from the odd local flare-up. The testing and tracking machinery had finally been bedded in, and it seemed unlikely that there would be another spike in infections and deaths. The prime minister appeared on prime-time television, patted himself on the back, praised the unique fighting spirit of the British people, and declared victory over the virus. Shops, cafés and pubs were gradually springing back to life. The financial markets were in full recovery mode, and wealth was being created yet again. As it turned out, the celebrations were premature. The virus came back with a vengeance, and we were back to wearing face masks and being wary of people in the streets.

Our nuclear family had institutionalized the post-dinner time being set aside for conversation. Each one had to describe the activities and events of the day and then give a rundown on what was on the agenda the next day. Then, we asked each other what had made us happy that day, or sad, or angry. Hasina was hardly ever angry, but she could be saddened when the university fell down on its lack of pastoral care. I was habitually enraged by the news bulletin, while Eden took a dim view of being fouled on the football pitch. He was happy when his essays got high marks and when there was caramel ice cream for sweets. He would usually wander off to bed with a book after the regulation kiss on the forehead.

At one level, our lives had returned to their regular beat within a month after we had returned from the meeting with Khan in Karachi. We were back to the daily grind of teaching, writing, and talking to students and colleagues. I was still expected to go to meetings but had long since abandoned my involvement at the IISS in London. At another level, we were acutely aware that our lives were about to change beyond recognition and never to return to the old state. It was time to begin work on the agenda from Karachi.

* * *

During the weekend, when Eden was out and about with his school friends, Hasina and I went out for a walk along the Oxford Canal. We needed to talk, and it seemed to us that discussions worked best when on foot.

"We are in charge of deciding on the target locations, and then the scouting, and finally working out the details of access and security in the target areas."

I was reminding myself and Hasina of what had been agreed in Karachi. Hasina continued.

"We decided that we should find two targets: one in the USA

and one in Russia. Those two countries have the majority of nuclear warheads. The USA is essentially in charge of the world economy. The old saying is: 'When the USA sneezes, the rest of the world catches a cold.' Even though Russia is a pale shadow of its former status as a superpower, it still remains significant by being a disloyal opposition. Aside from our two relatively humble warheads, they are inviolate against any type of attack from any other country.

"The centre of financial and political gravity is on the East Coast of the USA, with the epicentres being New York and Washington DC. Metaphorically speaking, the people who consider themselves to be the masters of the universe should be in sight of the mushroom cloud but not targeted directly. When it comes to Russia, the Kremlin is very much where the power is located. It is impossible for us to get anywhere near Moscow. St Petersburg, by virtue of its great symbolic value, is the next best target if one is going to attract attention from the decision-makers in the Kremlin. The contribution of Russia to global warming is modest, aside from it being a major exporter of coal, oil and gas but merits being a target as a demonstration that Russia is a victim but not a perpetrator."

I was impressed. "What you say makes sense to me. So, we have identified the rough locations of two targets. Now for the specifics."

"I have never been near either of the two places. I have been to the West Coast of the USA for a workshop, but I have never been to Russia. Have you?" she said.

"Many years ago, I did a postdoc in the US and drove hither and yonder just to see what was there. In the end, I decided it was not my kind of place. I have visited the USA several times since then, mostly on nuclear business, before and during my years at the IAEA. Once I went to the UN in New York as an aide to ElBaradei. In recent years, I have struck the USA off my visiting list. A long time ago, before the USSR imploded, I decided that I needed an adventure and travelled on the Trans-Siberian Express from Germany to the Pacific Coast. I shared a compartment with a nuclear submarine captain who was on his way, with his family, to take up a command with the Pacific Fleet in Vladivostok. I stopped in several places along the way. It was very interesting but tedious at times. I have never been to St Petersburg. I think we need to start with Google and then invest in some maps. We will need to visit while masquerading as sight-seeing tourists. I have been to Long Island many years ago and visited Brookhaven National Labs to talk about the disposal of nuclear waste."

We had turned around and were heading home for coffee and croissants. Eden was probably not far away, and we did not want him to think that he had been abandoned. Also, Google was waiting.

During the next two days, we both went searching on the internet and came to remarkably similar conclusions. Nassau on Long Island was the sort of place where a yacht was one amongst thousands and could come and go without attracting much attention. There was also some scope for anchoring up for one or two days outside designated harbours. The internet had very little to say about marinas near St Petersburg. The delta of the River Neva looked more promising on the map. There were also some islands in the bay offshore from the city. It definitely needed a visit.

Hasina was not wildly enthusiastic about a visit to the USA, so I volunteered to go to Long Island and do the scouting. Neither of us had ever been to St Petersburg. We decided on a joint expedition during the term break. We had mixed feelings about the likelihood of being involved in a plan to devastate one of the world's greatest treasure troves of architecture and works of art. There was a consolation of a kind that, in common with Venice, St Petersburg would not survive global warming and rising sea levels before the end of the century. The other complication was that there were few notable alternative targets in Russia that were within our reach or of sufficient importance.

It was too late to allow emotion to interfere with what we believed was necessary. In weak moments, we wished that the world community would join forces and embark on a credible and executable plan to limit global warming to less than two degrees. But rationally, we could not see any likelihood of that kind of action. It seemed that we were the last best chance for long-term survival.

The travel industry had fallen on hard times during the first onslaught of the pandemic. For a while, we were concerned with the possible total shutdown of flights across the Atlantic. I was fortunate to be eligible for a relatively early vaccination. By early April, I had got my second jab and was permitted to fly to the US, subject to being tested at both ends.

There was a gap in my regular life of 10 days in the middle of the university term. I booked a return flight to JFK and a week in a hotel on the waterfront, roughly in the middle of the territory to be investigated. I took the precaution of paying for the tickets in cash and using one of the passports and identities supplied by Qadeer Khan. The time might come when the travels of an Oxford academic might raise eyebrows in certain quarters.

On the first day, I booked a full-day cruise and joined an assorted group of domestic tourists in order to get a good feeling for the landscape and the anchorages. There were a lot of them, but I was particularly interested in the ones where the 50 to 60 feet ocean-going sailing yachts were moored offshore. There were a couple to choose from. The next day I found a shop near the hotel that seemed to stock every nautical map known to humankind. I also invested in a guide to Nassau and another book that claimed to be the bible of ocean cruising along the Atlantic coast of the USA. After lunch, I found a strategically located outdoor café; it overlooked the anchorage of a large number of sailing vessels. Later in the afternoon, some of the empty mooring sites were gradually being occupied by arrivals. There were numerous international registrations and flags to be seen. There did not seem to be any obvious policing of the area, or any security arrangements, such as CCTV cameras. There was a sign informing visiting sailors that moorage was free for the first three days. It all seemed fairly laid-back. I waited until dusk and then went off in search of dinner. The following morning, I went back to inspect the area at close quarters. A 15-metre sloop named Boudicca, claiming to be from Plymouth, could be seen next to a buoy, and another advertised itself as St Lucia from Stockholm. Further out, there was one from either Australia or New Zealand – at a distance, the flags were too similar. In the afternoon, I did a similar survey of another marina filled with assorted yachts. The arrangements seemed comparable to that of my first choice, although a greater percentage of the vessels were smaller and were moored in designated bays. Presumably these were reserved for local residents.

On another day, I signed on with a cruise to the nearby islands. There were certainly bays where a vessel could find undisturbed anchorage for a night or two. Back on shore, I sat down with my guidebook and maps and marked the areas I had investigated and added a few annotations. The final day was devoted to a ferry ride to Manhattan, just for old times' sake. The Empire State Building was still there, but it did not seem as impressive as I remembered from my youth. I had a look at the site of the 9/11 attack and then a walk around Times Square. It was less tacky but still very American, as I remembered. Then, it was home to Oxford.

A few days before the end of term, Eden came home from school with a letter saying that a week-long trip to France was being organized for him and his classmates during the long summer break.

The first wave of the pandemic had petered out, and Eurostar was back in action. Teachers were going along, and the idea was to introduce the students to French culture as well as giving them an opportunity to meet French students of the same age. We thought it was a wonderful idea. It was time for Eden to discover that the world was his oyster. Two weeks later, Eden, after a couple of hugs and kisses, was on his way to Paris. The same day Hasina and I were on our way to St Petersburg. We had made a booking at a hotel on the banks of the Neva. We travelled with false passports, courtesy of Khan, just to be on the safe side. The densities of tourists coming and going were relatively low, and it was just possible, but unlikely, that a bored immigration official might chase us back to the IAEA if we had decided to travel with our real identities. We did not want to be on the record as having visited.

On the first day, we simply put on our running shoes and went walking in the centre of the town. In the 1700s, Peter the Great lavished his attention and treasure and let the architects and artisans loose. We agreed that he had matched Louis XIV, the Sun King, for splendour and excess. A harbour cruise was on the agenda the next day. We had a guidebook and kept track of the sights as we covered the network of waterways that made up the delta of the Neva River. There were two areas that could be classified as marinas. Both of these seemed to belong to a club. There was an old and downtrodden one and a much larger marina known as the St Petersburg Central Yacht Club near the mouth of the Neva and in sight of the city centre. We visited the latter and discovered that there was a section devoted to visitors, some from far away. Near the mouth of the Neva, there were several small islands known as the Kirov Islands. We booked an all-day harbour cruise to check out the possibility of finding places to anchor for a day or two. The Kvestovsky and Vasilievski were the two main nearby islands. Both turned out to be developed as tourist traps. There seemed to be yachts and other vessels anchored in various places, but these could belong to residents. Another possibility might be to remain in the Gulf of Finland within 50 kilometres of St Petersburg and then make the final approach to the target area two days before detonation.

We took two days off from the scouting and became regular tourists. We joined an excursion on a river boat with a mixed group of sightseers up the Neva as far as Lake Ladoga. It was a nice sunny day and was definitely worth doing. Finally, we returned to the yacht club for another look. Some of the visiting yachts had left in the meantime, and there were some new ones. There was a shop and office inside the compound that sold all manner of nautical things. We came across nautical maps of the Gulf of Finland and of the local area of the approach to St Petersburg. We bought those. The man behind the counter had good English, so we explained that we had a good friend in the UK who was thinking of sailing into the Baltic Sea as far as St Petersburg later in the summer. We were assured that our friend would be most welcome and well looked after. Then we went back to the hotel and packed our bags.

* * *

We got back a day before Eden returned from France. He was brimming over with excitement about Paris and France. He thought the Louvre was "cool" but a bit tedious after a while. The group had stayed in a real French chateau with a moat and a secret tunnel. They had met up with a group of French students while at the chateau. They were really nice but beat Eden and his team at football. Unhappily, they had declined a rematch of rugby. Back in Paris, they had a day of lectures on French history and culture. They were told that it was just bad luck that Napoleon had lost at Waterloo. He thought that Paris was more interesting than Oxford, and we tended to agree with that. We confessed that we had been to St Petersburg on a holiday while he was away. He did not appear to mind.

* * *

Several encoded messages from Khan were waiting for us. An unlisted shell company had been set up in Karachi, named Bengal Bay Cruising Ltd. The company had bought two cruising yachts from private vendors in Kolkata, and the vessels would be delivered within two months. The two crews had been dispatched to the Maldives to be trained up. Finally, a message said that our two "devices" were being assembled. We responded by sending a report of our investigations in Nassau and St Petersburg. Two parcels containing nautical charts and other useful information were then dispatched to the address of the shell company. Progress was being made.

According to the *Financial Times*, the world economy was recovering, albeit very gradually. Central banks and governments were continuing their policies of pumping vast sums of money into the financial system in order to stimulate economic activity and ensure adequate liquidity for the financial institutions. The totality of sums was comparable to 10% of the collective GDP of the world, and national debt levels were projected to approach 130% of GDP within the year. The one saving grace was that money was cheap, and the servicing of the debt was manageable for the rich world. The balancing act of keeping a lid on the pandemic death rates versus economic recovery was gradually shifting towards the latter. Many of the less developed countries had given up on the death rates in favour of keeping the population in work. There were signs of politics getting increasingly ugly.

During the height of the pandemic, lifestyles did change for the better from the point of view of those that were concerned with global warming. In the developed countries, close to half of the working population was either asked to stay at home non-working, or was working from home. Large sections of industry simply closed down for the duration. In order to suppress the infection rates, many lifestyle activities, such as hospitality, tourism, sport, education, entertainment and retail were forcibly shut down. The consequence was that energy consumption and other contributions to greenhouse gas emissions plummeted. The activities were gradually brought back on stream as the infection rates decreased. Life was returning to "normal". Established industries were bailed out even though they had been accounting for disproportionate contributions to greenhouse emissions. On the other hand, investing in new 'green' industries was neglected. It was beginning to look like the old "normal" was going to be restored at exorbitant cost, thus starving a new "normal" of funds for the foreseeable future. We thought that by the time global warming had worked its way to the top of the agenda, Western countries would still be mired in incomplete recovery and in austerity imposed by the debts remaining from the cost of the pandemic. These were the gloomy views one would gain from the daily news bulletins and from modelling of the future. The year 2020, when the pandemic hit, turned out to be the hottest on record. It was also the year when unemployment and workers laid-off reached heights not seen since the 1930s. The large corporations shed employees in the tens of thousands, while most of the chief executives continued to award themselves bonuses. It became increasingly clear that we were not in it together. Poverty and hunger were stalking the streets of the slums, and the middle classes had become downwardly mobile and found themselves living on the overdraft and frequenting food banks.

It could have been worse. At least Trump lost the election, and most of the single-issue political parties and movements were beginning to fade while the green parties were gaining in strength. Maybe we were not going to have a rerun of the 1930s after all. Our worry was that the "deep" state would once again ensure a reversion to the old "normal".

We had to wait and see.

The Decision is Nigh

Christmas 2021 was approaching. We had just come out of a short cold spell, which ended with an unusual snow fall of 10 centimetres. The South of England had ground to a halt, and there were mutterings about: "So much for global warming!" We knew better. Eden had long since realized that Santa Claus was a myth, but he had prepared a wish list, just in case. Our hardy Siberian pine, which had lived mainly outside in a pot for many years, was getting ready to be carried inside once more for a couple of weeks. The cardboard box with decorations had been taken down from the loft. We were getting ready for Christmas. I went off to the supermarket and collected the goose that had been ordered. While in Vienna, we had become accustomed to doing Christmas like the Austrians. Therefore, Christmas Eve was the time for eating oneself silly to the accompaniment of Mozart while polishing off a better-than-average bottle of red wine. This year we had decided that Eden was allowed his very own glass of watered-down wine. I suspected that he would rather have had some juice, but it was nice to be inducted into adulthood. We finished the meal with homemade ice cream that Hasina had made especially for the occasion. Then, Eden had to wait for the presents while we had coffee. Finally, there was time to hand out the presents. As expected, Eden ended up with the greater number, which included a new backpack, a boxed set of Pippi Longstocking books, another book entitled *Why is it so?* a steam engine and his very first semi-smart mobile phone. There were also the regulation clothes. He had grown out of the ones he got last year.

Hasina got a proper eiderdown padded jacket, a new food processor to replace the one that had died recently, and the latest historical novel written by Hilary Mantel. I was pleased to get a new electric shaver and my very first tablet, plus six pairs of socks. It was probably very much like the kind of Christmas that was being had in every house up and down the street. Each time Hasina and I looked at each other, we recognized the same thought: "Will there be another one like this?"

Eden was beginning to flag, and I followed him upstairs. He was clutching his spoils. Once tucked into bed, he looked at me and said, "Why did you give me books about Pippi Longstocking? Is it not a book about a girl?"

"Yes, it is," I said. "I read the books when I was your age. They changed the way I thought about life and the world. Pippi made her own rules, and the world was hers for the taking. I hope you will like reading about Pippi."

"I'll let you know," he said and nodded off alongside the steam engine.

I went down again and found Hasina curled up on the sofa. "I wish we could bottle today so that it would last forever. How is Eden?" she said.

"He was not entirely sure about Pippi Longstocking, but the steam engine was a hit. I think we may have a budding engineer on our hands. Do you think we should seek professional help for this problem?"

"You're being silly," she said. "Engineers aren't all bad. After all, I married one."

Neither of us wanted to talk about the future, much less about the next year. At least we had each other and a mutual tacit agreement to let each day bring whatever it had in store for us.

Later on, in bed, Hasina whispered into my ear, "Promise me

that you will remember this day forever."

"I promise that I will."

* * *

On Christmas Day, we were invited to lunch with our friends and colleagues. Sheila and Stephen had a son, Anthony, of roughly the same age as Eden, and we had a long-standing reciprocal arrangement to play hosts to each other's offspring whenever academic duties sent either set of parents away. The two boys got on very well and did not mind being sent into exile from time to time. Today Eden brought the steam engine in his new backpack. The two of them soon had the engine running and had lost all interest in the older generation.

The traditional British Christmas Day luncheon generally lasts until early evening and involves near-continuous eating and drinking. Given that we were four academics belonging to the same institution, albeit in different departments, much of the conversation dealt with the mysteries of Oxford University and how bureaucracy was driving us around the bend from time to time, and how difficult it was to get anything done. These kinds of conversations usually ended with an agreement that Oxford was a wonderful institution in which to work. Yet again, I made the observation that each day I could enter a parallel universe populated by a different species, with institutional memories and traditions going back nearly a thousand years.

By mid-afternoon, we were on the third bottle of red. The boys upstairs had forsaken the steam engine in favour of computer games. Downstairs, the conversation was getting deeper.

The four of us had one thing in common. We were at the stage of our lives and careers when we were beginning to question the meaning of life in general and our own lives in particular. We were past the stage of thinking that this was the best of all possible worlds, but not past the stage that it could not be improved on. Most of our lives had been devoted to being at one or other intellectual frontier, and from time to time, we had been able to push a tiny part of it an inch or two forward. We had given ourselves a licence to question everything, and to harbour unconventional thoughts and views, especially after two bottles of red. In our different ways, we agreed that 2020 had been a dreadful year – but only marginally worse than many earlier years that had also been pretty bad. Stephen was a political scientist who thought that the state of politics and governance in the English-speaking nations had reached a new nadir. Sheila was one of the rare high-flying female economists who could mix it with the best. She was in the mould of the likes of Stiglitz and Piketty. Her work dealt with the origins, effects and amelioration of economic inequality and was highly regarded even by those who were supporters of the status quo. Hasina was the kind of historian who had branched out from dealing with the nuts and bolts of regional history, to examining the impact of history on nationalism and current political trends. I wondered where I fitted into the intellectual territories of the group. Technically, I was a hard-boiled nuclear engineer. I had changed in recent years under the influence of Hasina and Khan, among others. What we had in common was the belief in change. None of us believed that a return to the old normal was a viable option. Rather than descending into silly parlour games at the end of an alcoholic day, we decided to state our cases, in a wine-sodden mini-workshop on the banks of the Thames, for a better new year.

Sheila was elected to open the proceedings.

Sheila had made a living out of demonstrating that the main factor in driving inequality was the increasingly unequal accumulation of capital and wealth. She decided to share with us some of her thoughts on inequality and how to deal with the problem.

"Investment of surplus capital has generated a typical return of 8% per annum in recent years. A wage earner could on average do no better than expecting an annual rise in income of roughly 3%, equal to the increase in GDP. The compounding effect would predict that ultimately one person would have all the wealth, and the rest of us would have little, or no, wealth. In 2020, there were 89 billionaires in the UK with a combined estimated wealth equivalent to 30% of the total annual economic output of the UK. The richest person in the UK in 2020 had a personal wealth of £16.2 billion, while one needed a mere £120 million of wealth in order to get on the list of the thousand richest individuals in the UK. For comparison, the median household income in the UK in 2019 was £29,400, which was £400 (1.4%), up on the year before. Some 30 million households had an income less than that and generated a trivial increase in wealth. There are a variety of ways to avoid paying much tax on the annual increase in wealth, where some ways are legal and others are at least morally dodgy. I am one of several economists who are proponents of a wealth tax or possibly a levy on the annual increase in wealth. Some countries have tried, and failed, to introduce such a tax. There are numerous problems. Some could be fixed by having a universal identity card and then using the secure knowledge of identity to link all financial transactions to the identity. A large, but unknown, proportion of wealth resides in tax havens in accounts that are effectively anonymous. In this case, one would need something akin to a bounty scheme. A person, or entity, that leaked information of interest to a taxation authority would receive a share of the spoils, thus encouraging revelation of untaxed assets. There are, of course, a great number of loopholes that would need to be plugged. A typical wealth tax might be a levy of 3 to 4% on the annual gain in wealth, in combination with a rebate for loss of wealth. Could it happen? I think it might, after a major collapse of the world economic and financial system."

It was the turn of Hasina to air her latest thinking about history.

"I will begin with the restatement of the famous saying, 'Those who do not learn history are doomed to repeat it.' My current project has the working title of 'Modern History – Myth, Fabrication, Half-truth, or Factual. Does it matter?' A couple of years ago, I bought a copy of the high school history syllabus from various countries that had been involved in WWII. Between my dear husband and I, we have a working knowledge of most of the languages, or we sought help from some friends and colleagues. I then categorized the relative importance, as measured by the fraction of total pages in each syllabus, relating to particular events in modern history for each country versus that devoted to the entire period of 1850–1950. This was then further sub-divided into the relative numbers of words for the five years leading up to WWII, the five years of the war, and the five years after the war. Then, for each country, I identified the single most important wartime event, in terms of word count, for each five-year period. From these events, I isolated the one single event with the greatest historical impact in terms of word count for each country. I also identified the extent of commemorations of events in WWII for each country in the year 2000 as a measure of long-term impact of the war in the chosen countries. The study is in its infancy, but it is already apparent that there are as many versions of the history of WWII as there are countries. I can take you through a couple of examples. The retrieval of the British Expeditionary Force from Dunkerque at the beginning of the war is commemorated in the UK each year, but the siege of Stalingrad does not rate a mention in the UK syllabus. The bombing of Guernica by the

Luftwaffe is commemorated in Spain, the bombing of Dresden is commemorated in Germany, but neither gives comparable space to other events. Let me finish with the observation that learning from history can work in different ways. For instance, the lesson of WWII for Europe was 'never again', which led to the EU, social democracy, and relative peace in Europe for three generations, so far. The lesson for the English-speaking countries was that 'might is right' and 'capitalism rules OK'. Therefore, the latter nations carried on going to war in the developing world while being terrified of Marxism and command economy. The lesson for the USSR was that 'the invasions from the West had to stop'."

A slightly different historical slant on political science came from Stephen. He started with a brief rundown on democracy.

"As a system proposed by Montesquieu in the 1700s, it was intended to replace tyranny such as the monarchical arrangement where all power was vested in one person, be it a king, queen, emperor, dictator, etc. A better democratic system had separation of powers, such as being vested in an executive, a legislative assembly, and a judiciary. These were intended to be independent of each other. The legislature would be elected by an informed and thoughtful electorate that represented the will of the people. The executive would be charged with implementing the decisions; the legislative body and the judiciary would be charged with the enforcement of the laws based on a constitution. The underlying justification of such a system was that it was more likely to be in tune with the needs of the nation rather than be determined by the needs and wishes of the monarch or the tyrant. It now seems that democracy has fallen into disrepute and disrepair. There has been a steady trend towards increasing the power of the executive at the expense of the legislature and the judiciary. Accordingly, the separation of powers, and the checks and balances, are weakened.

Democracy is increasingly being defined by politics, where policies are defined by what is good for the party rather than what is in the interest of the nation. An election is typically won by accumulating more than half of the votes that are being cast and after a turnout of less than 70% of eligible voters casting a valid vote. Another problem is that parties have become tribal and are increasingly becoming adept at manipulating the electorates by focussing on so-called 'dog-whistle' messages or on promises that often are merely aspirational rather than intended to be deliverable. There is a clear intention by parties to mislead rather than inform and enlighten the electorate. Social media have, on balance, made the situation worse and play a major role in giving powers to the national governments that they have not deserved. I will finish by saying that Hasina and I have a lot in common in our views of what is wrong. We also agree that the EU has gone further than others in constructing a viable post-democratic model."

Then, it was up to me to lay out my intellectual wares.

"I will begin by reminding you about how the explosive eruption of Krakatoa in 1883 caused a measurable change in the global climate for a few years. I will also remind you that for all practical purposes, the earth has been treated as an infinitely large rubbish bin for humanity from the time when we entered the industrial era some 200 years ago. There is a burgeoning database, and overwhelming scientific evidence, that human activities are changing the global climate, mainly due to a greenhouse effect caused by some billions of tons of CO_2 being pumped into the atmosphere each year. On average, the earth is now more than one degree warmer than in pre-industrial times. The last 10 years have been the warmest on record. The warming effect is magnified in the polar regions by a factor of two to three. There are other manifestations of climatic change, and these were predicted by modelling, such as shrinking of glaciers, melting of sea ice at the North Pole, and net melting of the ice covers on Greenland and on the Antarctic continent. Droughts and floods are becoming more severe, and storms are becoming more ferocious and damaging – again, as predicted. There is good evidence that the world's climate will reach a 'tipping point' at an average temperature rise of 3 degrees, when the Arctic tundra begins to thaw, thereby releasing vast quantities of locked-up CO_2 and methane, where the latter is a more potent greenhouse gas by a factor of 30. Beyond the 'tipping point', there is no going back. Extrapolations of the present economic growth model, and of promises made by the major contributors to global warming, suggest that the generation of our children will inherit an unliveable world unless we begin to think seriously about removing greenhouse gases from the atmosphere. I will finish by saying that my remaining hope is for a severe shock to the existing system that will set us on a new course for humanity. It is interesting, and maybe hopeful, that the four of us have come broadly to the same conclusions concerning the ills of the world, even though we start from different parts of the intellectual territory."

Sheila opened another bottle and said, "After all of that, I feel that I ought to be thoroughly depressed, but I am an optimist. I think, somehow, the human species will muddle through. What do you think, Hasina?"

"I think it will be painful beyond anything we have ever known," was the quiet answer.

Sheila put her arms around Hasina and said, "In the meantime, let us drink and be merry. We have lived charmed lives so far. Let us make the most of it."

The boys reappeared and accused us of being tiddly. We could only agree with that observation but claimed that it was a necessary part of the Christmas tradition. It was getting dark outside, so we had a strong cup of coffee and found our way home.

Eden decided it had been a really good day. He had read the first two chapters of Pippi Longstocking that morning. And had decided that he liked it.

"She has red pigtails, can lift her horse, has a chest full of gold coins, and she has been everywhere with her sea-faring dad. Including Surabaya. Where is Surabaya?"

I told him that many years ago, I had travelled through Indonesia and had slept on the side of the road when the minibus broke down outside Surabaya. The mosquitoes were ferocious. Eden was suitably impressed. He promised to keep reading. Then, he got his regulation kiss on the forehead before bedtime.

Quality time for Hasina and me on the sofa was all that was left of Christmas.

"In case this is our last Christmas together, I will imprint the day in my brain," said Hasina. I nodded in silent agreement.

* * *

The New Year came and went. Hasina reminded me that I used to claim that it was not a new year we were given but a second-hand one. I responded, not with much joy, that this time it was going to be a genuinely new and different year, but it would be devoid of happiness for most. We were both dealing with a sense of foreboding but trying desperately to act as if nothing had changed.

* * *

We had scored a win. The Trump presidency had been consigned to the scrapheap of history, with Biden getting a hard-fought majority. There was optimism in the air. Three of the many groups that had been working day and night to develop a reasonably effective vaccine had made good headway. The concoctions had passed the required trials, and production was being scaled up. One unhappy sign of a return to business as usual was that the first batches were reserved for the countries that had funded the R&D. Europe, P. R. China and North America triumphantly claimed victory in the war against the dreaded virus and promised that the rest of the world would get their share as soon as possible, and at concessional rates. The virus was not yet finished with us. Two weeks before Easter, a mutant strain appeared, this time in South America. The recently developed vaccines turned out to be reasonably effective against the new strain, but the rates of vaccinations were outpaced by the virus. Borders were closed, and vaccines were hoarded by the countries that made them.

I had begun to think about what Sheila had said during the wine-sodden conversation at Christmas. It seemed to me that inequality was in the same category as global warming. Something had to be done about an unsustainable economic model. The solution to global warming was inextricably intertwined with a model that made a tiny minority obscenely wealthy, and left the majority to be either a herd of consumers on soma or trapped in never-ending poverty. The pandemic had the perverse effect of increasing the inequality, at least in the short term, and of setting the stage for an even more dramatic redistribution of wealth in the longer term, to the overall detriment of the majority of nations, and to the 90% of the world's population that went into the pandemic with little, or no, wealth. Within a year after the arrival of the vaccines, the markets had substantially recovered – even though the world's population living in absolute poverty (on less than $1.9 in purchasing power parity per day) had increased by more than 100 million. On the other hand, during the pandemic, the 10 richest individuals in the UK had doubled their wealth, while well over 4 billion had now fallen back into relative poverty. The effect was described as a disconnect between the markets and the real economy; this was deemed by some economists to be a mystery.

There was at least one explanation for the capitalists taking advantage of Black Swan events. The financial world was awash with cash as the pandemic struck, being hoarded by corporations with strong cash flows, by wealthy individuals, and by private equity funds. As well, debt was extraordinarily cheap. The amount of cash looking for profitable investments was well above 10 trillion dollars. When the markets crashed, the equities became cheap. Many well-established and normally profitable companies ran into problems with cash flow and were either forced into bankruptcy or were available as cheap takeover targets. The financial scavengers with ready cash could acquire distressed assets at bargain-basement prices. Once the financial system had recovered, as it always did, the investors would have doubled their money. Such opportunities were not available to the humble wage earners, many of whom were no longer earning a wage. The financial world was cruel for most but a gold mine for a very few with apartments in Monte Carlo or private islands in the Caribbean. It seemed to me that it was yet another reason to bring down the temple. The pandemic had been a useful Black Swan. We were about to unleash another. This Swan was aimed at the jugular of those that thought they were immune.

* * *

During the Easter long weekend of 2021 and the following two weeks, several messages arrived from Khan. He had been watching the news as avidly as we had and had come to the same conclusions. His recommendation was that we should act. Hasina and I had talked the issues through to the bitter end, and we agreed.

The next message said that construction of the two "devices" was complete. They were of the type where the cores consisted of highly enriched uranium surrounded by a blanket for enhanced yield estimated to be equivalent to 70 kilotons of explosive power; this was two to three times the power of the nuclear weapons that had devastated Hiroshima and Nagasaki in 1945. The message brought home to us the enormity of what we intended to unleash on the world. I had read about the bomb tests in the 1960s and 1970s, before the testing was done underground, and was able to visualize the likely devastation that could be inflicted on a metropolitan area.

A week later, we were told that the two crews were back from training in the Maldives. It had gone well, and the crews had received their certificates of competence in open sea navigation and in the handling of small sailing yachts. As if on command, a tropical storm of modest strength had come along during the period, and both crews had demonstrated that they could handle adverse weather conditions. In order to improve security, the two yachts had been registered in Myanmar and purported to be owned by a shell company there. The recent military coup in Myanmar had been a bonus for us. There would be no chance for anyone to trace the provenance of the yachts in a country that was essentially lawless. Khan had used such companies before as a transit point for nuclear-related hardware during the sanction-busting days. He was now in the process of acquiring a semi-derelict boathouse in Karachi so that the final modifications and outfitting of the vessels could be carried out in secret. When it came to security and secrecy, Khan was a master practitioner, it seemed. We congratulated him on his work. During the next couple of months, the vessels and crews would be cruising in the Bay of Bengal to make sure that the yachts were fully seaworthy and to allow the crews to become aware of any unexpected problems.

Then it was time to think about time, motion and distances. A quick look at the map showed that there was a lot of sailing ahead of the two crews. It seemed clear that the quickest route would be around the Arabian Peninsula, through the Suez Canal, and into the Mediterranean. From there, the two yachts would keep company through the Strait of Gibraltar. One crew would then head north-east through the Channel and into the Gulf of Bothnia. The other would turn west from Gibraltar across the Atlantic to the East Coast of the USA. It would be a long journey for both crews. They would need to arrive in the target areas at the same pre-determined time. At that moment, one could think in terms of departing Karachi during the autumn of 2022, after the September–October storm season, and arriving at the destination no later than the summer of 2023. I needed to do some legwork on serious ocean sailing.

Several yacht clubs have compiled useful information about routes and durations of stages. The route from Karachi via the Suez Canal to Gibraltar was rated as 4800 nautical miles requiring 45 days of sailing at an average speed of 5 knots. The stages from Gibraltar to St Petersburg, and Gibraltar to Nassau, were of distances 3200 and 4300 nautical miles, respectively, and of durations 30 and 35 days, again on the assumption of 5 knots average speed. In principle, the journey might not involve much more than three to four months of actual sailing days. However, one would need to accommodate adverse weather conditions from time to time, some rest and replenishing of provisions and supplies in harbours along the way, and include a margin for illness and repairs. For instance, the transit of the Suez Canal could involve a delay of some days. The approach to St Petersburg could be a major constraint. During the period from December to late April, the Bay of Finland would be icebound. Ice breakers generally kept an open access channel, but passage was treacherous, at best, for fragile sailing vessels. My judgement was that the crew should defer entering the North Sea until early May 2023. Departing Karachi in late autumn, we could reasonably expect the two yachts to be in the target areas in the mid-summer of 2023. I added a suggestion that the crews should have credible cover stories with suitable documentation in the case that officialdom took an interest along the way. We sent the information and suggestions to Khan to be checked and for agreement by the two crews. Then, there was a lull in the action.

* * *

The timings of the various stages of the operation could now be fleshed out. In consultation with Khan, we agreed that the crews should have a further outing to ensure that all was well with the vessels and that the crews were used to long periods of steady sailing under various weather conditions. We thought that a non-stop return journey from Karachi to the mouth of the Suez Canal during the month of March 2022 would be a suitable shake-down run. In the meantime, the boathouse in Karachi would be renovated and prepared for installation of the fake freshwater tanks. The intention was to have the work done before the autumn storm season. The vessels would then be taken to a safe anchorage. The last thing we wanted was for the vessels to be exposed to, and possibly damaged by, a tropical storm.

War in Europe

In late February 2022, Russia launched a full-scale invasion of Ukraine. Within a few months, the character of the hostilities had changed from an anticipated rapid and decisive Russian victory to a messy and bloody conflict with no clear winner. For those with long memories, the conflict began to have all the attributes of an old-fashioned European war.

Ukraine was neither a member of NATO nor of the EU. Accordingly, the carnage was confined to the Ukrainian battlefields, but the sympathies of NATO and EU member states were definitely with the Ukrainians. Political and economic sanctions against Russia had the effect of widening the cost of the conflict. The economies of the Western industrialized economies that had begun to recover from the Covid pandemic were now faced with rampant inflation and a potential worldwide recession.

Hasina and I had followed events in Europe with particular interest from the collapse of the USSR in 1997. On the grand geopolitical scale, it signified the end of the Cold War and the transition from a bipolar to a unipolar world order. From time to time, we had speculated on what would come next. We tended to agree that the rise of China would be the most prominent and defining trend. The main events were the unification of Germany and the many countries of Eastern Europe cutting their links to Russia in favour of the beckoning bright lights of Western Europe. Most joined NATO for reasons of security and gradually became members of an enlarged and prospering EU. There were a few exceptions. Belarus and Ukraine had been foundation members of the USSR and remained within the Russian sphere.

Neither of us felt that we had done sufficient homework to fully appreciate a rationale for a war between Ukraine and Russia. Hasina went off to the Bodleian Library to search the historical records while I went walking along the River Thames while Eden was in school.

One evening, Hasina and I decided to share our thinking. We were sitting in the lounge in semi-darkness with cups of coffee. Eden had gone to bed after doing his homework, followed by two chapters of Pippi Longstocking. I looked at Hasina and invited her to give me a short lecture on the history of Ukraine.

"What was to become Ukraine was the area where the great migrations to and from the heartland of Eurasia passed through the centuries. The Roman Empire had disintegrated into its western and eastern parts in Rome and Constantinople, respectively. The Vikings came rampaging from the west, and the Mongols came marauding from the east. Empires were created by conquest and subjugation but did not last for very long. The modern history of Ukraine began in the 1700s during the reign of Catherine the Great. By this time, Russia was an established empire. The Habsburg empire and Russia carved up Poland, and Catherine the Great acquired Crimea by conquest. A status quo in the areas that included the modern Ukraine then reigned for a century until WWI and its aftermath.

"In 1812, Napoleon and an army of 500,000 soldiers made an ill-fated attempt to launch a 'blitzkrieg' invasion of Russia. He was victorious in the battle of Borodino and entered a deserted Moscow, which was then set ablaze. The oncoming winter, and poor logistics, forced a retreat during which the bulk of his army perished from hunger, exhaustion and disease."

Hasina stopped to draw breath. My comment was to observe that

Hitler's invasion of the USSR was a rerun of Napoleon's disaster. In both cases, "King Winter" saved the day for the defenders, albeit at an enormous loss of life. Hasina then moved on to summarize events leading up to WWI and to describe how Russia fared during the war and its aftermath.

"The literature of the period occupies several shelf metres in the Bodleian and represents the work of a generation of historians. The best I can do is to give a brief summary of the outcome for Russia. One might describe WWI as the battle of the empires for pre-eminence in Europe. After a period of shifting alliances, Tsarist Russia found itself in bed with France and the British Empire, against the rest, with Germany being the most formidable foe. Russia could field an army of impressive size, but the leadership from Tsar Nicholas II at the top down to the senior military brass turned out to be inept and incoherent. The lack of functional logistics and the inadequate industrial support for a major campaign were fatal shortcomings. After a number of unsuccessful skirmishes with lesser enemies, the bulk of the army was deployed in the trenches in France. The Russian troops were no match for the German artillery and firepower and were decimated. By now, the national mood in Russia had changed for the worse, against the war and against the regime of Tsar Nicholas II. There were riots in the streets, and factory workers were downing tools. The Bolshevik party under the leadership of Lenin and Trotsky, with support from segments of the armed forces, gained control of Petrograd, which became Leningrad and, finally, St Petersburg. From there, the revolution spread to other cities and parts of the empire. In provinces with large non-Russian ethnic majorities, there was considerable resistance to the Bolsheviks. Some regions took advantage of the revolution to press for independence. It took a civil war lasting more than four years and costing millions of lives to consolidate the revolution and stabilize the Soviet-Russian regime. Ukraine was a case in point. Russia withdrew from WWI by signing peace treaties with the Central Powers. The Allied Powers intervened during the Civil War by occupying large areas of the former Russia until 1922. The fear of Marxism as an alternative model to capitalism had emerged as a geopolitical factor that would ultimately lead to a Cold War and a bipolar world order."

We needed a mid-evening snack and a coffee break before Hasina went on to WWII.

"The 1930s was a grim decade for most of the world due to a deep depression. Russia became the USSR with a focus on industrialization, collectivisation, russification and the healing of wounds from the civil war, starvation and deprivation. The Third World remained in the grips of colonial powers, and the European powers were still at each other's throats. Fascism, nationalism and xenophobia were on the rise. By the end of the decade, it was no longer a matter of if, but when the next pan-European war would come. It began with a civil war in Spain, with Germany playing a defining role on the side of the Falangists. In 1938, Germany annexed Austria. In the same year, a part of Czechoslovakia, Sudetenland, was also annexed by Germany. The Finnish-Russian Winter War raged for a few months in early 1940. By this time, Germany had invaded Poland, and WWII was underway. The Molotov-Ribbentrop treaty was signed in August 1939. It gave the USSR a period of grace to prepare itself for the inevitable German invasion of the USSR, but at a cost to Poland which was partitioned between Germany and the USSR. During the 1930s, Ukraine was a well-established and integrated member-republic of the Soviet Union but had suffered during a period of famine that may have killed some millions of Ukrainians and Russians.

"Germany invaded the USSR in the summer of 1941 with the

intention of emulating the blitzkrieg tactics that had given it near-total control of Western Europe in a matter of months. The size of territory and the willingness of the USSR to sacrifice lives slowed the advance down, and 'King Winter' came to the aid of the USSR. By the end of the war, the Soviet death toll during the war had reached an estimated 27 million (equivalent to some 15% of its pre-war population), while German losses on the eastern front were estimated at 4 million. There is a sense in which it could be said that WWII was won on the killing fields of the USSR. For comparison, the respective death tolls of the USA, France and the UK were roughly 300,000. The Chinese deaths, principally inflicted by Japan, before and during WWII, are estimated at just under 20 million."

The numbers quoted by Hasina left us with a sense of incomprehension and numbness about the scale of misery and suffering visited on some countries in an age when Europeans professed to be civilized and sophisticated.

Hasina had one additional piece of history that she thought might have a bearing on the reasons for the war in Europe in 2022.

"During the German occupation of Ukraine in WWII, the Ukrainian sense of nationhood re-emerged as a wish for independence. A Ukrainian Insurgent Army fought against both Germany and the USSR. The collapse of the USSR in 1997 gave Ukraine independence. A period of recession lasted while Ukraine made a transition from a centrally planned to a market economy. Its politics remained leaning towards Russia until the overthrow of the Yanukovych regime in 2014. Russia then reclaimed the Crimea and responded to unrest in the Donbas region by supporting a break-away secession by the Donbas region with a majority Russian population."

It had been a long evening. We decided to call it a day. I promised to do most of the talking about a possible analysis that could explain the Russian invasion of Ukraine. Later in the week, we had another session. I was primed to go into my lecturing mode.

"Near the end of WWII, when the outcome was reasonably certain, three meetings were held, in Tehran, Yalta and Potsdam, with the leaders of the Allies: Franklin D. Roosevelt, Joseph Stalin and Winston Churchill, and their advisers, in attendance. The one at Yalta was the most important. It was when the shape of the post-War world was decided. National borders in Europe were redrawn. Extents of punishment and rewards for bad and good behaviour were decided. Spheres of influence were defined. The UN was to be an over-arching organization, with the 'winners' in perpetual control. A collective framework for security in Europe, based on self-determination and democracy, was proposed. At best, it was a wish list with some glaring shortcomings. The Third World did not rate a mention; neither did colonialism nor mechanisms for dispute resolution.

"The friendship between the allied partners did not last. Having seen off Nazism, it was now a question of who was going to be the 'Master of the Universe'. There were only two credible contenders: either the USA or the USSR. There were two contenders, but with irreconcilable ideologies – capitalism, free markets, democracy and individualism versus communism, dictatorship of the proletariat, central planning and collectivism. Reciprocal demonization became the order of the day. Both sides dealt with real or imagined enemies within. Senator McCarthy launched a crusade to root out prominent Americans who were deemed to harbour communist sympathies, while Stalin sent ideological deviants to the Gulag. In the geopolitical arena, there were plenty of issues where the two sides could disagree.

"At the end of the war, Berlin was sub-divided into three zones, as was Germany, but found itself fully inside the Soviet zone that was to become East Germany. There were disputes between the former allies about access to Berlin through the Soviet zone. The acrimony got to a stage in June 1948 to the extent that the USSR blockaded all access by land. This triggered the first Berlin crisis of the Cold War. The US and UK proceeded to set up an air bridge in order to supply their Berlin zones with food and fuel. This went on for a year, at which point the USSR relented and reopened land access to Western Berlin.

"A legacy of past colonial times had left the Korean Peninsula partitioned into a North and a South. North Korea invaded the South in 1950, with support from the USSR. The intention was to rid the South of an authoritarian and corrupt regime and thereby achieve reunification. The USA intervened and a 3-year bloody Korean War ensued, with China entering the fray. The result ended as a pre-war status quo. The war in Korea was to be a foretaste of subsequent 'proxy wars' where former colonies suffered most of the loss of lives due to two or more groups of insurgents who fought a civil war while being supported by the USA and the USSR.

"The North Atlantic Treaty Organization (NATO) was enacted in April 1949 as a follow-on to the Marshall Plan of 1948. Both were US initiatives. The Marshall Plan was promoted as a scheme to rebuild the post-War economies of Western Europe. NATO was explicitly concerned with security and was implicitly to be a defensive bulwark against the USSR and as a means for Western Europe to be within the sphere of influence of the USA. Some years later, the USSR reciprocated with the enactment, in 1955, of the Warsaw Treaty, which brought the countries of Eastern and Central Europe into a defensive alliance with the USSR as the dominant partner.

"What became known as the Truman Doctrine was a policy that dove-tailed with that of NATO. In 1947, Truman enunciated the principle that the USA should offer support to countries or peoples that were threatened by the USSR or by communist insurgents. The doctrine was seen by the USSR as a declaration that would lead to a Cold War.

"After the collapse of the USSR in 1997, Russia could no longer be described as a communist country and an ideological threat to the security of the USA. Most of the countries in Eastern and Central Europe, formerly aligned with the USSR, joined NATO and the EU. Russia had to contemplate a new reality of NATO forces camped on the Western border of the 'Motherland'. By the end of 2021, Ukraine was the last buffer state that protected Russia from a sworn enemy in the West. The Russian fear was that, yet again, history would repeat itself, and armies would come from the West and would, once more, devastate Russia."

It was time for me to step down from my lectern and let Hasina have her say.

"You have made a good case for how the world might be viewed from the Kremlin. I remember the saying: 'Even paranoiacs can have enemies'. Thinking back to the rhetoric some months ago, it seems that the members of NATO were encouraging Ukraine to take a hard line in the confrontation with Russia. There was a sense that the various sides to the dispute had not thought through the consequences of talking themselves into a war. The NATO countries gave the impression of wishing to stand up against Russia without realizing that Ukraine would be the proxy doing the fighting. As it has turned out, the misery has been spread around by sanctions and disruptions to trade and commerce, rising inflation and increasing poverty. In game theory lingo, it has been a negative sum game. I have many questions. How, and when, will the war end? Does the war affect the project we have planned with Qadeer Khan? We may need to have a session with him."

Hasina was right. We needed to consider the new circumstances and how they would affect our plans. One certain outcome of the war was to change the rank order of issues. Headlines about global warming had disappeared from the front pages and from news bulletins. Additional resources were being allocated to defence and would not be available for investments in renewables and low-carbon industries. Rising costs of living were having the effect of relegating global warming to the luxury category. At the moment, there was little we could do about the war in Ukraine. I could speculate about Hasina's questions, however.

"Exhaustion of human and material resources could force Ukraine to accept defeat on the battlefield. For instance, the capture of Kharkiv and Odessa by Russian forces could be a major blow to Ukrainian morale. There was no immediate likelihood of such an outcome. The USA and its allies could decide that an ongoing war is in no one's interest. The US has experience with everlasting wars, such as the ones in Vietnam, the Middle East and Afghanistan. Ukraine could be offered a latter-day Marshall Plan as a carrot for reconstruction in exchange for neutrality and a non-aggression treaty with Russia. In addition to the carrot, there might have to be a stick involved to the effect of winding back military and diplomatic support for a continuation of the war and a winding back of sanctions against Russia. There might have to be some territorial adjustments. The second-worst outcome would be an open-ended war that would leave Western Europe and the world economy destabilized indefinitely. There is yet another scenario. There are signs that the USA and its allies will continue their support to Ukraine with advanced military hardware and financial assistance. The underlying rationale is to engineer an economic collapse in Russia and a regime change. The absolute worst case would be the spread of the war to other European countries, with the spectre of tactical nuclear weapons being used. Variations in the possibilities include the extent to which China maintains its support for Russia. It is to its advantage that the USA is preoccupied with events in Europe. Almost all of the scenarios would leave Ukraine as the meat in the sandwich."

I had not dealt with our planned contribution to the mayhem. That might have to wait until we had been in touch with Qadeer Khan. Hasina had not enjoyed my thoughts about the future. We decided to let things rest for a few days and then get input from Qadeer.

Decision

Hasina and I tried to carry on as usual with our lives at home and at work. Hasina was close to finishing her latest monograph dealing with 'bad' history being the cause of 'bad', or even disastrous, decision-making. She was having a second look at the argument that those who did not know history were condemned to repeat it and then take it one step further. Her conclusion was that being steeped in bad history was even worse than not knowing any history at all.

I found it difficult to focus on science and technology. Students were allowed to come in for their tutorial sessions while lectures were delivered online. I did my best to sound interested and enthusiastic, but my heart and soul were not really on the job.

* * *

We had two encrypted online sessions on the dark Web with Qadeer Khan. He had followed events in Ukraine as avidly as we had and had been thinking along lines similar to ours. We agreed that the war in Ukraine was between the USA and Russia, with Western Europe playing support roles in a game manipulated by the puppet master and with the luckless Ukrainians doing most of the suffering. Qadeer Khan had prepared his statement.

"The war between Ukraine and Russia will contribute to the inflationary pressures initially stoked by the post-pandemic recovery, cheap money and excessive financial stimulation. The recession will temporarily adversely affect worldwide economic activity. There will be a brief period of lower emissions of greenhouse gases, followed by a return, once again, to rising emissions. In the meantime, the policies, regulations and investments that could possibly meet the net-zero goals by 2050 will be deferred. The chances of any agreement on concerted collective action on global warming in an increasingly polarized world seem unlikely, at best. On the other hand, the war has added to the worldwide political and economic instability following on from the pandemic. Yet another shock to the system could be enough to permanently set the global community on a new course."

We compared our thoughts with those of Qadeer Khan and came to the conclusion that our project was the last best opportunity to prevent global warming past the "tipping point".

* * *

In the back of my mind, I could not escape the gravity and consequences of what we were planning. Suppose that I and Hasina and Eden had now been living in St Petersburg or on the East Coast of the USA in blissful ignorance of what was about to happen to us? Would it be that I, the living, could not bear so much guilt and would come to envy the dead? The two voices in my mind had come back to life, and this time the rational "me" did not have the upper hand. I needed Hasina to help me resolve what was going on in my mind.

She reassured me that something had to be done for the greater good. We had talked it through, setting emotions aside, and come to a conclusion about the means and ends. It was as if we were chosen because, together with Khan, we had the means. For us, there was no other choice. Hasina was right.

* * *

Easter was coming up, and we decided that the family deserved an outing to an interesting place. We booked a week on Malta in a nice hotel not too far away from a waterpark. Every second day we went to the waterpark so that Eden could get his fill of aquatic activities. One of the other days was devoted to exploring the battlements and alleyways of Valetta. We also had an outing by ferry to Gozo and walked up to the fortified medieval castle. Then, we took a bus ride and visited the pre-historic remnants of a temple that was dated to have been built 6,000 years ago. Eden realized that the world had a lot to offer, aside from Oxford, Paris and Chittagong. We told him that one day it was all going to be his. For the time being, he had a story to tell his classmates when he got home.

Not long after Easter, we were back in Oxford and heard from Khan that the shake-down journey had gone well. The yachts were now going sequentially into the boathouse to have the modified freshwater tanks fitted, each containing a nuclear warhead securely in place. The refurbishments would involve taking the mast down and temporarily removing some of the rigging while each vessel was indoors. Also, it was decided to add an attachment for an auxiliary outboard motor to make for easier manoeuvring when in harbour.

In addition, each vessel would be fitted with a short-wave transmitter. These were designed to be activated one hour before the detonation of the warheads and would broadcast a message about global warming and a warning that a shock would be administered to the world community. The message would stress that the sole objective was to encourage the world to adopt policies and procedures that would prevent further release of greenhouse gases into the atmosphere.

Khan estimated that the work would take two months. In due course, we got the all-clear. The yachts would now spend four to six weeks at a safe moorage until the end of the autumn tropical storm season.

In the last week of October, when the storm season was on the wane, the crews were getting ready to weigh anchor and set sail. Khan, Hasina and I had a lengthy discussion with Qadeer Khan about when the vessels should be in the target areas and precisely when to set the triggers for detonation of the warheads. The triggers needed to be pre-set and synchronized before the two vessels left Karachi. We settled on the first day of July 2023. That was to be Armageddon, eight months later. A bail-out mechanism had been included in the planning. A code could be transmitted by Khan to the two crews, which would allow the crews to deactivate the warheads and then return to Karachi. We were comforted by that option.

The two yachts and their crews left Karachi early in December 2022. Hasina and I began to think about what our lives would be like eight months later.

Countdown

The two yachts and their crews had departed as planned from the anchorage in Karachi. The last couple of weeks before departure had been devoted to checking and double-checking everything from spare sails to a complete assortment of spices for the galley. The communications equipment was tested to make certain that the crews could be in regular two-way encrypted communication with home base at Rawalpindi. The trigger mechanisms fitted to the warheads were given a final once-over to ensure that the timing was set correctly and that it would work when required. Likewise, the permissive action link was checked in case it was decided to abort the mission by sending a coded message to the crews. As far as it was humanly possible, nothing was left to chance.

The first stage of the journey went from Karachi to Suez at the bottom of the Red Sea. Aside from being asked to identify themselves by a Saudi patrol boat, when they turned the corner into the Red Sea, the journey was largely uneventful. The weather was good, and a predominantly easterly wind was relatively favourable; they arrived in Suez early in the new year. Both vessels were measured and scrutinized by the harbour staff, and they were made to wait three days before entering the canal proper, while convoys of larger ships had preference. Using the auxiliary outboard motors, it took the yachts just over 20 hours to transit and then arrive at Port Said. They anchored up there for a week of R&R for the crews to stretch their legs and enjoy the familiar cuisine on offer.

The next port of call was Limassol on Cyprus. A pre-arranged rendezvous had been arranged. I was going to pretend to be a tourist in dire need of some winter sun and was, therefore, to spend a week there. The actual purpose was to meet up with the two crews and to find out if all was well. I estimated that the journey from Port Said could take roughly 10 days. I booked a week in Limassol and left Heathrow on the 12 January. This time, I thought it was safe to use my "real" identity and my old passport. The Old Port Hotel sounded promising. As it turned out, I got there one day after the arrival of the two crews. We made contact by phone and agreed to meet at the nearby marina. I would arrive there at 6 p.m. and be wearing a pale blue sunshade and carrying a *Times* newspaper and a duty-free plastic bag.

Four lean and weather-beaten sailors were waiting for me at the agreed time and place. As I expected, and was promised by Khan, they were impressive specimens and had impeccable command of the English language. Yet again, it was apparent that Khan knew what he was doing. We went off to a sparsely occupied café and found a secluded table. It had been decided that none of us would know each other's real names. As an additional layer of security, we decided that I would know the crews as Abdul 1, 2, 3, and 4, and they would know me as Paleface. It appeared that we had all retained our sense of humour. The pre-planned stop-over at Limassol served to replenish the freshwater and to top up the supply of fuel, with the added bonus of long warm showers, washing the salt out of the clothes, and having a break from the on-board diet.

The crews reported that the journey had gone well. On two occasions, they had been asked to identify themselves: once to the Saudi patrol boat and then to the pilot that took them through the Suez Canal. Here in Limassol, we were just one of many yachts, most of which were far more noteworthy than ours. They had checked for CCTV cameras and had moored out of the line of sight of the cameras that were visible. We had known that there was ample time for the rest of the journey, and there was an ill-defined plan to spend six weeks in the Mediterranean. There were plenty of Greek islands to visit. Malta and Sicily were possible destinations where visiting yachts would not raise any eyebrows. I proposed that we would meet up again in Algeciras, next door to Gibraltar, toward the end of February. By this time, we would know the state of the ice conditions in the Bay of Bothnia.

Before we parted, I asked if they would mind if I was a passenger on the yacht that was heading for St Petersburg from Algeciras as part of the last leg. In my youth, I had crewed with a friend on a few occasions, but I promised to be a passive non-interfering passenger. I would leave them somewhere along the coast of Sweden and then move on from there. They seemed surprised but agreed to have me along. Then, we went our separate ways. I became a proper tourist for a few days. The day before leaving, I checked the harbour, and the yachts had gone.

* * *

Back in Oxford, I was debriefed by Hasina, and then we reported to Khan. I also had a session with Eden, apologizing for being a generally useless absentee father. I tried to be as truthful as possible by saying I had been to a conference in Cyprus. He accepted the story, having heard a variation of it before.

Hasina said we needed to have a long and serious conversation about our lives. I was not looking forward to that. We had already realized that once the mushroom clouds had risen, the greatest manhunt in history would get underway. No effort would be spared, and no quarter would be given in order to find the perpetrators. The search would probably begin with those countries that were known to be nuclear armed, followed by the small number that were suspected of considering their nuclear options. Some countries were in possession of dual-capable technologies and materials, such as spent fuel reprocessing facilities or centrifuge technology. Then there were legitimate suppliers of yellowcake, heavy water or industrial radioactive isotopes. Was there an illegitimate trade in such commodities? There were many thousands of people who, at one time or another, had worked in military establishments and were now retired or retrenched or had changed careers. These would need to be traced and interrogated in case they had joined up with sub-national groups with the necessary funding and connections to construct two crude devices. Could it be an inside job involving one or more renegade employees who had managed to divert two nuclear warheads for ideological or remunerative reasons? It was a long list, but there would be a powerful incentive to find who was responsible for the greatest terror attack of all time.

We sat down in the evening for a review of the operation and made some guesses about the next couple of months. Everything seemed to have gone according to the plan so far, and we could not think of any good reasons for encountering problems during the final phase. The question was: what would happen to us afterwards? I began to think aloud.

"We have to face the possibility that we – including Khan – are likely, sooner or later, to be the most hated individuals since Adolf Hitler. One thing is certain. If we are identified and caught, our lives would not be worth living. I have been trying to think of the weaknesses in the security. It is difficult for us to judge the security in Rawalpindi and Karachi. A fair few people have been involved at that end. Khan is an old hand at maintaining security, and he did get away with setting up a complete nuclear programme and then taking it to the point of live testing of devices and warheads. There were certainly rumours about a Pakistani programme and a lot of guesswork, which turned out to be largely correct. There was a conspiracy of denial that protected him, partly from the world community, which essentially thought that Pakistan was entitled to go down the nuclear road, and partly from the Pakistani government, who protected the nuclear programme. I am guessing that the government would continue to protect Khan with all means at its disposal. It is possible, but unlikely, that our involvement would have the same protection."

I stopped to let Hasina get a word in edgewise. She posed serial questions.

"Can we be found? How would they hunt us down? What would then happen?"

"These are questions for which there are no certain answers. If the hunters thought that Khan and Pakistan were involved, then they might check up on everyone who has ever been associated with him and the laboratory at Rawalpindi. They would certainly find us through the IAEA from the time when we acted as inspectors of the activities in Rawalpindi. These visits involved both of us visiting under our real identities. From there, they can track us to Oxford University – and we would soon find the house surrounded by men in balaclavas brandishing automatic weapons. It is possible that the NSA and GCHQ would have a log of encrypted messages going back and forth between Rawalpindi and the UK. Another method would be to search through the lists of people with known associations with nuclear establishments. Sooner or later, I would be found on such a list, and that would be correlated with persons known to have been in contact with Khan. Once again, the balaclavas would be on the doorstep to ask questions under duress. The two yachts arriving at St Petersburg and Nassau, respectively, would be one of very many in each location. Both yachts would be vaporized and would yield no information. The two crews would hopefully have vanished with false identities and would be untraceable. In due course, they would get back to Pakistan, and Khan would ensure that they would effectively vanish into thin air somewhere. I think we are the most vulnerable ones."

"So, what do we do?" asked Hasina. "Do we just sit here and wait for the balaclavas, as you call them, to turn up?"

"I am afraid we are vulnerable. Here in Oxford, we are sitting ducks. We are also lacking in protection. Once we are on the radar, it is inconceivable that the UK would protect us. We are alone and friendless in what would become an extremely hostile environment. Our best hope is to vanish and leave no trails. I have thought about this for a while. If we remain here, or even stay in the UK, or even in a Western country, there are far too many ways to track people down. As of today, we have two months before the baying of the wolves begins. You and Eden must disappear, at best without a trace, but at least with a trace that cannot be followed. I will try to do the same. The one and only thing I can now wish for in life is to know that you and Eden are safe somewhere."

For what seemed an eternity, there was silence, and I could see the tears welling up. "What happens if I say no?" she whispered.

"If we are deemed to be involved, we might find ourselves in Guantanamo Bay or in a gulag in Siberia being waterboarded for the rest of our lives. The life of Eden would be hell on earth. We must not let that happen."

"Why can we not go into hiding together?"

"The three of us will always stand out in a crowd. I am just another white European and would blend into the scene in any Western country. You would blend into the masses anywhere on the Indian sub-continent. So would Eden, being more like you than me. If I get identified as a person of interest, the trackers will look for a family of two adults and one child when they wade through miles of CCTV footage. I really do want you and Eden to be safe. I won't want to know where you are, just in case."

"I need to think this through. We might never see each other again or even be aware of what has happened to each other. How could we bear that?"

"It is for the sake of Eden and for the sake of an ultimately better world. We are just the expendable pawns that did what was necessary – but Eden is our future life after death."

I had been speaking softly to Hasina and to myself.

* * *

We let things rest for a few days. Every moment of togetherness was to be treasured and remembered. Now and again, we reminded ourselves of our lives together and promised each other, without words, that the memories would remain.

Then, practicalities kicked in. We told our respective departments that we wished to take time out with unpaid leave of absence for an unspecified duration. There were raised eyebrows and expressions of hope that "you will return to the fold and continue the good work". We cleared our offices and said goodbye for now. It was actually nice to get the feeling that we were wanted and would be missed. We had our neighbours, Stephen and Sheila, over for dinner one night. The boys went upstairs, as usual, to play the latest computer game. We broke the news about disappearing from Oxford. The explanation was that we wanted a break from academia and from the unique parallel universe known as Oxford University. They were surprised and sympathetic. I explained that we were beginning to realize that the university was a bit like the US Marine Corps. You joined it and had your personality and view of life rebuilt so that you could never really leave the institution. In the end, you became an Oxford University person. We were rebelling and going in search of our old and real selves. They thought it was an interesting theory, but it had some merit. We parted to the tune of: 'Good Luck' and 'We hope to see you again'.

We had one last exchange with Khan through the dark Web. I explained to him about Hasina and Eden needing to vanish and asked for passports and documentation for Eden linking him to Hasina. The papers duly arrived two weeks later, with best wishes from Khan. He hoped we would meet again. Inshallah.

It was time to have a long talk with Eden. We dreaded that. After dinner, I announced that we needed to have a family meeting. This had been our custom for two or three years, and Eden liked to feel that he was being consulted on issues that affected the whole family. Hasina started it off.

"Daddy and I are beginning to think that we have been in Oxford long enough and that we all need to see other places and learn about what other people are like and how they conduct their lives. There is so much to see and experience, and the more you see and learn, the more you understand about the world. Daddy always talks about the world being his oyster. It is time for you and me to find out what he means."

I was watching Eden, and he seemed to take it in his stride. He had always been curious about everything and everyone. Maybe it went with the territory in the household. Once he had mastered "yes" and "no" the next word was "why?" Now it was my turn.

"I think you and Mum should go back to Chittagong, for a start. It has been a long time since Kualeda and Mujibur were taken by the ocean. We promised we were going to remember them forever. You and Mum will lead the way in a few weeks. I have some work to do here, and then I will follow after you. After Chittagong, the whole world is ours. Maybe we will get a large map of the world and throw darts at it. Wherever the dart lands, that is where we go next. How is that?"

Eden liked it. "Then we will be like Pippi Longstocking," he said.

* * *

We now had less than a month to deal with the winding up of our lives in Oxford. A day was spent in the office of a real estate agent. We insisted on putting the house on the market at a price well below its market value. Our explanation was that we were leaving the country and wanted a rapid and clean break from the UK. Then, we hired a car and took most of our personal belongings to the rubbish exchange. The Salvation Army would collect the furniture once the house had a new owner.

We would need to have access to cash. We would not be able to use the banking system, and there was a limit to the cash one could carry. We could, in principle, use our access to the anonymous store of gold that had been set up by Mujibur and Kualeda. I had also been thinking about an additional anonymous account in Pakistan.

We would realize a tidy sum from the sale of the house. That would initially go into our joint account in Oxford. Some of the proceeds we could keep as cash. In the meantime, I had consulted Khan on how to move most of the cash into an untraceable account. We needed a facility similar to the way that the gold was held securely and anonymously in what was effectively a numbered account.

Two days later, we had a message from Khan. He would arrange a fake real estate investment in Rawalpindi and then set up a numbered account for us. The details of access would follow.

Several offers came within days from clients with cash. We met some of the interested parties during the viewing process. One gentleman from Hong Kong was desperate to have a bolthole in the UK for himself, his family and his money. Hasina and I agreed that we lived in interesting and useful times. The gentleman even offered to pay a bit extra if he could have the furniture as well. We signed a contract later that day.

All that was left was to remove all signs that we had ever been there. Every bit of paperwork was shredded, e-mails were deleted, accounts were closed, and subscriptions were cancelled. All files on our hard drives were deleted, and we made certain that anything stored in the cloud was retrieved and deleted. I took the hard drives out of our two PCs, put them into the microwave at maximum power and then smashed them with a hammer. Memory sticks and backup discs got the same treatment. All that was left of our memories of a past life were what lived between the ears and what was left on two laptops and two smartphones; these were coming with us. A hypothetical forensic examination of the house would find fingerprints and strands of hair in various places, but there was not much we could do about that.

It had been decided that Hasina and Eden would fly out to Dhaka at the beginning of the spring term holidays. This would give Eden a chance to wind up his UK education in an undramatic manner – at least for the time being. A few days later, I would head off to Algeciras to join one of the crews for a leisurely journey into the Bay of Bothnia. Then, I would make my way through Sweden to places as yet undecided. Our family had two weeks left before we were going to be torn asunder.

* * *

The two weeks were the most traumatic of our lives. Every hour brought us nearer to an inevitable separation and had to be survived somehow. Every night we clung wordlessly to each other. There was nothing else we could do. We were locked into a chain of events that had begun many years previously – from the moment of the conversation with Khan in Rawalpindi – and had progressed inexorably. Now, there were two nuclear warheads on their way to targets. Three months later, we would be the architects of unimaginable death and suffering. The sorrow and misery filling our solitary bubble seemed that much the worse because we had tinkered with fate and were not innocent.

We tried as best we could to keep things together, but Eden sensed that life had changed. He was aware, as we were, that joy had left the household. We reassured him that the love was still there, especially for him.

Eden had a few days in school before the term break. Hasina and I went for walks along the canal or the Thames, partly to talk and partly to give us something to do. She was thinking about how it had come to this.

"I am seeking refuge in fate," she said. "This makes it easier to bear. Looking back, it seems as if it was destiny that I was sent to Oxford as a child, then to the university where people told me I was special and that I was going to do great things. Somehow it came to me that I should join the IAEA, get an office not far away from yours, and fall in love with you. Now it all seems preordained. What do you think?"

"My life is now about finally having found order and meaning out of chaos. In the beginning, I had no fixed point to cling to. At university, I discovered natural laws. Apples always fall down, and there was a rational explanation for that which did not depend on faith, opinion or luck. For a while, I looked suspiciously on every apple tree to make sure that no apples ever fell up. From then on, my existence was conditional on natural laws. This was the first glimmer of order in my life. I continued to remain standing outside and looking in on a world that seemed profoundly chaotic, but maybe there was order on the other side of some hill. So, I embarked on a search and became a vagabond: 'have knowledge, will travel'. I think it was largely luck that took me to Vienna and the IAEA. Then you came, looked through the shell into my soul, and taught me that there was another dimension to life. You and Eden have changed everything for me. It is no longer just about laws, order and numbers. It is also about love and caring for a family, and about a future beyond my lifetime, and of how I will have a measure of immortality."

We walked on in silence for a while. Hasina was the next to speak.

"Whatever happens, you will always be with me. But rivers of tears will be shed – by me and by the many who will have lost loved ones. I promise you that Eden will know one day that whatever world he grows up in, we had a part in making it. I promise to be the lioness that protects our cub when the lion is no longer with us."

Then, we turned around and went home. Eden was on his way home from his last day at school in the UK.

Two weeks later, in early May, I walked Hasina and Eden to the bus stop that would take them and two backpacks to Gatwick and then onwards on a PIA flight to Dhaka. It was a sombre and melancholy moment. We embraced, and I told Eden to look after Mummy. When the bus turned the corner and disappeared from sight, a feeling of total loneliness and abandonment struck me. For what seemed an eternity, I stood there, unable to leave the spot where I had seen Hasina and Eden for the last time. After a while, I was able to go to the place that had been our home but was now a shell full of memories and nothing else. I had to pull myself together.

$$* * *$$

At what had once been a home, I decided I had to leave. I did some tidying up, packed a few things and handed the keys over to a real estate agent, and then booked myself into a B&B. The next day, a large amount of money landed in our joint Barclays account. I booked a session with an advisor upstairs and explained that we were moving to Pakistan to be closer to Hasina's family. I requested that they please transfer most of the proceeds in our account to the institution in Rawalpindi that had been set up by Khan. We were long-standing and trusted customers, and the paperwork was organized. I also got some cash and did the rounds of several banks to buy a selection of pre-paid anonymous money cards to keep me liquid for a while. Later in the day, I sent an e-mail to Hasina, telling her about the transfer.

I had intended to stay in Oxford a few more days but decided that I needed to make a clean break from my old life. I would rather have a few extra days in Algeciras waiting to be picked up by the yacht crewed by Abdul 1 and 2. I booked a cheap flight to Malaga two days later. There were frequent buses from the airport to Algeciras. Two days later, I was installed in a hotel near the port, having a Mediterranean dinner with a view of the Rock of Gibraltar ahead while watching the setting sun.

The yachts arrived four days after my arrival. I met up with the crews in a café. They reported that there had been no complications and that they had enjoyed a leisurely cruise meandering through the Mediterranean. According to the latest information, there was a clear passage, with no ice, all the way to St Petersburg. As well, the long-range forecast for the North Atlantic suggested that there was no immediate danger of foul weather. We agreed that all systems were go. This gave the crews roughly six weeks for the last stages of their journeys. I reminded the St Petersburg crew that I would like to be a passenger as far as the coast of Sweden. They said that was fine. Two days later, I brought my backpack, freshly bought water, a wind-proof suit and a new pair of running shoes down to the harbour and clambered aboard. The living quarters were surprisingly spacious below deck. I got the sofabed to myself and was told that I was allowed a weekly shower in recycled freshwater. Then, we set sail and headed north along the coast of Portugal. The other yacht headed in a north-westerly direction and was soon out of sight.

The Bay of Biscay was somewhat lively, with heavy swell coming in from the Atlantic. I began to feel queasy out of the weather below in the cabin but recovered upstairs in the fresh air. Once we were past Brittany and into the Channel, I got my appetite and my sense of humour back. We stopped in Plymouth for two days to get some fresh food. I was allowed to have a night in a B&B and took the opportunity to have a warm shower. Then we weighed anchor, passed through the Channel and along the coast of the Low Countries before circumnavigating Denmark and on through the narrow strait between Sweden and Denmark into the Baltic Sea. There was now three weeks until the crew had to be at ground zero. I had looked at the map and decided that I would leave the yacht at Nynäshamn, just south of Stockholm, and then find my way to a place where I was unlikely to be found. On arrival, we stayed offshore until early evening. I was rowed ashore in the rubber dinghy and deposited on the dock. We shook hands, wished each other good luck and "see you again". I had become quite fond of the two Abduls and felt mildly sentimental about leaving. I knew that I would never see them again. The journey with the yacht had left me with a seriously unshaven look and a sunburn. Sweden was still struggling with the tail end of the pandemic, and a face mask was in order, but it was no longer mandatory. Even Hasina would have struggled to recognize me. I found out from a local youth that the railway station was within easy walking distance, and I set off on foot. My first impression of Sweden was that the locals spoke better English than some native English speakers I had known. An hour later, I found myself in the middle of Stockholm. I wandered around for a while and then picked a hotel at random. I had actually entered Sweden without even waving a passport in the air. It was nice to be in a civilized place. I decided that I might as well stay there for a few days while I was thinking about what to do and where to go.

*　*　*

Three days of walking the streets of Stockholm gave me my land legs back. It also allowed my brain to freewheel while I was waiting for something to pop out of the nether regions of my subconsciousness. I thought that if I engaged in random planning, then that would result in additional survival value in case I ended up being tracked. Suddenly, the word "Wittgenstein" appeared in my conscious inbox. Why?

As a student, there was a time when I believed, mistakenly as it turned out, that I could ultimately know everything. I went through a philosophy phase, beginning with Socrates and worked my way up to Ludwig Wittgenstein, whereupon I realized that I had reached my limit in comprehension. In the late 40s, Wittgenstein was diagnosed with aggressive prostate cancer that had begun to spread. In early 1950, it had reached the stage of preventing him from working. For some months, he and a friend retired from the world to a small island off the coast of Norway. He did return to civilization and died later that year. I suspected it was the idea of hiding on a small island that was the trigger. Or, maybe it was the notion that a wounded animal goes into hiding and waits for the end?

I took the train to Oslo, which involved showing one of my passports at the border. It did not raise any eyebrows. As is the case in most cities, there was a tourist information office near the central railway station. I told the nice lady that I wanted peace and quiet during the summer while working on my book. Passing myself off as an eccentric writer was probably a better cover than most. A log cabin in the mountains would be perfect, as long as I had internet access. She showed me a selection. I specified access by public transport and a supermarket within reasonable walking distance. We settled on a place called Sjusjøen at an altitude of just under 1,000 metres and with access by train and bus from Oslo. I paid for the summer in advance and got a set of keys, a map, and a list of what to do and what was expressly forbidden. The fresh air would do me good. The next day, I was ensconced in new surroundings and had been to the supermarket. I was already feeling better. I hoped that Hasina and Eden were safe and well, but I might never know.

* * *

During the next week, I went for walks in different directions in order to get oriented. There were a few easy hills nearby to climb and several lakes with places to stop and devour sandwiches and drink coffee from a Thermos and to feel at one with nature. I rarely saw anybody on my walks and did not mind the solitude. There were a lot of thoughts to listen to and process.

A short message came from Khan, telling me to watch the news on the thirtieth of the month of June. I wondered why. The target date was supposed to be the 1 July. Had something changed? I decided to wait and see. Khan had always seemed to know what he was doing. It was just under two weeks to wait.

Ragnarok

Life in the mountains had settled into a pattern. I would wake when the first photons crept over the horizon. Breakfast was next on the agenda before catching up on the latest news from half a dozen sources around the world. The internet was very good, and the world was available to me. There was also a TV that offered fare from half a dozen local channels, but also CNN and BBC World Service. Far too often, the watching of the world was not good for digesting sandwiches. The war in Ukraine accounted for at least half of the airtime, followed by gloomy news about the economy. Then it was time for my daily walk, unless the rain was bucketing or if there was a howling gale. I would usually get back mid-afternoon, sometimes via the supermarket, for cups of coffee and another round of world news. This gave me an hour or two for contemplation of the meaning of life and for talking to the stray cat that had appeared one day and had decided I was a soft touch. At the end of the day, there was dinner and a last session of news. It had taken a few days to get used to the sound of silence, broken only by the whistling of the wind through the pine trees that were eking out a precarious existence at the tree line.

The news was not any more cheerful than at any other time in the recent past. The Trump administration was gone, unloved and soon to be forgotten, but the incoming Biden team was not even pretending to make a break with the past – failed – policies. Polarization, demonization, blame-shifting and fake news dominated the agenda. Failing policies and systems were being propped up – and justified by the manufacturing of enemies and malevolent "others" such as Vladimir Putin. As usual, I was treated to platitudes, such as "this is not the time for change" and "if it ain't broke, don't fix it". Any attempts to deal with real underlying problems, such as global warming, glaring inequality, and lack of effective universal health care, were kicked into the long grass after being described as unaffordable or un-American or not in the national interest. A new Cold War, with China being the dreaded wicked enemy, was being institutionalized. The rest of the world was given a clear choice of either being on "our" side or being sanctioned to death. It was becoming yet another negative sum game where the costs were being transferred to the most vulnerable and the least deserving.

Temperature records were measured in the Russian Arctic, and forest fires of epic dimensions were predicted. Some glaciers in Iceland were in the process of disappearing, possibly forever. An ice-free North Pole was on the cards, and a team of intrepid explorers were planning to paddle their kayaks to the North Pole later in the summer. Australia was yet again in the grip of drought: the temperatures in Melbourne and Sydney during the southern summer had exceeded 40 degrees on successive days. The Antarctic and Greenland ice sheets were 'calving' at rates greater than ever observed. The facts were indisputable. Politicians were given tongue-lashings by Greta Thunberg and were chastised somewhat more politely, but with equal passion, in sermons by David Attenborough. The responses were soothing words and a great deal of hand-wringing, as well as promises of targets to be met by 2050. Business as usual was going to rule OK.

There did not seem to be any good reason to abort our operation. Khan had been silent since his message about the thirtieth. This was not the time for flurries of electronic messages.

* * *

After a week of splendid solitude, I needed a change of scenery and took the bus to the nearest town, Lillehammer. It hosted the Winter Olympics in 1994. The one main street offered several cafés. I chose one at random and ordered a double espresso and a waffle with jam and cream. The place was crowded, and I ended up sharing my table with an elderly gentleman, who turned out to be a local. Lillehammer seemed to be the kind of town where it was mandatory to strike up a conversation when sharing a table. He soon realized I was not a Norwegian, and I confessed to living in the UK but was currently escaping from modern life to a cabin in the mountains. He thought that was very wise of me. He thought modern life was too complicated, with change happening too fast and not for the better. He said that the fabric of his community was unravelling and that it was in the process of losing its sense of identity, purpose and belonging. Amen, I thought to myself.

"The old certainties have gone or are going. In my youth, we had a metre of snow down here in the city before Christmas. This year, there was hardly any snow at all in the city, and up in the mountains, the skiing season was a month shorter than normal. I blame global warming – and the politicians are useless!" He was into his stride and holding forth.

"How do you think it will end?" I asked.

His pale blue eyes stared straight at me. "It will end with Ragnarok."

When I seemed to be uncomprehending, he realized that I had no idea what was meant by Ragnarok. He apologized for not remembering that I was a foreigner. He told me that he was retired from his job as a teacher of history at the high school just up the hill.

He asked if I would mind if he was to give me a short lecture on Norse history and mythology. I assured him that I would be honoured.

"Before Christianity replaced the polytheistic regime in Scandinavia around 1,000 AD, a multitude of gods and semi-gods were in charge of the natural world and its Norse inhabitants. There were similarities with the Greco-Roman hierarchy of polytheism and its godly personalities.

"For instance, Odin was the father of all other lesser gods. His wife, Freya (or Frigg), was the goddess of beauty and fertility. Baldur was the handsome god in charge of kindness and innocence. Hel was the goddess in charge of the dead and the afterlife. Loki was the tricky one who could never be trusted to behave. Njord was the god of the sea and of its powers for good and worse. Thor was the warrior god with magical powers and accounted for thunder and lightning. Skadi was the anti-god. She was in charge of winter, cold, darkness and death, as well as mountains and the wilderness. There were others – but you get the idea. As well as the gods, there was a variety of evil creatures such as jotuns, dragons, snakes and dwarves. These were a constant threat to the gods and to humans. The mythology speaks of a great battle in which the gods succumbed and died. The world was then consumed by flames before finally being submerged by the sea. This was Ragnarok, a cataclysmic end to the world. Fortunately, two humans survived and started the world anew. It is a description of a cyclical death and rebirth of the world. So endeth my lecture. Maybe Norse mythology has something to tell us."

My memory was triggered by Wagner's epic, *Ring Cycle*, that I had watched some years ago in Vienna. The last opera of the cycle was entitled Götterdämmerung, the death of the gods, which draws on Norse mythology. I mentioned this to my new friend in the café, and he was clearly pleased to have struck a chord. We agreed that Ragnarok was waiting for us when global warning reached the tipping point.

I had to catch the last bus of the day. We said our goodbyes and "hope to see you again". He told me that he was in the café every day at lunchtime.

* * *

The last week of June was the longest of my life. Even going for the regulation walk could not settle me down. I was constantly checking the news and my e-mail to make sure that nothing untoward had happened. I was torn between wishing that the warheads would fizzle and hoping that our plan would work to perfection. In between my mood changes, I had imaginary conversations with Hasina and Eden in my mind. Were they safe? What would the rest of their lives be like? What would my life be like? Why had Khan told me to check the news on the thirtieth? During the night of the twenty-ninth, I could not sleep; my mind was working overtime. When I eventually nodded off, the nightmares of my childhood returned. In the end, I gave up and sat on the doorstep, watching the sun rise. The cat came for a piece of cheese and did its best to calm me down. What time was it in St Petersburg? In Nassau? We had been planning for afternoon and morning, respectively, in local time, in order to get the synchronization right. The seconds became minutes which then, one eternity after another, became hours.

A few minutes after noon, CNN went into overdrive. A mushroom cloud filled the screen to the accompaniment of a breathless voice announcing a nuclear strike on Long Island. Other voices came and went telling of shock waves and of total devastation, JFK being out of action, possibly destroyed. Then, came the recorded message we had prepared. A few minutes later, the news came of the strike on St Petersburg, and there was another view of a mushroom cloud. A state department talking head came on air and went on about despicable and evil acts by unknown perpetrators. An anonymous security expert held forth about the two main nuclear powers being hit simultaneously in a highly sophisticated manner. There were speculations about what would happen next. Obviously, all retaliatory and defensive systems would now be on red alert. Would the USA and Russia be talking to each other on the "red phones"? Could an all-out nuclear conflagration be avoided? Aerial images taken by a high-flying SR-71 spy plane showed that the northern third of Long Island was affected, as well as some of the nearby boroughs of New York. Subsequently, satellite images confirmed these observations and showed that St Petersburg and environs had suffered a similar fate. Traffic out of Long Island had ground to a halt as frantic survivors were attempting to flee or seek medical assistance. Conversely, medical crews and rescue services were being mobilized but struggled to reach the affected areas. Fallout shelters had fallen into disrepair since the end of the Cold War. Many of them had been decommissioned, and their locations were unknown to most of the people who were looking for the shelters. Communications were badly affected, and chaos reigned.

Within minutes of the strike, financial markets had plummeted by 30% and further trading was suspended. Banks had closed their doors for fear that they would run out of cash. Shops were being boarded up in anticipation of panic buying, and looting was reported. Widespread societal breakdown was a very real possibility. The National Guard was mobilized and were beginning to guard strategic buildings and facilities.

An ashen-faced President Biden addressed the nation from the airborne command centre in the early evening. He said that he grieved with all Americans for the loss of life that had been caused by as-yet-unknown assailants. He said there could be no justification and no forgiveness for such an act of perfidy. He was using quotes from FDR after Pearl Harbour. The nation would endure and overcome as it always had. He vowed to find the evil enemy wherever he might be hiding and exact a terrible retribution. Whoever was offering shelter or support would be considered a mortal enemy and would suffer the consequences. Then, he invoked the blessing of God in this endeavour. It was not too dissimilar to the oratory of George W. Bush after the 9/11 attack. We were treated to excerpts from a similar tone of speech in translation from President Putin to the Russian nation. As well, there was a chorus of support and commiserations from the majority of nations, including North Korea and Iran.

There was a report that a passenger plane in a holding pattern near JFK had witnessed the characteristic double flash of the nuclear blast and then experienced the initial shockwave, followed by the fireball and the rise of the mushroom cloud. There was a similar report from St Petersburg. A low-flying plane approaching the airport had been caught in the shockwave and had crashed in the centre of town. The fireball was followed by a local tsunami wave going up the estuary of the Neva that had submerged large areas of the city.

I was still confused by the timing. We had agreed at our last virtual meeting that D-Day was to be 1 July. Why, then, the thirtieth of June? The obvious answer came to me. The plan had been that the yachts should arrive at ground zero two days before the first day of July. The crews then planned to leave the yachts anchored and head for the nearest airport. They intended to catch the first available planes to anywhere. Ultimately, they would have found their way back to Pakistan. Instead, the yachts ended up as vaporized and dispersed single atoms. Khan was not leaving anything to chance. He knew that dead men can tell no tales. Therefore, the warheads had been set to ignite one day early. I had come to know the crews – especially the two men, Abdul 1 and 2. I had lived with them from Algeciras to Sweden. My initial reactions were a mixture of grief and guilt. Somewhere there would be families whose sons, brothers and husbands would never come home. They were fine men who had done a good and vital job and did not deserve to die. I probably would never meet Khan again and would not be able to tell him what I thought of him. He would probably tell me that it had been a necessary act. It occurred to me how different my reactions were to the deaths of the four people I had known in comparison to the remorse about the millions of others. It seemed to me that empathy works only on a personal level. On the other hand, guilt worked on the macroscale as well as on the microscale: I did feel guilty about the deaths of the four men and about the millions of others. Somewhere, Hasina was undoubtedly sharing my thoughts. I wished that we could have been together to share the guilt.

* * *

That evening I sat at the kitchen table doing calculations on A4 sheets of paper to get a rough idea of what we – Khan, Hasina and I – had done.

The energy released in a nuclear explosion was roughly equivalent to that released by tens of thousands of tons of TNT. The devices that were detonated at Nassau and St Petersburg were rated at an explosive yield of 70,000 tons – equivalent to a few shiploads of TNT. The energy came from splitting a heavy nucleus, such as

Uranium or Plutonium, into two fragments. The sum of the energies that held the separated fragments together was less than the energy that held the original heavier nucleus together. The difference was the explosive yield per fissile atom. The energies involved in rearranging bonding within a nucleus were typically a million times greater than the energies involved in rearranging chemical bonding between atoms. Pound for pound, one got a million times greater explosive energy from a nuclear reaction than from a chemical one.

There were four main consequences of the enormous release of energy from a nuclear detonation that caused death and injuries to people and destruction of structures.

Somewhat less than half of the energy was dissipated as blast. The initial fireball had temperatures close to that at the centre of the sun. It expanded outward in all directions and vaporized and ionized everything in its path. The air in its path was superheated, leading to underpressure. Buildings initially collapsed in on themselves, and there was serious damage to people due to the collapse of internal bodily cavities. Of greater consequence was the formation of the subsequent overpressure of the wave that travelled outward, initially at supersonic speeds, leaving death and destruction in its wake. The speed of travel gradually subsided away from ground zero but still had speeds and overpressure greater than that of the most lethal storms.

Thermal radiation was a close second in the causes of death and destruction from a nuclear explosion. The expanding fireball was an isotropic emitter of heat and X-ray radiation. The intensity and temperature decayed with distance. Flammable materials were set alight due to absorbed radiation at km distances from the original fireball. Individuals exposed in the open suffered fourth-degree to minor burns, depending on distance and on sheltering effects.

Prompt ionizing radiation emitted from the fission processes accounted for some 5% of the total energy release. The neutron flux and gamma radiation had long mean free paths in air, and unprotected individuals could be exposed to doses that ranged from being lethal, at close quarters, to causing delayed radiation sickness further away.

Another 5–10% of total energy release was due to delayed radioactivity. Many of the fission fragments were radioactive isotopes with half-lives ranging from seconds to tens of years. The long-lived isotopes returned to the biosphere as fallout and became a long-term hazard for the wider community. The neutron flux was the source of activation products due to absorption of neutrons by materials in the target area. The products had half-lives from seconds to years.

For purposes of carrying out some rough calculations, I assumed a ground burst of a 70 kilotons warhead and a flat terrain in the target area.

These assumptions gave me a radius of 1.5 km, within which the overpressure would have been greater than 20 psi. Such a pressure was taken to imply that no structures were left standing inside a circular area of 7 square km, and the death toll would be 100%. Within a larger area of 20 square km, defined by a pressure contour of 5 psi, most residential buildings would suffer major damage, and there would be a significant death toll. Buildings within an area of 100 square km would suffer moderate damage. Thermal radiation would result in lethal burns for unprotected victims over an area of 30 square km. Less severe burns would be the result of thermal radiation over an area greater than 100 square km. Deposition of thermal energy would trigger fires in areas where there are combustible materials.

Exposure to ionizing radiation could be lethal for individuals sufficiently close to the fireball, but the cause of death would be dominated by blast and thermal radiation. Survivors at distances far enough away from ground zero could be exposed to ionizing radiation at levels that, over time, were life shortening. Fallout in the immediate aftermath of the nuclear attack would have a longer-term effect on victims, such as a propensity for excess prevalence of cancers.

It was midnight by the time I had finished working out the rough estimates. By this time, CNN had brought in a range of experts for comments. I actually recognized a couple of the talking heads from one of the many laboratories where I had worked. Their numbers were in rough agreement with what I had worked out during the evening.

From the aerial images, I deduced that ground zero had been offshore from the north-west corner of Nassau County, in close proximity to the Queens and Bronx boroughs of New York City. This was consistent with the images showing major damage of the coastal regions of all three counties. CNN reported calls for urgent but orderly evacuation from areas as far away as Manhattan due to a moderate wind from a north-easterly direction. This would possibly bring significant fallout over some of the most densely populated areas of the Eastern seaboard of the USA.

Within hours, the highways were gridlocked, and tempers were fraying. There were pleas for calm but to no avail. All available helicopters were scrambled and airborne, bringing casualties from the worst affected areas to hospitals that became overwhelmed within a few hours. Paramedics were brought in to areas more than 10 kilometres from ground zero to administer first aid on the spot. There was talk of a possible death toll of 500,000 and well over 1 million seriously injured.

From time to time, I checked BBC World Service to get the latest news from St Petersburg. My impression was that ground zero had been in the inner harbour at the mouth of the Neva River. Aerial images after the explosion showed that most of the compact inner city had been flattened. The population of metropolitan St Petersburg was somewhat greater than 5 million, but most of that population lived well away from the core of the city. Official information about death toll and injuries was sparse, possibly due to communications being disrupted.

* * *

By midnight, the news was becoming repetitive. I was taking stock of what had happened. As we had hoped and expected, the twin attacks had not been the trigger for an immediate beginning of WWIII and an all-out nuclear exchange. It was likely that the President, Vice President and Speaker of the House had been transferred to their separate airborne command centres within 15 minutes of the strikes, while President Putin had probably retreated to a deep bunker under the Kremlin. All early warning systems had immediately gone into red alert modes. The launch crews for silo-based ICBMs had been scrambled and placed on a war footing while stealth bombers carrying nuclear-tipped cruise missiles were ordered to take off. Naval assets had been ordered to move to offensive positions. Submarines carrying nuclear missiles were told to stand by and to wait for permission to fire volleys of long-range missiles at pre-determined targets. The two presidents were patched into direct communications with each other within 15 minutes. I could only guess how the conversation unfolded. The absence of any further nuclear strikes was proof that the two men had managed to convince each other that the strikes were bolts from the blue and that neither side had been involved, either directly or indirectly. As expected, when it came to a nuclear war, rationality had won out.

My best guess was that Russia and the USA would join forces to track down and identify who was behind the attacks. "The enemy of my enemy is my friend" is one of the most important laws of international relations. It was after midnight, and the sun was thinking about rising for another day. I went to bed.

* * *

Another day had come for being glued to the television and for monitoring news updates online. The markets were still plummeting. The US dollar was not doing well. The conspiracy theorists were having a field day on social media. The more extreme proposal was to round up environmentalists and hang them from the nearest lampposts. Greta Thunberg and family had taken refuge inside a Swedish army base. The left was pointing the finger at the right and vice versa. China had, during the last few years, been elevated to the number one enemy of the West. Both sides of the political spectrum thought that China should be wiped off the face of the earth. Later in the day, the moguls of social media, under pressure from the authorities, pulled the plug on everything that was not vetted and authorized by governments. The mainstream media outlets – such as CNN, Fox News and PBS in the USA, BBC World in the UK, CGTN in China, RT in Russia, and so on – were allowed to continue broadcasting, subject to government monitoring and authorization.

I had to make my own guesses about what was happening behind the doors of the national security agencies in the US and Russia. Likewise, there would be furious activity in countries that were either nuclear capable or had dual-capable programmes underway in order to demonstrate clean bills of health and total innocence.

It seemed blindingly obvious to me that someone would draw the conclusion that in both cases, ground zero was close offshore. If so, there were only three possible ways to deliver a warhead: a midget submarine carrying a warhead, a small surface vessel, or a nuclear-tipped torpedo launched from a stand-off submarine. The latter could be ruled out. Enemy submarines were closely monitored and were most unlikely to get anywhere near a harbour. A midget submarine would need to be launched from a mother ship somewhere within the territorial waters and would need to be operated by either a robot or by a small live crew on a suicide mission. Again, this seemed implausible due to the necessary presence of a mother ship. That left a 15-metre yacht arriving one morning and blowing itself up. Virtually all major ports in the world have small ships' harbours where vessels of all kinds would come and go. At best, the marinas are supervised by one or more harbour masters, and there may be security towards the land side. There may be CCTV monitoring and occasional patrols looking for unauthorized visitors and checking for delinquents who have stopped paying the mooring fees. A medium-sized sailing yacht that arrives one morning, or during the night, and then blows itself up after a few hours, might not attract much attention before the bang. At Nassau, it would have been one amongst thousands. The numbers in the inner harbour of St Petersburg could have been more manageable, but whoever and whatever had been doing any noticing would no longer be amongst the living. Likewise, live witnesses would be thin on the ground at Nassau.

I was certain that over the next few days, the fallout would be analysed by air sampling for radioactive "fingerprints". It would be readily apparent that the devices were of the highly enriched uranium variety rather than being based on bomb-grade plutonium. The implication was that the bomb makers must have had access to output from an ultra-centrifuge plant configured for U-235 enrichment to 90+%. Fast fission fragments from U-238 would show that the yields of the devices were boosted by the U-235 cores being surrounded by layers of lithium deuteride and U-238. My guess was that the analyses of the fallout would show that the devices were quite sophisticated and were not cobbled together in the back of a bicycle shop. They had to be begged, bought, borrowed or stolen from a well-established and mature nuclear programme. I hoped that Khan had covered his tracks sufficiently well. From my days as an inspector from the IAEA, I had not been able to find much wrong with his set-up – even though he was widely suspected of having passed information and hardware to various "customers". He had the advantage of the Pakistani government protecting him from a truly intrusive inquisition.

From the 1940s and onwards, a couple of hundred thousand workers, technicians and scientists had been involved in the pioneering nuclear weapons programme in the USA. In the 50s, some 6,000 people worked at the Harwell Laboratory on the British nuclear weapons programme. Many of those were no longer alive; some of them had been working at the periphery or had limited experience and knowledge beyond particular aspects. At the top of the nuclear food chain were the ones who knew everything, and then there were the ones who knew a lot from sharing offices, canteens and drinking sessions with the highest flyers. There were also a few, like me, who had not been formally engaged but had talked to a lot of people who had been involved, and finally, the ones who had read a fair portion of the open and classified literature. I was probably on some lists, but not anywhere near the top. During the years at Oxford, I had been out of the game – unless the encrypted exchanges with Khan had been cracked or if somehow my visits with false identities to Karachi had rung the alarm bells somewhere. If so, then I would be a person of great interest. For the time being, I was probably safe. But soon I would have to keep moving and leave only the faintest of trails.

* * *

The news during the next few days focussed almost exclusively on body counts and assessments of destruction. The emphasis was very much on demonstrating that the authorities were moving heaven and earth to deal with the vast numbers of injured victims and to bring medical and other forms of aid to areas where they were most needed. Reasonably orderly evacuations from areas of the Eastern coastal communities in the USA continued as the fallout was spreading. The situation in St Petersburg followed a similar pattern, although it got less airtime. A change in wind direction took some of the fallout into the southern coastal areas of Finland, and that was noted by the Norwegian NRK news.

There were signs that disaster fatigue was setting in. Covid-19 had hit first and had so far killed more than 7 million people. Several vaccines had come onto the market and had put a lid on infections in Western Europe and in North America. Countries with weaker economies and less well-developed health systems, and worse infrastructures, were still trying to access and deploy vaccination in a systematic manner. In addition, a mutated virus, named Delta, with higher infectiousness but similar lethality, had appeared in Europe and was spreading globally. In early 2022, a new variant, the Omicron, came out of Africa. It was the most transmissible so far but not as lethal. The vaccines were finally putting a lid on the death rates in the countries with high vaccination rates. As well, the approach to herd immunity, in combination with booster shots, was beginning to have an effect on curbing the death toll. The war in Europe was an additional distraction from focussing on the virus.

Then, before the virus had been dealt with, came the two nuclear attacks. There was a palpable sense of, "What have we done to deserve this?"

After the initial shock, the world was beginning to take notice of the claim that the attacks were not an end in themselves but a wake-up call for the world to deal constructively and effectively with the coming apocalyptic global warming. After all, what else could be the purpose of subjecting the world to nuclear terror? At the beginning of the aftermath, a coalition of the ruling classes and big business took control of the airwaves and mounted arguments to the effect that holding on to liberal democracy, free markets, and capitalism was the only viable solution for dealing with global warming. Other voices were pointing out that Liberal Democrats and capitalists had been the architects of the mess the world was facing. There was hope for the emergence of a pragmatic technocracy that could deal with the twin global evils of inequality and warming without shedding any more blood. In the meantime, maximum efforts were being devoted to finding the evil culprits and to exact retribution.

Down in the streets and around the suburbs, and in the favelas and slums, other schools of thought were brewing. The system was broken, business as usual was unsustainable, liberal democracy was just another version of kleptocracy for the few, and so on. The marches were getting bigger by the day, the demands for change became louder, and moral power was filtering down to the multitudes of dispossessed. The Bidens and Putins of this world were calling for calm while sending the security forces into the streets. Increasingly, the forces imposing law and order were coming to realize that they were the people, as well. They began to stand back and, in some cases, change sides. In Austin, Texas, a group calling itself the Confederate Army took control of the Capitol building and the local TV station. They declared independence for the Republic of Texas. Federal troops moved in later in the day. After a brief firefight, order was restored, and a shaken governor went on air to declare a state of emergency and to reassure the population that the USA remained intact and in business. The army changed sides in Venezuela, allowed President Maduro to flee in a helicopter, and then declared martial law and announced the formation of an interim government to restore law and order. The EU closed its borders, declared a curfew, banned assemblies of more than 10 people, and required all law enforcement agencies to be on standby. Two days later, the highest legal authority, the European Court of Justice, declared the measures illegal. All social media was shut down for a period of 30 days, however. The Chinese government cut all electronic links and other means of communication with the outside world. Change was in the air – for better or worse.

It was getting increasingly difficult to keep track of what was happening from where I was watching and listening in a log cabin in the mountains of Norway. CNN and BBC World Service were still alive and well, but I had the feeling both were exercising self-censorship in accord with official wishes. It was early days, and I could not tell whether or not the world was finding its way to a new normal, much less what that might be. I needed to check the pulse of life in a city.

* * *

From where I had listened to a lecture on Norse mythology, it was a two-hour train journey to Oslo. Civilization was a shock to the system after the rarefied air and overwhelming peace in the mountains. I had been to Oslo a few times in the past: once to inspect a couple of aging reactors and twice for conferences. It was not one of my favourite cities. It did have a nice harbour overlooked by an ordinary late medieval fortification, a brutalist modern city hall, and a pleasant redevelopment of what once was a shipyard and some factories. Around a promontory, there was the opera house that seemed to be in the process of sliding into the sea. Since my last visit, I noticed a post-modern building that was intended to be an art gallery featuring most of Edvard Munch's works. I sat down next to a fountain and watched life. There did not seem to be any whiff of fear in the air or even a smidgen of apprehension. People were wandering past, seemingly without a care in the world. There were no signs of a new "normal". It occurred to me that after three generations of being drunk on oil and having amassed a sovereign wealth fund with assets of more than 1 trillion dollars, one might feel relatively bulletproof. Oslo was not the place to judge the mood of the world.

My immediate problem was that I did not know what to do now or where to go next. I stayed in Oslo for a few days and was none the wiser. The TV in the hotel was no more informative than the one in the mountains. I did buy a selection of foreign papers and a copy of *The Economist* at the railway station, and that helped. The extent of deaths and injuries on the East Coast of the USA and in St Petersburg were still mounting, and the two affected nations were still in shock. The rest of the world seemed to be watching and waiting for what was going to happen next. *The Economist* had a whole issue devoted to the reasons for, and consequences of, recent events. The tone seemed to suggest that there was a powerful case for change but that the USA was unlikely to come to that party. The international edition of *The Wall Street Journal* was interesting, in the sense that a survey of the CEOs of the 100 biggest corporations were in favour of a new "normal", where global warming was seen as the greatest threat to the future of prosperity. So, maybe all is not lost, I thought. The *Financial Times* reported that the EU was going to strengthen its internal carbon tax regime and was considering the introduction of a tariff on imports; the tariff was to be based on the inferred carbon footprint for each imported item. The internal combustion engine was to be phased out within the next 10 years. Short-haul flights within the EU would be banned within six months in favour of ground-based public means of travel. There were predictable howls of outrage from various vested interests. The dark art of compromise would probably need to be exercised, but the EU was a master at that. Similar sentiments had surfaced after the 2008 financial collapse and once again after the Covid-19 pandemic but had as yet not been converted into action. There were signs that this time it would be different.

I returned to the mountains after a week in Oslo to consider my options. How would I get out of Norway and across a border to anywhere without leaving a trail? There was another problem. I had been in a manic mode for over two years, and I had a feeling that I was coming down with a thud. We had accomplished what we set out to do. Now, I could only sit back and watch. I had persuaded myself that the future would evolve in a particular way, given the initial conditions that we had set in place. I recalled that Hasina had talked about the unpredictability of change. Suppose the worldly system was too complex, and the future turned out to be brutish, nasty and chaotic. Then, we would have inflicted death and destruction beyond imagination and for reasons that were totally misguided. Such thoughts were sufficient to bring on depression to the sanest of minds. In my case, the mind was in a fragile state. I wished that Hasina and Eden were here and could talk to me. As it was, the cabin was going to be my black hole for a while, into which I would retreat and pull down the lid.

* * *

The weeks went by. The black bubble was my private hell in which I was trapped. All I could manage was a short walk now and again. The highlight of the day was when the cat came to talk to me and to get its treats. Twice, I dragged myself down to the supermarket to get some much-needed food. I thought about taking the bus to town, but it seemed to require far too much willpower. The barriers were too high.

Then, one night, Hasina came to me in my dreams. She stood and looked down at me with tears running down her cheeks. In a whispered voice, she said, "Please don't leave me. I need you the way you were. Please listen to the survival instincts."

In the morning, the vision was still with me. Hasina was right; I needed to be the way I had been. Most of the morning, I sat on the steps outside and looked out over the valley to the lake below. The world began to make sense again. I decided I could do life once more. It had been a long night of total darkness. Now, the sun was shining again, and I could start thinking about getting a grip.

The rest of the day was spent catching up on news. The death tolls had risen. The financial markets had fallen further. There had been serious rioting in the streets in the US with exchanges of live fire. Government buildings were protected by military cordons. In Russia, most cities were in total lockdown, and the Kremlin was protected by a ring of tanks. Europe had turned relatively quiet, and the war had gone on the back burner. The external borders of the EU were still closed, but travel within the EU/EEA was permitted. The EU Council of Ministers had been meeting and had managed to cobble together a vision for a new world without inequality. There was a promise of a new EU where quality of life was going to replace the traditional obsession with GDP and where the future was going to be based on sustainability. China was keeping its head down inside closed borders. I could discern a few glimmers of hope. The electronic media seemed to be mainly preoccupied with the aftermath of the nuclear strikes and only fleetingly with who had done it.

I took the bus to town to see if I could learn more from the print media. The best I could do was a recent copy of *The Economist*. The bastion of liberalism had come to life. The issue had several lengthy articles in defence of liberalism, but with a twist. This time it purported to accept that it could be reinvented with a human face and as a custodian of the environment. There was also an article speculating on who was responsible for the nuclear attacks and how it was done. The conclusion was that a sophisticated warhead could only have been sourced in the laboratories of one of the known nuclear powers. *Right on*, I thought. Also, unnamed sources in the CIA were confident that the weapons had been delivered by sea, in yachts. *Quite right*, I thought. The writer of the piece must have done some homework and concluded that the hypothetical yacht heading for St Petersburg must have passed through either of the Danish Straits from the North Sea into the Baltic Sea. *Well done*, I thought.

Thinking back to my cruise a couple of months previously, I remembered thinking that it would be a miracle if we had not been noticed. There were a lot of other pleasure vessels with sails or motors in the area at the time, and we were not conspicuous. The question was, were we photographed? Could such a photographed image be matched to another photograph taken in St Petersburg? A more important question: had anyone noticed me being set ashore south of Stockholm?

I needed a cup of coffee and went to my favourite place on the main drag in Lillehammer. There, I found my friend who had told me about Ragnarok. He nodded to indicate that he remembered me, and I sat down at his table. His immediate comment was, "We live in unhappy times." I agreed. He continued. "We are seeing the end of the old world, but a new world will rise from the ashes of the nuclear blasts, as predicted in Norse mythology."

I asked him, "Do you think it will be a better and kinder world?"

He did not think so, again, according to mythology.

"Let me tell you about my father. He lived through WWII as a machinist in the engine room on the Murmansk convoys. Twice he was torpedoed but survived, very much against the odds. For the rest of his life, he was waiting for the next torpedo that he knew would kill him. My father thought that after the lessons of the war, a new and kinder world would rise from the rubble. Sadly, he was disappointed."

My friend shook his head and said he had to go, but he would be back the next day. He then said he was like his father and was waiting for the next torpedo. I never saw him again.

* * *

Back in the cabin, I took stock of my situation. I knew enough about the world to realize that sooner or later, the wolfhounds would get a sniff of the trail. When they came, it would be without any warning. All I could do was assume that they were not far behind. I needed to keep moving.

In Scandinavia, everyone has an identity defined by a so-called person number. From cradle to grave, everything you do of any significance is linked to your person number. I had no such number and no legitimate identity in Norway, but anything I wanted to do could end up on a database. I had one real identity and three fake ones. If I crossed a border, I could only do so by using an identity. There would be a time when I would run out of identities. I had to use them sparingly. At that moment, I was probably safe where I was. The only written record of my existence here was the signed contract in Oslo for rental of the cabin. I had then used one of my fake identities. My real identity, complete with one or more photos, was on the internet from the time when I went to conferences and addressed learned audiences. This gave the hunters data for face recognition. In the mountains, there were no CCTV cameras, except possibly in the supermarket. In Lillehammer, there would be plenty, and in Oslo, one on every corner. So far, I had used cash everywhere and had avoided leaving a financial trail. Clearly, flights and airports had to be avoided. This left me with buses, trains and ferries as means of getting around. I could, of course, go for a long walk and cross the border to Sweden by following the wartime refugee trail. My beard was the best I could do to confuse the face recognition software. As well, I hid behind a face mask and wore a baseball cap whenever I was out and about.

In the end, I decided that the EU was the most promising place to hide. Once inside the Schengen area, I had a lot of territory to choose from with an identity card. Also, I did not fit the profile of an illegal migrant or a hard-boiled terrorist. My German, with an Austrian accent, was perfectly passable, and my English was fluent. I had a bit of Dutch from my two years at Almelo and enough French to pass as a tourist. Either Denmark or Germany seemed to be the obvious first port of call. It was just as well that the virus had not come a year later. If it had, I would have been stuck in Sweden or Norway for a while.

I cleaned up the cabin, said goodbye to the cat, locked the door, and took the train to Oslo. There, I handed the keys to the lady agent and told her that the book writing had gone well. Then, I checked myself into a hotel next to the combined bus and train station. I had the choice between a ferry or a bus to either Germany or Denmark. I had to find a weak point in the security at the border. It took me three days at the bus station to check on buses to the continent. It was near the end of summer, and the holiday time was at an end. The passengers who boarded buses were a mixed lot, ranging from students to guest workers. There were a few customers like me who took the buses. They might have fallen on hard times. Then, I surveyed the ferries to Kiel in Germany and to various ports in Denmark at the two ferry terminals. Both of them seemed to attract a high percentage of pensioners. Presumably, the attraction was a long weekend away, a bit of shopping and unlimited duty-free boozing. I sat in the departure hall and watched the passengers going through turnstiles waving some form of identity card under the nose of a disinterested immigration officer. It looked like my sort of place; I settled on a one-way ticket to Kiel.

The Fugitive

The journey to Kiel was uneventful. After inspection of my cabin in the bowels of the ferry, I spent most of the evening in a semi-deserted lounge. As soon as we had crossed an imaginary line into international waters, the lounge emptied completely. The bar had opened, and duty-free alcohol was on tap. I took the opportunity to find the cafeteria. The dinner was not memorable, but it would keep me alive.

Before arrival, I had done some internet leg work and had identified a modest hotel near the railway station. I had worked out how to get there, courtesy of Google Maps. The town was remarkably deserted. Then, I remembered that the main claim to fame of Kiel was the Kieler Woche earlier in the summer – when the town hosted thousands of sailing boats, a greater number of sailors, and an even greater number of spectators and revellers. There were non-stop regattas for all the known classes of vessels. After a couple of weeks of drinking and cavorting, the town went back to sleep until the next year. The checking of roughly 2000 disembarking passengers was perfunctory at best. I inflicted myself on a group of pensioners speaking Norwegian and was waved through. The pensioners were presumably there on a weekend cruise. My intentions were different, but I did not tell anyone. Numerous buses were lined up dockside to take the pensioners to the city centre. I followed my pensioner friends and found myself being deposited not far from the railway station. On the spur of the moment, I abandoned the thought of the hotel and boarded a late train to Berlin.

I had been to Berlin several times in the past and had enjoyed the place. Once, I had been to the Free University for a workshop on the disposal of high-level nuclear waste. On another occasion, the IAEA had sent me to hold forth on the topic of nuclear proliferation. Early in my formative nuclear life, my supervisor had sent me on a course dealing with the technology of pressurized water nuclear reactors. I had made some dimly remembered friends on each occasion but had no intention of refreshing the friendships. I made sure to minimize any chance of meeting a former friend or colleague by heading for the Turkish quarter, where I booked myself into an innocuous hotel for a few days.

* * *

The next day was a shock to the system. In the morning, I picked up a copy of the *Frankfurter Allgemeine* on my way to the nearest café. A pot of coffee and two Hörnchen appeared while I began to turn the pages of the paper. In the middle was a two-page spread of the candidates who might have been involved in the nuclear attacks, and there was a ranking according to capability to produce and deliver two nuclear weapons. All the usual suspects were on the list with a series of pros and cons based on having the motivation to do so. Each candidate was rated according to technical, political and ideological criteria by the respective number of stars. Pakistan was high on the list with four out of five stars. None of the other major nuclear states managed more than three stars. One column was devoted to the connection of the attacks to global warming. The paper speculated that possibly the two warheads had been handed over, or diverted, to a sub-national group concerned with mitigation of global warming as its sole objective.

Another column speculated that it was no coincidence that the

Covid-19 pandemic had resulted in a measurable, but transient, decrease in global emissions of greenhouse gases. As well, there had been a significant upturn in thinking about a sustainable future, even from quarters that traditionally had not supported such views. The *Frankfurter Allgemeine* was not, by any stretch, considered to be a left-wing rag, and had clearly decided to focus on the issues rather than foaming at the mouth about evil and despicable terrorists. *Good on it*, I thought.

On the next page was a much shorter piece on Qadeer Khan and about his wheeling and dealing in nuclear technology and materials that had resulted in Pakistan becoming a declared nuclear state and that indirectly had helped North Korea to develop nuclear weapons. The article asked the rhetorical question: Had he continued his activities and sold a couple of warheads to an as-yet-unknown customer? There were good reasons for this to be unlikely, according to the paper, as Khan had recently suffered a stroke and was reported to be in a coma in a military hospital in Rawalpindi. Possibly he could have carried out his last nuclear deal while he was alive and well.

I finished my breakfast, bought a copy of *Die Welt*, and hurried back to the hotel. The news required some thinking and possibly a measure of mourning.

* * *

The rest of the day I sat in my room, reread the papers, searched the internet, and tried to decide what it all meant. *Die Welt* did not shed any new light on the matter. The internet was replete with theories that made little sense, but any hard information was thin on the ground.

Hasina and I had last met up with Khan nearly three years

previously in Karachi. He was then in his early 80s but seemed to be in full command of his physical and mental faculties. He knew exactly what he was doing and why it had to be done. There were two possibilities. Either the stroke was genuine – given his advanced age, the news could be based on fact. Or there was another possibility: the Pakistani security service might have smelled a rat and decided to remove Khan from the market. One cannot interrogate a comatose subject, especially in a well-guarded military hospital. If this was the case, then the Pakistani security services could also have removed all traces, down to the last milligram of unlogged highly enriched uranium and any signs of clandestine work on undocumented warheads. Any personnel involved in such work would have been sent to obscure guard posts in the Himalayas or taken out of circulation by other means. It might even have been that Khan was alive and well but undercover in the hospital. Would there then be a remaining link to Hasina and me, aside from the legitimate one, when we were working for the IAEA? How many of our footprints had Khan had to reveal or been able to eradicate before hypothetically being forced to confess to his sins? If it came to a choice between my well-being and that of Pakistan, I would be thrown to the wolves. It seemed possible that Khan, in particular, and Pakistan, in general, would endeavour to deal me out of the game. Alternatively, I could be made to disappear. A dead man cannot rat on his friends and enemies. I would have to assume the worst. Would the fake identities be known to the Pakistani security service, ISS – and would the ISS need to ensure my silence? Could it be that the Russian security service, FSB, the CIA and the Pakistani ISS could all be after me? I could not think of satisfactory answers to these questions. I felt vulnerable and friendless. All I could do was remove the encryption software from my laptop and smartphone, along with any other incriminating information about websites that had been visited. Later in the day, I bought a new laptop and a new SIM card for the mobile phone from a hole-in-the-wall shop. After dark, I went for a walk along the River Spree. At a quiet stretch, I threw the laptop and the old SIM card into the river. Afterwards, it occurred to me that it might have been where the dead body of Rosa Luxemburg had been floating after she had been killed by Hitler's Brownshirts. It was a sobering thought. I hurried back to the security of a main street.

Once Pakistan and Khan had become a country and a person of interest, it would not take long, courtesy of the IAEA, for my name to be noticed. I had been the chief inspector of activities at Rawalpindi for several years until 2010 and, on occasion, had been accompanied by Hasina. A cursory search of the internet would then find us at Oxford University. Inquiries would reveal that we had taken a leave of absence and seemingly vanished into thin air. We could be on the radar. We would be known from published works and conference presentations to hold and express unconventional views on geopolitics and on the rationale for having nuclear weapons. Once the hunters had drawn blanks in Pakistan, their attention would turn to secondary targets. Hasina and I could be on the list.

I was hoping that Hasina was now in a part of the world where she would blend into the background and where the worst of modernity had not yet provided the means to keep track of people and their movements.

Superficially, I could blend into the street scene almost anywhere in Western Europe. The difficulty would be to avoid leaving an electronic trail. CCTV cameras had become omnipresent in recent times, covering street scenes, as well as most private and public establishments, while keeping tabs on virtually all modes of transport and travel. Face recognition had made great strides in recent years. Most financial and electronic transactions would end up on a database that could be interrogated on command.

I had a few things on my side. I was decidedly able to pass as an average male person of indeterminate age. A bushy beard, in combination with a face mask and dark glasses, would make the AI algorithms struggle to match the current me to the clean-shaven images from my past life.

The best I could do was to make life difficult for the hypothetical pursuers. I had to assume that my identification papers, real and fake, were compromised. I could cross borders only as an illegal migrant or by avoiding checkpoints. My past face was relatively well known. It was just possible that top-of-the-range face recognition software on a supercomputer could match my present likeness to past images, given access to sufficient databases. I knew enough about the software to be aware of its limitations. Within the EU, the sample size was far too large to make a definitive identification of a single particular person, but artificial intelligence software could possibly correlate multiple hits with other information, such as a path followed by a moving target. One target that followed the same path each day could be discarded, while another target that changed hotel three times in a week would be a promising hit. It was fortuitous that I had access to untraceable cash in any denomination, courtesy of Mujibur and Khan. I could therefore steer well away from any bank and avoid being known to the electronic transaction systems. I could make the geometry of my cheeks marginally different with a couple of cotton balls. Occasionally, a heavy-duty mouth guard would distort the facial geometry sufficiently for the recognition software to pair me with another group of individuals. Otherwise, I had to fall back on the uncertain strength of privacy legislation within the EU.

During the next few weeks, I changed hotels every so often,

always choosing modest places in backstreets away from the city centre.

Christmas 2023 was approaching, and it was getting colder by the day. Usually, I spent most of my time in my room checking the internet for the latest news or in cafés hiding behind a newspaper. Sometimes I would inform the concierge that a friend might come and inquire about my presence. Could the concierge please take a message and let me know? I usually approached the hotel each time from a different direction and looked for suspicious activity, such as men sitting in parked cars or loitering outside shops. Maybe I was getting paranoid, but even paranoics may have real enemies, I said to myself.

Christmas came and went. The saying that one is never as lonely as amongst a crowd in a city began to weigh on me. As well, I was beginning to get bored. Sitting in my room on New Year's Eve made me question the meaning of my present life. What else could I do? The possibility that I had inadvertently left a track somewhere, and somehow, in Berlin was a thought that brought the survival instinct back to life. I was not ready to just sit and wait for the hunters to come for me. It was time to move on. Maybe I could leave a false trail.

One evening at the end of January 2024, I told the concierge that I was leaving the next morning. I had received an invitation from a friend in Düsseldorf who had a flat just off the Königsallee, and I could stay there.

Having planted a false trail, the next day, I boarded an overnight bus to Hamburg. I sat in the back of the bus behind my newspaper. My furry appearance and face mask were doing nicely as camouflage for a good part of my face. The top was partly obscured by the baseball cap. For part of the journey, I pulled the cap down and nodded off.

The bus rolled into Hamburg early in the morning and dropped me off near the city centre. I had checked out the hotel situation and walked to the centre of St Pauli. As usual, I booked myself into an innocuous place away from the main streets. It was time for a short walk to orient myself before finding a quiet place for dinner. The bright lights had to wait for the next day.

The festive season was at its end, it seemed, when I headed outdoors in the morning. Covid-19 had presumably taken its toll on the hustle and bustle of St Pauli, which claimed to be the liveliest place in Germany. I had always been partial to harbours and rivers and went for a morning stroll along the Elbe toward the sea. As expected, it was no longer a working harbour and its Hanseatic architecture had been obliterated at the end of WWII by some of the heaviest allied bombing inflicted on Germany. Nevertheless, it was a pleasant walk. I found a café and treated myself to a leisurely coffee and Hörnchen. Somehow, for once, I felt at peace with myself and with the world. The morning walk along the Elbe, in combination with coffee, Hörnchen and the daily paper, became my routine during the next week.

The *Frankfurter Allgemeine* had another shock in store for me. It announced that Khan had died in hospital without regaining consciousness. I wondered if he had been given an overdose of morphine and wished I had been able to have a look at what had been sown into the traditional white cloth. It was reported that the demise of "the father of Pakistan's nuclear bomb" was mourned throughout the country. I still could not stop thinking that maybe he was alive in a well-guarded military outpost in a mountain valley. I would probably never know, but he was one of the few people I had admired and liked, and I would miss him.

It was time to change hotel. I found another in a street close to Reeperbahn, the centre of the red-light district. The man at the desk looked at me as if to say that I did not seem to be much like the usual customer. The room I was given had red décor, an oversized well-sprung bed, and a mirror in the ceiling. *Never mind*, I thought. The management was likely to be discreet and non-committal in case there were any questions concerning one of his customers. I realized later on from the creaking of beds that some of the rooms were rented by the hour.

The days in St Pauli stretched into weeks. I got used to my over-sexed room and looking into my mirror image as I was dozing off. A good part of the day was spent in cyber-space checking the news from around the world. One report had two yachts passing through the Suez Canal. The paperwork said that both were registered in Myanmar, but no trace was found in Myanmar of the yachts ever having existed. Khan had done a good job on that score. Further investigations suggested that the yachts had spent the winter in the Med. I recognized one of them in a grainy image. It would not require much intelligence to realize that they must have gone past Gibraltar, and one of them would then have headed through one of the narrow straits past Denmark and then along the south coast of Sweden in order to get to St Petersburg. The other yacht must have crossed the Atlantic. There was no mention of a middle-aged non-descript male being involved. So far, so good, but it was probably just a matter of time. This kind of information was almost certainly planted in order to involve the public, who unwittingly might have useful information. The question then was, what other information was known but not revealed or leaked? Had the wolf pack started to look for an Oxford academic who had taken a leave of absence and disappeared, presumably with his academic wife, who also had disappeared? If the fake identity papers were known, then I was in serious trouble and was potentially traceable at least in Norway and possibly as far as Germany. I wished I knew.

The nearest café to my hotel was just around the corner from the reddest part of Reeperbahn. I began to go there for my morning shot of caffeine and two Hörnchen. This was roughly the same time as the ladies of the night congregated after a hard night's work. Fishnet stockings and low-cut blouses seemed to be the most popular uniform. It was a varied clientele, ranging from fresh-faced apprentices to seasoned pros. Much of the conversation was about the men who had most recently availed themselves of their services. These seemed to range from rank youngsters who needed to be helped, to middle-aged professionals looking for variety and uncomplicated sex, to the older generation needing reassurance that they still had it. There was occasional talk about difficult customers when the muscle had to be called. It was a world very far removed from academia. I recalled once reading a book by Arthur Koestler in which he described academics as call girls, with reference to the ones who spent their time on the conference circuit. I had known people like that.

One Sunday morning, the café was particularly busy. As usual, I sat by myself up against a wall. One of the fresh-faced ones asked politely if she could share my table. I nodded and continued to read the newspaper. When I looked up to deal with my waffle, she was looking at me intently.

"Are you looking for a girl?" she said.

I smiled and responded, "I am too old and tired."

She smiled back. "I doubt that. Are you from Austria?"

"I used to be. I think you are an Ossie. Maybe somewhere near Dresden?"

We were showing off our respective linguistic knowledge. I looked at her more closely. She was probably in her mid-20s or early 30s, with blonde hair, probably real, tied back in a ponytail, taller than average in high heels, dressed in the regulation fishnet stockings and a low-cut blouse. There was a haunted look about her. I wondered what she made of me and if it mattered to her. Maybe she recognized the haunted look in me. She stood up and collected her coat.

"Dresden is near enough. I have to go now. It's been a long day."

She got up and left. After another cup of coffee, I did the same.

A few days later, I was engrossed in the morning paper at the usual table by the wall. Suddenly I had the feeling that there was someone close by. She was back again and pulling out a chair without asking permission.

"What are you doing here?" she said.

I thought about that for a few seconds. "I'm hiding." I had not intended to say this, but somehow the words had escaped.

"Can you tell me what from?" she asked.

It was turning into a game of questions and answers. I felt a great urge to be truthful.

"I think I'm fleeing from myself and from not wanting to think about what I've done, what I've lost, and what I can never atone for."

"Are you a danger to me?" she asked. I thought the question was conditioned by her profession.

"Not at all. I could never look anyone, you included, in the eye and wish to inflict harm. If anything, I am the victim of not being able to escape the inescapable. It is my turn to ask a question. Can I?"

She nodded.

"What is your name?"

"Ursula, and yours?"

"Call me Johannes. It is not my real name. It's best that you don't know that. We now have labels. Now we can get personal."

I continued. "What brought you to Reeperbahn? Please forgive me if you would rather not tell me."

She closed her eyes, as if she needed to look into her soul before answering. Then, she began talking.

"My mother died in childbirth, on the day I was born, and my father was left with a newborn baby girl. He was a good man, a good father, and a good citizen. He worked for the Volkspolizei in a small town, and he believed in the system. He had read *Das Kapital* in the same way as his forefathers had read the Bible. The Communist Manifesto made the same sense to him as the Ten Commandments had made to others. Most of the time, he chased thieves, flagged down speeding cars, and wagged his finger at drivers. Once there was a killing, and he was happy when detectives from the city took over the case. Each month he would report to the Stasi. Then, the Wall came down, and he felt that his hope for a better and fairer world had been shattered. He took to drink and stopped talking about his visions for the future. A few years later, the Stasi archives were released to the world. His name turned up somewhere in the miles of dusty folders. The entries under his name seemed to suggest that conversations he had with others had found their way to superiors, and lives had been ruined. My father became a pariah and an outcast in the small town. People called me names and threw rocks at me. One day, when I came home from school, he was gone. He had hanged himself in the woodshed. The priest and I were the only ones present at his funeral. This happened when I had just finished high school, and I could run away. In the autumn, I enrolled at the University of Karlsruhe with the intention of studying psychiatry. I think the need was to get myself together again. At the end of the second year, and after two failed relationships, I took an inadequate overdose and was institutionalized for several months. I had no money, no skills, no self-confidence and no prospects. This is how I came to Reeperbahn, where I met many other women who, like me, had been on bad journeys in life. It is my first year living off my vagina. This is my story." She stopped talking, looked away, and I recognized a wounded soul.

There was silence between us. She had laid bare her soul, and I did not know how to respond. In the end, I could just mutter that no person should have to endure what she had lived through.

"I admire you for telling me about your life. That takes courage and strength. Once you have got to the point of revealing yourself to a stranger, you are well on the way to resurrection."

She accepted that this was the best I could do and then continued. "I have become a master at judging people. I seem to know who can hurt me and who will not. You will not hurt me. Therefore, I can tell you my story. This will help to heal my wounds."

We stopped talking. At this stage, there was nothing more to be said. We wished each other well before she left. I went home deep in thought, and for once, I did not think about my own miserable situation.

* * *

Another day, and another visit to the café in the morning for my breakfast. Ursula was there ahead of me. We greeted, and I had my coffee and Hörnchen. I broke the silence.

"I would like to tell you a story, but not here. There is a park where we can talk in private."

She agreed, and we left together. A couple of other ladies of the night looked at us as we walked out and probably concluded that Ursula had landed a client. As we walked, I rehearsed in my mind what I was going to say. I had to be economical with the truth.

We found a park bench, sat down, and I began my prepared speech.

"I am like you, wanting to bare my soul. I told you earlier that I was running away. I was not entirely truthful. I am actually a fugitive from my own life. All governments engage in activities that are deniable. Many of these activities never see the light of day, and if they find their way into the public domain, they are denied by those who are in power and give the orders. I can give you many examples. The system needs people who work in the shadows, and they are the ones that do the dirty work. I have been one of those. I did not like what I was doing. It often involved working for two masters who, on the surface, were enemies but colluded behind the scenes when it suited their purposes. There were consequences that in many cases were intensely distasteful. In the end, I decided to go public. I was in possession of a great deal of hard evidence. One day, I handed it all over anonymously to Wikileaks, which then ensured that it ended up in the public domain. As a result, the careers of some very senior public figures came to a deserved and abrupt end, and I became a wanted man. The security services of two major nations are now looking for me. So far, I have stayed ahead of the wolf pack by changing my appearance, by not leaving financial or identity trails, and by moving randomly from one place to another. Two months ago, I crossed into Germany without having to identify myself. The time has come for me to cross another border anonymously."

I stopped talking and waited to see how Ursula would react.

"I think you are telling me this for the same reason that I told you about my life. Am I right?" she said.

"Before I explain myself further, I would like to ask you a couple of questions. What do you want to do with your life? How much money do you make from working on the Reeperbahn? I would understand if you choose not to answer either of the questions."

"I have a plan. It is to remain at the Reeperbahn for two years to make enough money for me to go back to being a student. I think I could then finish the degree in psychiatry so that I can help people like me to turn their lives around. At the moment, I think it is possible to save about 25,000 euros per year from what I am doing."

She looked at me as if waiting for me to continue.

"The people who are trying to find me have a motto: 'We always get our man.' I have seen them in action. I would like to make you a proposition. The reason for doing so is that I want to change my profile from being a loner on the run. I think it is the survival instinct that keeps me going. At the moment, I feel in my bones that it is time for me to move on and keep running. I would like to offer you 25,000 in cash per year, paid monthly, to be my companion and to be a cover for me by turning us into a two-some. You will be a part of my survival strategy. I do not wish to be your sugar daddy. I would promise to act with you in the way a good father would. You will be free to leave at any time of your choosing. My immediate plan is to cross the border into Austria without being noticed. If at any time I think you are in danger, I will pay you out for the year and do my utmost to ensure that you will be safe. Please go away now and think about my proposition for two days. Then meet me here again."

Ursula nodded and left without another word. I hoped that I would see her again.

* * *

Ursula had come before me when I arrived at the park bench. She smiled and said, "When do I start?"

"Unless you need some time to extricate yourself from the Reeperbahn and other commitments, you can start today."

She said that her line of business did not require any advance notice. One simply said Auf Wiedersehen and walked out after collecting personal items from a locker. She had a bedsit nearby with a microwave for a kitchen and a shared shower and toilet down the hallway. This could be abandoned at the end of the month.

I gave her two envelopes: one containing 1,000 euros for expenses; the other 2,000 euros for one month in advance. We shook hands, and the deal was done.

It was only later that I began to think about how this had happened and came to the conclusion that we were two of a kind – lost souls who had recognized each other. We had both needed to talk about ourselves and parade our demons.

On the Run with Ursula

We had agreed to meet in a café in the centre of St Pauli, some distance away from Reeperbahn, to change our pattern of movements. This was to be our first planning session.

I told Ursula about threats – how to recognize them and then take evasive action. I also told her about the various methods that were used by security services to track down people who were wanted for various reasons. It was difficult to remain unseen and anonymous in a modern society.

Then, I told Ursula about her role in my survival strategy. I needed to change my profile. From being a lone middle-aged male, I would become the older member of a couple. Ursula would be a younger companion, either a partner or a daughter. She would also be a second pair of eyes watching for signs of danger. If necessary, I could remain hidden while Ursula dealt with activities in public.

"What should I do at the moment?" asked Ursula.

"I would like you to find us a two-bedroom flat in an area popular with immigrants. My potential enemies would stand out in such an area. I would like you to sign a contract for two in your name with me as your partner. My name is Johan Cruyff, in case you are asked. You should ask for an initial contract of two months with an option to extend. We would prefer the flat to be on a corner and on the second floor. It needs to be at least partially furnished with access to Wi-Fi."

"Give me three days. I'll meet you here with a collection of offers. By the way, I am really happy to have a purpose in life," she said.

"Consider it to be the first tentative step in your resurrection," I responded.

* * *

We met again as agreed. Ursula showed me half a dozen pamphlets with details of flats for rent. We looked through them, chose the two most promising prospects and set off to the agents to arrange viewings. By the end of the day, we had made a decision, signed a contract and got the keys. German efficiency could not be faulted. Ursula headed off to collect her belongings while I invested in two sets of bed linen and some towels. Then, I went back to the hotel and announced that I had just this morning had a message that my father in Cologne had suffered a stroke. Yet another false trail had been laid. With my meagre belongings in the backpack, I returned to my new home and waited for Ursula. It was going to seem strange to share a house with another person.

She returned an hour later, dragging a suitcase on wheels. I welcomed her home. For a few brief moments, we stood in the living room and looked at our few belongings. I think we thought that somehow our lives had changed, and it had come to this.

Later on in the evening, we walked off to the Aldi down the road and stocked up on food for the next few days. I made my favourite pasta and salad dinner while Ursula sorted herself out in her bedroom. Then, we uncorked a celebratory bottle of Merlot. It was probably the first dinner either of us had enjoyed with another person for a long time. After dinner, we sat down with cups of coffee, and it seemed to me that life was near-normal again.

"What happens now?" Ursula said.

"I am hoping we can stay here for two months, maybe longer. Then, we can move on to Munich. The trick is to keep moving and try not to leave any tracks. My plan is to cross into Austria without going through a border check. There are trails through the Alps that will take us across the border without being noticed. We have to wait for late spring or early summer to do this. I think Innsbruck is the best destination. I lived in Vienna for many years. In Innsbruck, I am very unlikely to be recognized by anyone. That is as far as I can plan at the moment. We have to be ready to move on short notice, if necessary."

I could see that Ursula was thinking about what we would do from one day to another when nothing seemed to be happening. I needed to fill in some gaps.

"There is a condition called cabin fever. During the pandemic, there were periods of total lockdown, when people found themselves marooned indoors with nothing to do aside from daytime TV or computer games. As the weeks of total boredom went on and on, depression set in for some, while others sought relief in alcohol. The secret is to discipline oneself with routines and activities.

"Lately, I have been seeking refuge on the internet, partly to keep busy but also to keep track of my enemies. I will probably continue this regimen. Now there is a big difference; you will be a vital part of my daily life."

"If I am going to be cooped up for weeks, I would like to know more about you. For instance, are you married, or have you been married?" she asked.

"I appreciate the need for the question. Yes, I am married, and I have a son. I have been on the run for two years. Sooner or later, I will be found, and that will be the end of my life. There was a high likelihood that the pursuers could get to me through my family. So, my wife and I decided that we should go separately into hiding in places where we would be unlikely to be found. It was the most difficult decision I have made. Even I do not know where they are, in case I get caught and am made to tell everything. I cannot reveal what I don't know is the idea. I don't expect ever to see my wife and son again."

"Thank you for telling me this," she whispered, then came over, embraced me, and began weeping, just as Hasina had done before we parted for the last time. She kissed me on the forehead. "Good night, Daddy; you are not my real father, but I will still love you."

That night, Hasina and Eden came to me in my dreams. Maybe the conversation with Ursula had been the trigger. They were not happy dreams. In the dreams, I was running and looking everywhere, hither and yonder, hoping desperately to find them, but I never did. In the morning, I woke up feeling dreadful. I told myself that I had to keep going, for my sake and for their sake. Ursula had not seen me like this. She did not say anything but made me cups of coffee. Life was going to go on, I decided.

* * *

A week passed, and we were getting used to each other. We made dinner on alternate days. She had her shower in the morning; I had mine in the evening. In the afternoon, we walked along the Elbe. I stared intently at my laptop for two hours after breakfast while she was engrossed in a textbook on mindfulness. We decided that we should exercise our minds. English was my second language and it was fluent, while Ursula's high school English was getting rusty. Every second day was devoted to speaking English. On the alternate days, Ursula would take me through a chapter on mindfulness. We were becoming a good complementary team and were beginning to enjoy it.

* * *

I felt that I was starting to get an overview of the current state of the planet and of the effects of the triple shocks from Covid-19, followed by the war in Europe and then the twin nuclear attacks on the East Coast of the USA and on St Petersburg. One day I went into one of my rare optimistic modes. After breakfast, I thought long and hard about the future.

There was ample evidence for global lungs having benefitted from a dramatic economic dislocation. The consumption of goods and extraction of resources had gone down initially by more than 30%. The recovery had turned out to be much slower than anticipated, with the possible result that lifestyles might be undergoing a permanent change. The millennial generation in the rich countries now appeared to favour accumulation of experiences rather than collecting ever more "stuff". There seemed to be a trend toward expenditure on services rather than on things in cardboard boxes that would ultimately end up as landfill. Recycling was becoming a way of life, and consumers preferred products that could be repaired and packaging that could be recycled. The benchmarks were moving beyond 60% of "stuff" being recyclable.

Many of the mature industries had been the bedrock of the developed economies as well as directly, or indirectly, being the major contributors to greenhouse emissions. They were now at, or beyond, their peaks. For instance, the annual contribution to the global GDP of manufacturing new cars had been in the neighbourhood of US$4 trillion. If one added to the annual GDP the contributions from servicing and repairing the total fleet of cars, then an additional US$2 trillion was a reasonable guess. Sales of new cars had plummeted precipitously during the pandemic and after the nuclear attacks. The sales might recover slowly, and only partially, with time. In addition to the diminishing number of cars being built and sold, automotive technology looked set to undergo dramatic changes. The diesel engine was being consigned to history, and by 2030, fully electric cars were likely to dominate on the forecourts. The self-driving cars would then be seen more commonly on the highways. By that time, the private ownership of the car could be on the vane. Mobility would probably be available on command by ordering a self-driving vehicle with an electronic chauffeur that never slept, always stayed sober, did not get paid, and rarely made mistakes. The 40% of land in a typical city devoted to parking stationary cars could then be converted to more productive and environmentally friendly uses.

The contribution of the fossil fuel industry, from extraction of oil, natural gas and coal, was worth approximately US$4 trillion to the annual global GDP. In all three cases of the main fossil fuels, the world was awash with actual and available supply while the demands were declining. Renewables were now the fastest-growing components of the energy budget. Coal, being the dirtiest fuel, was increasingly being spurned by consumers and investors. Natural gas was seen as an energy supply of choice during the transition to the time when zero net carbon was reached. Oil was substantially a captive of the demand from the transport sector, but that was diminishing. During the period of the pandemic, the aviation industry fell off a cliff. It might recover but was unlikely to reach its former peak.

The finance sector had seemed to occupy a parallel universe that was decoupled from the "real" economy. Down at the micro-economic ground level, small and mid-sized businesses were going bust, unemployment was high, tenants were struggling to pay their rents, food banks were finding it difficult to cope with demand, many new entrants to job markets were unlikely to get beyond zero-hour contracts. This was the current reality in the so-called rich countries. In the emerging economies, absolute poverty was rising, and starvation was becoming a real reality. At the macro-economic level of the financial universe, stock markets were hitting new highs after the pandemic, the central banks were flooding the system with freshly printed cash, and private equity funds had seemingly inexhaustibly deep pockets for take-overs, mergers and buy-outs. Apple became the first company with a market value in excess of US$3 trillion; the personal wealth of the founder of Amazon, Jeff Bezos, reached a net worth in excess of US$200 billion. There was a gradual realization that the club of tech companies had excessive market power and were becoming too big to control. In effect, they were setting their own rules in terms of taxation, monopoly power, and influence on cultural and political discourse. Unlike in the case of the real economy, Covid-19 and the nuclear attacks had strengthened the control and domination of these companies. How had it come to this?

* * *

Ursula and I had been living together for a while and had settled into a routine. The English conversations were improving. I had begun to explain to Ursula what I thought about the state of the world. And then she told me in more detail about her life. I told her how my early life had some similarities with hers and how I had found some solace in talking to myself. She thought it was an alternative survival mechanism to mindfulness and a substitute for other forms of therapy. She suggested that we were good for each other when we were talking about our early lives.

One morning, I was doing my online visitations of the many sources of news. There was a new item in the online version of the *Washington Post* attributed to sources at the Pentagon. There was a near-certainty that the two warheads had been delivered by yachts.

The two yachts had come through the Suez Canal, each with a crew of two males with ethnicities consistent with that of the Indian sub-continent. The yachts had spent some time in the Mediterranean. There had been a brief stop in Algeciras, where a white male had joined the crews. The two yachts had passed through the strait at Gibraltar, and then presumably parted company. One yacht had been observed entering the Baltic Sea. The last sighting was off St Petersburg two days before the explosion. A passing pleasure cruiser was certain that the crew consisted of two people speaking accented English. What had happened to the fifth person, the white male?

The hair was rising on my back. Sooner or later, they would guess that I might have gone ashore on the coast of Sweden, and the timing would be narrowed down to plus or minus a few days. Every harbour would be checked for the arrival of an English-speaking white male. Almost inevitably, my image would be on a CCTV camera. Would someone have made the connection with a person who had been working with the IAEA in Vienna? The hunt was on, it seemed. How long would it take to follow the trail through Norway and then to Kiel, Berlin and Hamburg?

* * *

I had feared there was a possibility, indeed a likelihood, that the pursuers would get the scent of a trail, but I had tried to bury the thought in my subconsciousness while thinking about my current life in which I was a player in a silly game. Suddenly the game had become deadly serious, with the likely ending being my demise. Ursula sensed that something had changed. I had turned in on myself and had become withdrawn. My undivided attention was no longer a part of our daily life.

At dinner, she took matters in hand and gently implored me to tell her what had happened. I told her the bare bones about the pursuers who had found a trail to follow.

"Are we in danger?" she asked.

"There is no imminent danger. I have been running for close to a year. During that year, I have changed my location several times in a manner that is known as a random walk. At the moment, they know that I am a white male of interest. At every opportunity, I have tried to lay at least one false trail. I think we are safe here for a while, but yet again, I have to keep thinking about the next move and about the one after. There may be a time when I decide to give up, stop running, and wait for the endgame."

There was a long silence from Ursula.

"Please don't give up," she said. "For once, my life has meaning, but I need more time to put the past behind me. I realize that I have been in denial about the past and that I've been in a holding pattern, waiting for my demons to go away. Now I feel positive about myself, but I'm not yet ready to believe that it's going to last. I want to stay with you for a while longer. There will be a time when I can move on, but not yet."

The best I could do was to say thank you and offer reassurance that as long as she was not in danger, I would not ask for her to leave. Ursula was my one remaining connection to a normal life.

"This is my promise to you."

She went and found a bottle of red from Aldi and poured us a glass each.

"Let us drink to that."

And so, we did.

* * *

It had been a heavy evening, and I was in the process of nodding off when there was a soft knock on the bedroom door. The door opened, and Ursula came in.

"Please don't be angry with me. Let me be with you," she said. "Tonight, I feel like a bedraggled stray cat that needs to be stroked. I don't want to diminish what you feel for your wife and son, but tonight I ask you to be the person who can comfort me in my hour of need."

Suddenly the need to feel a warm body next to me, once again, was overwhelming, and I nodded invitingly. She climbed into bed next to me. For a while, we just enjoyed the closeness and warmth, and then, gradually, the lust took over.

There was a tacit agreement in the morning to accept the new sense of intimacy. Breakfast took on a new meaning, and the meeting of eyes said everything that needed to be said.

* * *

I found one new item of information. Someone had noticed a yacht coming in from the Atlantic and heading for Long Island. The description was matched against that from Algeciras. A picture was emerging of two yachts carrying nuclear warheads coming from somewhere in the Far East. I was surprised that it had taken such a long time to join the dots. There was nothing new in the story about the fifth man. I had come to the conclusion that the unconfirmed words from the Pentagon about the fifth man had been leaked deliberately in order to see what members of the public could contribute. It was possible, on the other hand, that the spooks knew a lot more but were keeping the rest under wraps. Possibly they were hoping that I would panic, get careless and make mistakes. The bonus of having teamed up with Ursula was that I could keep a low profile while she did what needed doing in the public arena.

Our relationship had reached a steady state. We knew that, in time, it would have to come to an end. For the time being, we did the best we could. Now and again, we would spend the night together to enjoy the intimacy and to pretend we were a couple, and for the moment, all was well with our lives.

Our two months in the flat was nearly up, and decisions needed to be made. We were now into May. We decided to stay another month unless there were signs that we were vulnerable. Ursula had struck up a friendship of a kind with an elderly lady diagonally across the intersection from our flat. The elderly friend seemed to have devoted her declining years to keeping an eye on the neighbourhood. Ursula made her an extremely calorific Black Forest cake, took it over to her, and struck up a conversation. We then concocted a story about a jilted ex-lover who was trying to track her down. Would the nice lady keep an eye out for a strange man loitering in the neighbourhood? If such a person was sighted, could our friend give us a phone call? In return, Ursula would bring a weekly cake and do her shopping, if needed. It was a good deal for both parties.

At the end of May, we decided to move on. The time together in Hamburg had been good for both of us, but it was time for another leg of the random walk. Ursula took another cake to our elderly friend across the street and told her that we were going back to her roots in Dresden. Our lady friend was sorry to hear that we were leaving but wished us good luck. Another false trail had been laid.

* * *

Munich was the next stop. Ursula had been there for a few days when she fled the former East Germany, or DDR as it was once called before the Wall came down. She had sought refuge in a cheap hotel and thought she could find it again. I had been there once, many years before, to visit the university. She was beginning to think I had been everywhere, and she was not far wrong. We thought that a bus was the safest way to go. There was only one CCTV camera on long-distance buses. Between dark glasses, the baseball cap, and a face mask, any images would be next to useless for the purpose of identification. In addition, we decided on the overnight bus. Ursula bought the tickets for both of us, and off we went. Before leaving, Ursula left a fictitious forwarding address of the physics department of the University of Oslo with our landlord in case there was any mail. It would keep a prospective pursuer occupied for a day or two.

It was just after dawn when the bus arrived in Munich. We grabbed our bags and headed for the first café that was open. Coffee and Hörnchen were on the agenda. The map on the smartphone suggested that the distance was walkable to the hotel that Ursula had once stayed at. Google was right, as usual. On closer inspection, we decided that another slightly less down-market hotel with Wi-Fi was preferable. Ursula checked us in as Herr and Frau Faisst and gave our home address as a flower shop in Cologne, and then we installed ourselves.

Once we had found our bearings, we went in search of a good outdoor shop to get information and maps. At one place, we talked to a man behind the counter who sang the praises of the Trans-Alpine Crossing, beginning in Germany at Tegernsee and then winding its way up and down through the Alps for seven days as far as Italy, but with a bail-out point to Innsbruck. We got the map and a pamphlet describing the scenic delights along the way and listing places to stop and rest.

That evening we sat and stared at the topographical map and read the description of the trail. It seemed doable. In my younger days, I had done some treks in Nepal and been on a couple of walks in the Austrian Alps during my days in Vienna. My knees were probably no longer in mint condition, but I thought that with a bit of care, they would last the distance. Ursula was young and healthy, and she was ready for a challenge. We decided to do a trial run of the first two days of the journey and then turn back. If that went well, we would come back and do the whole thing.

We went back to the man behind the counter. He supplied us with two pairs of sturdy walking shoes, a lightweight tent, two sleeping bags and ground mats, as well as a gas stove and a few portions of dehydrated food. We were ready. Aldi sold us a cheap pot for cooking and a few other necessary items.

We set off on 15 June, in accordance with our pamphlet that described that date as the start of the walking season. A local bus took us to Tegernsee. We pitched the tent there and cooked dinner, just to make sure that we knew what to do and had not forgotten anything essential.

As I was waiting for sleep to come, I realized that, for once, I felt safe and totally relaxed. The only sound was that of silence, with the wind gently rustling around the branches of the pine trees next to the tent. For once, I did not wait for the front door to be splintered and a stun grenade to be thrown in through the gaping hole, followed by men in black. Tonight, Ursula was breathing heavily next to me, and I felt safe.

Healthy portions of oat porridge got us going the next morning. It was a gentle walk to Wildbad Kreuth with a few moderate up-and-down hills along the way. We took our time to cover the 20 km with a lunch stop by the Weissach River, including occasional stops to take in the views. It was early in the season, and we had the mountains to ourselves for most of the day. We pitched our tent on a patch of soft mossy ground and polished off a double dose of rehydrated spaghetti carbonara. The pamphlet promised us a sterner test the next day. And so it turned out to be, with 800 metres of uphill and a similar downhill waiting for us. The path began with a climb from below the tree line up to open alpine terrain before reaching a crest which designated the border between German Bavaria and the Austrian Tirol. According to the pamphlet, this was the area where the Habsburgs came for the hunting and maybe even for the stunning views. It seemed like a good place for lunch and a long rest. We had ascertained that there was no border post, and one could simply walk from one country to another. We could now have continued downhill to Achenkirch. Instead, we checked the map and found another path down to a small alpine lake. This seemed more appealing, so we set off, found the lake, and pitched our tent there. It was a fine and sunny early summer's day. At the shallow end, the water was sufficiently warm for a wash, followed by air drying in the afternoon sun. We agreed that it had been a good day.

Ursula snuggled up and said softly, "This has been the best day of my life. Do you think we could stay in the mountains for the rest of our lives?"

"I wish we could," I replied. "For once, I feel safe and at peace with myself. You've given me a second lease on life. I wish that time would stop for us and that this moment would never end. Let's stay here for another day."

The next day was just as good as the first. On the third day, by the lake, we grudgingly decided that our moments of bliss had come to an end. We packed up and retraced our steps back to Munich.

* * *

Back in Munich, I booted up the laptop to see if we had missed anything while we were walking in the Alps. I had to deal with another shock. The headlines told of a large explosion and subsequent fire at the laboratory in Rawalpindi. Many casualties were reported. The area had been cordoned off in case nuclear materials had been involved. It had been in the back of my mind that Khan and the laboratory at Rawalpindi would be the most likely source of the two warheads once other and lesser suspects had been eliminated. My immediate reaction was that it might not have been a tragic accident. Alternatively, it could have been the work of special forces swooping in with helicopters from Afghanistan and planting high explosives. The layout of the laboratories would have been well-known from satellite imaging and from the files of the IAEA. I knew there was a bunker where several tons of conventional high explosives were stored. If I knew this, so would many others.

There was another possibility. It would have been perfectly obvious to Pakistan that Khan and his laboratory would have been at the top of the list of suspects. The government might have concluded that the best course of action would be to take pre-emptive action to remove all evidence. Blowing up the laboratory while claiming a tragic accident could be the best way to eliminate any possible traces of illicit activities and thereby get off the hook. The alternative would have been to succumb to comprehensive and intrusive inspections of all its facilities and the most rigorous interrogations of anyone that had ever been close to the nuclear programme. If this was the case, I would wish Pakistan the best of British luck. I would be looking forward to the aftermath.

* * *

My assessment was that the USA and Russia would be preoccupied with Pakistan for a while and that my existence would go on the back burner. We might as well remain in Munich for a while longer.

I went back to checking the world on the internet. The news was mildly disturbing but not unexpected. My pursuers had discovered that I had disembarked from the yacht heading for St Petersburg, somewhere south of Stockholm. From there, it was likely that I had headed for Norway. My guess was that the spooks knew more, but they were releasing some information in the hope that the public would join the hunt. A grainy image from a CCTV camera was included in the story. I found the story in all the major newspapers in Scandinavia and on the internet. Two days later, another story appeared. I was now identified as a person with links to Khan and having worked in numerous nuclear establishments, and more recently at the IAEA in Vienna, before taking up an appointment at Oxford University. Some eighteen months previously, the unnamed person of interest and his family had taken a leave of absence and vanished. A perfectly clear picture showed me looking straight into the camera. It must have come from my university ID card. It seemed that I was known by name, reputation and appearance but that the tracking was a year behind. It was possible that the spooks had tracked me as far as Norway or further. I decided not to tell Ursula. We would take one day at a time, and the future would have to look after itself.

We remained in our humble hotel during the week after returning from the mountains. We decided to stay in Munich until the end of the summer unless there were reasons to keep running. I stayed out of sight while Ursula went hunting for a two-month lease for a flat in a suitable location. In the evenings, we went out for dinner in one of the nearby restaurants offering ethnic cuisines. After a couple of days walking the streets of inner-city Munich, she returned with a stack of paperwork from real estate firms. We settled on a small flat in a neo-gothic converted townhouse that had survived the bombing during WWII. It was located just north of the so-called Englischer Garten, a large multi-functional park close to the city centre, allegedly designed by Count Rumford. The next day, she went off with a deposit and signed the lease. The following day, we got the keys and took possession. As usual, I left a forwarding address to a 4-star hotel at Jesolo near Venice in case there were any inquiries.

In the evening, we walked the length and breadth of the park and discovered running tracks, beer gardens and peaceful places for contemplation. We were ready for a few weeks of stable living and a minimum of worries. Even though we had been together for less than six months, we were at the stage in our relationship of being settled into a mutually agreed lifestyle wherever we found ourselves. The day began with cups of coffee and two Hörnchen. This was followed by a morning jog in a park or along a river. I would buy a copy of *Frankfurter Allgemeine* on the way home while Ursula dived into a corner shop for whatever was on the menu for dinner that day. Once home, we had a proper breakfast before a quick shower to get ready for the day. The remainder of the mornings were devoted to mindfulness for Ursula and the interrogation of the internet for me. Lunch was limited to coffee. In the afternoons, we conversed in English about the morning chapter from the current book on psychiatry while I held forth about the headline news of the day. We took turns making dinner on alternate days. One night a week, we had dinner out before going home to a bottle of red and then making love in the gentle manner that befits a staid couple. I think we were both making up for past chaotic and unsatisfactory lives. My past life with Hasina and Eden was beginning to seem like a distant dream that could never rematerialize.

In this manner, the weeks flowed as a quiet river of time. Mid-summer came and went. I had been tracked to a hotel in Oslo, according to a headline in *Aftenposten* and translated by Google, but seemingly no further. As usual, I suspected that the spooks might be keeping quiet about what else they knew. Maybe they had given up, or they were on summer holidays. Neither seemed very likely. I could only hope that they were too busy raking through the embers in Rawalpindi. Spooks never sleep, and they claim that they always get their man; ask Bin Laden in his watery grave. I hoped they would miss my stay in Lillehammer if for no other reason than I did not want my Ragnarok friend to get into trouble.

From time to time, the state of the world was not all about bad news. The Biden administration seemed to have rediscovered global warming – first, as a useful rhetorical tool, and more recently as an issue that required global action. The US decided to remain within, and to support, the United Nations Framework Convention on Climate Change. There was a tacit agreement that a multilateral approach was needed, and this included entering into a constructive dialogue with China and with the EU. There were now clear signs that the world had accepted a condition where peak oil and peak cars were likely to happen within a few years and where fossil power generation would be phased out within two decades. The one merit of social media being controlled by individuals with personal wealth in the 100 billion range was that they could become champions of mitigation of global warming by the simple expediency of tinkering with algorithms. In this manner, content involving denial of global warming could be given a much lower weight, or even be blocked, than that of factual information. The world economy was recovering marginally better than expected, with China being the main contributor to the health of global GDP, as had been the case after the financial collapse in 2008. Most remarkably, the war in Europe was still going on but inside a cordon sanitaire; the killing was much reduced to a level of intermittent skirmishing. Exhaustion had set in on both sides.

The pandemic was still with us, particularly in the Third World. Several vaccines were on the market, but some were of limited value due to providing only partial, or time-limited, protection. Nationalistic policies ensured that the best versions were available only in their countries of origin. The known death tolls had by now passed 12 million, while estimates based on excess mortality were a great deal higher, with the economically struggling nations bearing the brunt. As expected, we were not in it together. It was not all good news.

* * *

By the middle of August, we had to make decisions. We could remain in Munich over the winter and hope for the best. The alternative was to cross the Alps into Austria before autumn set in. The latter seemed the safer option. We had travelled through Germany by public means, and there was always the possibility that our images had been captured by one or more of the very many security cameras somewhere along the way. I had become adept at spotting surveillance cameras and avoiding being in their fields of view. Hiding behind Ursula, travelling at night, and finding seats oriented in the opposite direction to that of travel, were useful tricks. Unfortunately, I did not have an invisibility cloak. One of my past physics colleagues had been working on it but had not made much headway.

* * *

The beginning of the last week of August had come, and we were packing our bags and abandoning the flat. We were carrying food for 10 days, as well as warm clothes, just in case. The first two days were a straightforward repeat of the trial run earlier in the summer. The daily morning jog in the mornings ensured that we were well prepared for the hills on the second day up to the border.

At the actual border crossing, we stopped for lunch and a rest and then continued on an easy path down to Achenkirch, where we set up camp for the night. The next day was relatively short and easy. We followed an undulating path along the Achensee. We resisted a swim in one of the sandy inlets. The final stretch was on a gravel road and then along the tracks of an old railway to Maurach. We found a nice campsite by the lake and brewed up more of our dehydrated food for dinner, followed by coffee. The next day was yet again short in distance but included a good climb. We were now entering the Zillertal. In the morning, a gondola took us up to 1850 metres. From there, it was downhill to the village of Hochfügen.

The last day of serious walking started along the Zillertal Valley and was then followed by a steep climb up to Sidanjoch ridge. From there, it was a short stretch to the Rastkogelhütte hut. This seemed like a nice place to stop and give our knees a half-day to recover.

We were now close to the high mountain road from Kufstein to Innsbruck. The path to the road passed through pleasant terrain along numerous tarns. We were not yet ready to leave the mountains and rejoin civilization, so we pitched the tent half-way and spent the night in splendid solitude under the stars. On the next day, we walked out to the road and waited for a bus to take us to Innsbruck. It had been a memorable journey. I had a nagging feeling that this was as good as it was going to get.

The End of the Road

The bus deposited us by the railway station in Innsbruck. I was pleased to see that not much had changed since I visited last time, back in the days when I was working for the IAEA. I remembered it as a mildly overgrown small town, and it seemed to have remained so. A bit over 130,000 people lived at the point where the River Inn meets the Wipp Valley and was hemmed in by two mountain ranges with peaks of over 2,000 metres. The hosting of the Winter Olympics in 1964 and 1976 had placed Innsbruck on the map, but that glamour had long since faded. The annual German-Austrian 4-hills ski-jumping competition helped, but alpine skiing had remained the economic bread and butter. The town was sufficiently small to be liveable, big enough and far enough away from Vienna and Salzburg to have a vibrant cultural life of its own, as well as a university founded in 1669.

This time we had done some work on the internet before leaving Munich in order to have our living arrangement sorted out. We had found a cute cottage in the foothills within walking distance from the city and the Bergisel ski-jumping hill. It was located amongst a patch of pine trees at the dead-end of a short gravel road. Privacy seemed guaranteed, as well as offering a measure of secrecy and a feeling of solitude. On the day of our arrival, we had a quick look at the place before Ursula headed off to the real estate office, where she paid two months' rent, signed the contract, and got the keys. I was hiding out in a café behind my customary newspaper. By mid-evening, we were installed.

It took a week for us to feel at home in Innsbruck. There was one problem of some significance. The cottage had no access to broadband, and my trusty laptop was useless unless I went to a location with Wi-Fi. A solution of a kind was for Ursula to become the proud owner of the latest generation of smartphone. This allowed me to keep in touch with the world from home. Otherwise, we could return to our familiar routines.

My state of paranoia returned to its normal level of intensity. I realized that there were pros and cons associated with hiding in the midst of a small forest area. On the plus side, we were invisible to the rest of the world if we did not break cover. As long as I stayed at home during daylight, I was effectively non-existent. Ursula could come and go as she pleased on the assumption that she was not on the radar of ill-wishers. On the other hand, the cottage could be approached unseen and unheard from several directions.

High technology came to the rescue. I bought a dozen battery-powered motion sensors and installed these in strategic locations around the periphery of the forested area. The sensors were designed to communicate with a base station in our living room. We tested the sensors and they worked. Anything bigger than a medium-sized dog would trigger a signal of intrusion at a particular location and give us time to escape in a direction away from danger. It was the best we could do, aside from heading back to the mountains. Late in the summer, after a spell of drizzly rain, an elderly lady was out picking mushrooms and set one of the sensors off. Ursula went looking and ended up having a lengthy and friendly conversation about edible mushrooms. From then on, we shut the system down during daylight hours. My assessment was that the bad guys, such as special forces, would arrive under cover of darkness, complete with night-vision equipment and stun grenades.

Before the onset of autumn, we embarked on another walk in the

Alps. We started from the point where we ended in the summer and walked three days to the finish of the Trans-Alpine Crossing. This included a crossing into Italy and then on to Sterzing. Two buses took us back to Kufstein, where we stayed overnight. Another bus on the next day brought us home to Innsbruck, where we needed a few days to rest our knees.

* * *

The days were getting noticeably shorter. We had finished dinner and were concentrating on dealing with a bottle of Rioja.

"It's on days like these that I feel that I'm ready to take on the world. This afternoon I dropped into the university to talk to an advisor about psychiatry. I thought that maybe I could ease back into my unfinished education. What do you think?" said Ursula.

After a moment of thinking of how to respond, I said, "Watching you charging the hills of the Alps, I think you're ready for anything. When does the autumn semester get underway?"

Ursula could not possibly be on the radar as a wanted person as long as I was not linked to her. There was no reason for her not to lead a reasonably normal life.

"The first week of October. I thought I would enrol for two units. One on introduction to clinical psychiatry, and the other on psychiatry of trauma."

I nodded with a smile. "You could always come home and do field work on me. A very long time ago, I was accused of having an impenetrable soul and of being obsessed with rationality to the point of being borderline psychotic."

She turned serious and replied, "I wouldn't do that. I like you exactly the way you are, and I admire the way you're managing your own life. I wish that I could do for someone else what you've done for me."

"As one previously wounded soul to another, let us drink to that."

* * *

Three times a week, Ursula trotted off to the Department of Psychiatry for her lectures and came back bursting with enthusiasm and knowledge. This became the new routine. While I was making dinner, she told me about the events of her day. Memories of my first days at university came flooding back to me. Many years ago, I had finally discovered a new world in which I could flourish, just as she had. I found myself sharing in her joy at discovering new knowledge and the challenge of gaining understanding.

During the weeks after the last outing to the mountains, I began to feel increasingly tender in the area around my waist. My initial guess was that it was simply the aftermath of a week of walking up and down mountainsides. After all, I was no longer in the first flush of youth, and one should expect a longer recovery than in years past. But as the weeks passed, I was beginning to doubt that diagnosis. In addition to the nagging back pain, I was feeling decidedly lethargic and vaguely out of sorts. As an adolescent, I had gone through periods of what, at the time, were described as the winter blues. Maybe I was going through the mythical male menopause? Considering my recent life, I could be forgiven for experiencing a bout of mild depression. I had a couple of lengthy discussions with myself and came to the conclusion that my problems were more likely to be physical rather than mental. I needed to be checked out. My problem was that I was not known to the local health system – and could not afford to become known. I needed to talk to Ursula.

One evening, we sat down and worked out how to get me to a doctor to have a look at me. Ursula had not had a medical check since she left Hamburg. Being a card-carrying EU person, she was eligible to access medical services anywhere within the EU and EEA. She suggested that she should register with one of the local health centres. Ursula would then register me as her husband. Once she had been checked out, I would turn up a few days later. Remarkably, it worked. I described my problems to a youngish woman doctor, who proceeded to prod me in the region around where the spine connected to my lower half. Her verdict was that I needed a scan and possibly an examination by a specialist. While I should not be alarmed, there was a possibility that a tumour was hiding somewhere. A week later, a letter of appointment arrived from the local hospital.

A standard X-ray image revealed that there was a tumour nestling up against the spine. The preliminary diagnosis was soft tissue sarcoma, but more testing would be required to confirm the diagnosis. I was to come back for an MRI scan the following week. Assuming that a sarcoma was confirmed, a biopsy might need to be obtained in order to establish whether or not it was malignant. I walked up the hill deep in thought. Dinner was waiting when I got home. In response to the unspoken question from Ursula, I limited myself to saying that the hospital wanted me back for an MRI scan and possibly a biopsy. We decided to hope for the best.

The MRI confirmed that the tumour was hard up against the spine but on the inside. This made a standard biopsy difficult but not impossible. A CT scan guiding the biopsy needle past the spinal cord was suggested, and I was asked to come back a week later. I went home and reported to Ursula. I could tell she was worried. She had been to the library at the university and done some reading. The biopsy revealed that the tumour was malignant and probably not operable. Chemotherapy seemed to be the one viable treatment. I needed to do some serious thinking. But first, I needed an additional discussion with the hospital.

* * *

A seriously sombre group of four medical specialists and I met around a table in a small conference room at the hospital. The results of the diagnostic tests were on the table with a preliminary report. Each specialist took turns to describe the results, what they meant, and the implications. There was agreement that excision of the tumour by surgery was risky because of its location at the spinal column and likely to be of limited value given the high probability that the cancer might have spread to other organs in the abdominal cavity. There were similarly good reasons for not recommending radiation therapy from either an external source or from targeted internalized radioactive bio-constructs. The consensus among the specialists was that chemotherapy was the one remaining option. The objective would then be to shrink the size of the tumour, thereby clearing some space and giving access to surgical intervention.

It was my turn to have my say. I asked if there was a quantifiable probability that the cancer had spread. If so, then chemotherapy followed by surgery would, at best, be an interim solution unless additional biopsies could be carried out as part of the surgery. There was agreement with such a prospect. Then, I got down to the serious questions that needed to be asked. I explained that one option was to let nature have its way. What would then happen? The experts looked at each other and said, as gently as possible, that there was no simple answer. My next question was about the feasibility of tracking the progress of the cancer for two to three months. Would that be possible? I could tell that the team was not in favour of my proposal when they explained that the success of any treatment would be increasingly unlikely in the later stages of the disease. I agreed with that argument but said I needed time to decide if I really wanted to fight the cancer. The meeting ended with the agreement that I could come back at any time for further tests and then be in a better position to decide on treatment.

I walked around for a while and ended up on a park bench. Short of a miracle, my remaining lifespan was limited, possibly to some months or a year, or two, if I was lucky. Was there anything that I needed to do in the remaining time? Looking back on the last two years, they had been largely meaningless, aside from meeting and being with Ursula. During the two years, I had just been running and waiting for the day when I would be cornered. Was it just the survival instinct that had kept me going? Was this the only meaningful aspect that remained of my life? Maybe there was comfort in knowing that the cancer would get me before the pursuers caught up with me. Maybe there was a triumph of a sort to cheat the pursuers of victory? This seemed to be all that was left for me to do. All my life, I had wanted to know what was going to happen tomorrow. It was time to draw the line and acknowledge that the future was for others to know. Now, I had to go home and explain myself to Ursula.

For most of my life, a succession of people had entered my life and stayed for a while before either they or I moved on without grief or regret. Each time I simply turned the page and started a new chapter. Hasina had changed this. When she and Eden had gone from my life, the grief was without bounds or end. I was beginning to think of Ursula as being my second encounter with loss, grief and regret. It was going to be another difficult parting of the ways.

* * *

She was waiting for me. "Tell me what happened," she said when I had sat down with a cup of coffee.

I told her about the meeting and that the recommendation was to try chemotherapy to shrink the tumour and then possibly attempt surgery. If the cancer had spread, that would complicate things. I explained to Ursula that I wanted time to see how the illness was progressing and then make a decision.

"It sounds as if you have decided that the cancer will kill you in the end." Ursula was reading me like an open book. I told her that I wanted to think about the option of letting nature have its way. I was tired of running, and I did not want to be caught.

"Being with you since we met in Hamburg has made it bearable, but sooner or later, a time will come when the running has to stop. I think I have been traced to Kiel. I think I would rather succumb to the cancer than be cornered as an animal. If you stay with me, you will also become a de facto target. I don't want that to happen. I want you to be my epitaph and to be my final gift to a better future. Soon you must leave me, and we must make certain to cut all the physical links between the two of us."

The reply was halting and spoken softly. "In the back of my mind, I knew it had to end for us. I have hoped that one day you would be free to live a normal life. I know it cannot be. It seems we're destined to end up living separate lives. You would keep running as long as you could with the cancer. I would try to return to an ordinary life. We would both remember the special days together, even though we would no longer be together. I could write you letters and tell you that I was well and happy, even if I didn't know where to send the letters. Now I wish our remaining days to be gentle and thoughtful while we prepare ourselves for separation."

There was a tacit agreement to save the practicalities for another day. We made dinner together and found another bottle in the cupboard. We needed that night to be normal. It had been an emotionally draining day. We went to bed early and sought comfort by snuggling up together. Soon we were both asleep.

During the night, some of my old nightmares came back. When I first realized that I was one of the most wanted people on earth, I could not escape thinking about how it might feel to be cornered and shot on sight or how it would be to end up in a place of eternal darkness, such as Guantanamo Bay, or spend the rest of my life in solitary confinement while being waterboarded. The nightmares had hit me before and had lasted for many weeks. A combination of willpower and preoccupation with survival had made them go away. This morning I woke up totally exhausted and had to seek refuge in the certainty that the cancer would be an escape of a kind. It was going to be my final faithful friend.

In the morning, we sat in silence, looking at each other across the breakfast table. I finally understood the extent to which Ursula was struggling to process her thoughts about the future. It became obvious how deeply it had struck her when she said, "I would like to have a child with you so that when the time comes, a part of you will always be with me."

For a while, I could not find words with which to respond. Thinking about the parting from Hasina, it struck me that Eden was a reason for Hasina to embrace her fate. Ursula was seeking refuge the same way by grasping for a reason for being. I also realized that we were all alike. There had to be something, or someone, that would endure when we were gone.

When I surfaced from my thinking, I could see that Ursula was waiting and looking at me.

"I hear, understand and appreciate what you are asking," I said. "How could I possibly say no to your offer of giving me immortality?"

"In your own peculiar way, I think you are saying yes – is that right?"

"It is," was my answer.

"I will stop taking the pill, and we will stop drinking wine. Then, we will leave no stone unturned, beginning tonight."

* * *

A month went by. Ursula announced at dinner, showing me the thermometer, that she felt fertile. That evening, we did our very best.

I got a letter from the hospital inviting me to come for a check-up of my condition. An MRI scan was carried out, and we waited with bated breath for the outcome of the comparison with the earlier scan. There did not seem to be any major differences. Maybe my body was fighting back and keeping the cancer at bay.

* * *

From what I could tell, there were no indications that I had been tracked beyond Kiel. I searched my memory and decided that I had been scrupulous about avoiding surveillance cameras on the leg to Hamburg. As well, I had been wearing an oversize face mask in order to confuse the facial recognition software. The software works on facial geometry, hairline, moles, scars, eye colour, etc. In my case, I was one middle-aged Caucasian male among a large number of middle-aged male Caucasians. In any case, was I the kind of person who would go to ground in a red-light district in Hamburg?

There was another piece of good news. The independence referendum just held in Scotland resulted in a 60% yes vote with a turnout of 85%. Scotland was now entering into negotiations with a view to joining the EU, and there was hope that the Schengen Agreement could be extended provisionally to include Scotland within a few weeks. I was beginning to think about where I wanted to end my life. My happiest years had been in Oxford in the now-diminished UK. Schengen would now allow me to get to Scotland. From there, I could walk unnoticed across the porous border to England and then find my way to the banks of the Thames, where a merciful end could come. In the meantime, I would stay with Ursula for as long as possible.

* * *

We woke up to see the first dusting of snow to brighten Innsbruck after a wet and foggy autumn. Ursula padded off to the bathroom and checked the calendar. She returned triumphantly and announced that she had missed her period. After a cup of coffee, she rushed down the hill to the pharmacy and bought a test kit. She was pregnant.

"I insist that you return to bed so that I can make you marmalade on toast and I can watch your beaming face. All being well, we will become parents. Nature has been on our side."

* * *

It was going to be a race against time. The growth of the new life was going to be neck and neck against the growth of the cancer. My personal race was between feeling safe where I was, against the day when I was no longer capable of managing the last leg of my journey. The over-arching priority was to arrange a safe future life for Ursula and the child-to-be.

A new routine was established – both of us were going to the hospital, but for different reasons. Ursula went once a month to check on progress. She had reached the stage of seeing the new life on the ultrasound screen. I was being checked monthly for deterioration. It was less bad than predicted. The best estimate from the latest scan was that I would have a year unless I relented and asked for chemotherapy. The pain did not seem to be increasing much. The specialist kept asking if I wanted painkillers, but I wanted to save these for later. As expected, I was losing weight, but I felt that I was acting and looking my age. Ursula said that I was holding up well, but I suspected that she was making good use of her psychiatric training.

There were a couple of weeks when Ursula felt decidedly unwell in the mornings, but she passed through that phase. She kept going to her lectures at the university and was intent on sitting for the exams before Christmas.

* * *

We began to talk about the future. In a strange way, I was now entirely comfortable about that. "My future is obviously limited, but there is an up-side: there will be an end to the running, and I will be in charge of the end. I will be comforted by the thought that there is a future after me in which I will be playing a part. I will be remembered."

I was thinking of Hasina and Eden wherever they were and of Ursula and a child yet to be born. For the rest of my life, for better or worse, I had lived a lot and had done that which I thought was necessary.

During our discussions, I had been adamant that Ursula had to become totally dissociated from me and from our brief life together when the time came.

"If necessary, you can confess to having met me in Hamburg. We travelled together. Then, I left you when you became pregnant. There is nothing else that you should confess to. You did not know anything else about me except that I seemed to be a tortured soul. You could say that I had been diagnosed with cancer and had talked about going away to die."

Ursula had been following and accepting my arguments.

"Do you think there will be a time when our son will know who his real father was?"

"It's possible. The trail stops with me. So does the need for retribution. You and our child did not play any part in my sins."

There were other worries to be discussed, but that would have to be for another day.

Christmas and the 2025 new year were approaching. Ursula was getting ready for her exams. She had hunted down past exam papers and had done yet another review of lecture notes and textbooks. She was ready. As expected, she came home and said she thought it had gone well.

The good burghers of Innsbruck knew how to do Christmas. The centre of the city was a winter wonderland with oompah bands, children singing carols, and Strauss waltzes wafting through the air. There was a market by the inn where fresh-faced ladies in dirndl outfits with fur scarves and red hats served beer, sausages and gluhwein to flushed men with moustaches, frozen knees and lederhosen. As well as having mastered Christmas, Austrians knew how to do mid-winter feasting. On the main street, there were sleighs and reindeer made from straw and twigs. I took a photo of Ursula seated between two children on one of the sleighs. I had not seen her that happy for a long time. She took a photo of me with a beer in one hand and a sausage in the other, standing next to a dirndl girl. It was a good day.

I had another check-up just before Christmas. This time the hospital had a look at the liver and kidney functions in addition to the MRI scan. The conclusion was that the cancer was not as aggressive as expected. They thought they could give me at least six months, and possibly a year, of a reasonable quality of life. The news brought back the spring in my step.

New Year's Eve came and went. We walked to town and watched fireworks. Shortly afterwards, Ursula had her check-up at the end of the first trimester. All was going according to plan. On the way home from town, we stopped by a shop that had prams and cribs in the window.

Then, she got her exam results; it was top marks in everything. Her life was certainly on track. She enrolled in the spring semester courses with the proviso that another event might interfere with the next lot of exams.

I was sitting in semi-darkness. Ursula had gone to bed and was sleeping for two. I was letting my mind go into its free-wheeling mode.

There seemed to have been a lull in the action after the announcement that I had been tracked as far as Kiel. The Biden administration might have decided to focus on rebuilding the East Coast. After all, Khan was dead, and the laboratory in Rawalpindi was in ruins; Pakistan denied any involvement of the state, and there was no hard evidence that I had been more than a sleeping partner in the plot. It was certain that the warheads had been constructed in a secret laboratory in Rawalpindi by a small team of engineers, all of whom had vanished into thin air. No doubt the Russians had reasons to be aggrieved, but there was no way of knowing what they were thinking or doing. On the plus side, they had been able to cash in on the sympathy vote, thereby finding friendships in quarters where formerly they were demonized and ostracized. Maybe the world had lost interest in me. On the other hand, the US had never lost interest in Bin Laden, who ended up in a watery grave.

It could be that I was engaging in wishful thinking. The enemy could be entering Innsbruck at this very moment. Just because Ursula was on track with her pregnancy and I had been given an extension of life, I should not be lulled into a false sense of security. I so wished to be around when Ursula gave birth. Then, I could draw the line and wait for the end.

The weeks went past and then became months. We both had relaxed into our roles – as a pregnant student for Ursula and as a budding master of Zen in my case. I had decided to stop worrying about the future; it would have to look after itself. I had done my bit for the future. Now it was up to the rest of humanity.

Once the semester started, I provided moral support by walking to town with Ursula. She would go on to the university, and I would take the short walk to the railway station. Its main merits, as far as I was concerned, were that the coffee was good, and there were places to sit where I was just another lost soul seeking shelter from the cold. The main attraction was that the Wi-Fi was excellent. Trust the Austrians to be efficient. I could pretend to read the newspaper while checking the world on the smartphone. After an hour, I would usually stop worrying about the state of the world. The rest of the day could evolve in different ways. I could either walk back to the university and wait for Ursula to have her lunch break between lectures. Or, I could take my time shopping for staples and then return to meet Ursula when she was finished for the day. My life was totally relaxed and laid-back. The nagging pain in my abdomen did not seem to be getting worse. It was not a bad life for a condemned man, I thought.

We waited, with a mixture of expectation and apprehension, for the result of the check-up at the end of the second trimester. Ursula told me she felt fine, and she was right. I waited outside on a bench while she went in for the check-up. The midwife gave her the all-clear, and the ultrasound images showed that the foetus was going to be a proper human being – and a girl at that. Parenthood was not far away, and we needed to make preparations. The hospital offered us a starter kit for first-time mums. We bought a how-to book on parenthood that told us about what to do and when to do whatever was required. I began to recall what it had been like when Eden was born.

It was time for my check-up. The tumour was growing. The kidney function was deteriorating for the kidney on the left side, but the one on the right seemed to be OK. I was asked if I needed more potent painkillers, but again I declined. It was bound to get worse, and I did not want to get hooked on heavy drugs too early. The Zen would have to do for the time being.

* * *

The time was coming for me to think about how I was going to wind up my life with Ursula and then end my last run in a dignified manner. Equally important for me was to do my best to set Ursula up for a new and safe life as a single mother. I thought she needed an additional two years to become a certified psychiatrist. Then, there was the problem of how to decouple her new life from her past. As far as we were aware, there was no indication that any links between us had been established so far. My plan was to lay a trail to my dead body when the time came. The assumption was that the hunt would then come to an end. Hasina had been off the radar for more than three years, and there was no indication that there had ever been any serious interest in her. She was obviously known to the system through our associations at the IAEA and at Oxford University, but the focus of the hunt seemed to have been on getting "their man".

Ursula and I felt we would need to have several discussions

about how to manage our remaining months together, partly to take the emotional sting out of the situation and partly to agree on how to proceed.

"I've thought about where to finish my studies. I could continue here in Innsbruck, but I think I'd miss you too much. I don't want to go back to where I started; there are too many bad memories. I think I'd like to return to Hamburg, where we met. I understand Hamburg. Does this make any sense to you?" she asked. We were talking about life after separation.

"Yes, it does. I can visualize you there, back in St Pauli."

Another evening and we were talking about money. We had got to the stage where we could deal with such pragmatic matters.

"I have a way of moving money around without going through the financial system. I will arrange for 25,000 euros to be sent here as cash in 200-euro notes. I propose that you open a security box in one of the local banks here. For obvious reasons, you have to avoid the electronic banking system for a while, until you have a job and get a legitimate income. Another 25,000 euros will come here, again in cash in small denomination notes. These you can keep for ongoing living expenses that can be paid in cash. When you get to Hamburg, set up an account with a bank, and deposit a few thousand into that account. A couple of thousand will not raise any suspicions. From time to time, you can deposit additional small amounts. Later on, I will arrange for another 25,000 euros in cash to be sent to your address in Hamburg. The money here in Innsbruck is for an emergency. I have some spare money here. The cash is in different currencies. I will need some cash for my final run, but the rest I will leave with you. It is best that you don't know how these arrangements are made."

* * *

Ursula was half-way through the third trimester. Her bump was becoming ever more impressive. The midwife at the hospital made soothing and reassuring noises. I walked with Ursula each morning to the university and was on hand for when she was ready to come home. There were still a few icy patches on the hills, and this was not the time to slip.

Then, the exam time came. She agonized about asking for a deferment versus turning up and being impressively pregnant. The department was understanding and gave her the option to sit for the regular exams, sit at a later time, or both. She decided to turn out for the normal exams. I went with her on the day and paced up and down in the reception area until she had finished.

"I think I did OK. The baby was giving me a swift kick now and again, and that spurred me on. Let's go home and rest."

Two weeks later, she woke me up in the middle of the night, saying that the contractions had begun. We were prepared. I wrapped Ursula up in warm clothes while we waited for the taxi. Four hours later, a baby girl was born and had a lot to say. Ursula was exhausted but happy. I was overwhelmed and tried not to feel useless. The hospital kept her for two days, and then she and the baby came home. I had read the good book about how to deal with babies. It had been twelve years since Eden was born, and my skills in handling babies were rusty. The hormones had done wonders for Ursula's breasts, and the baby took to them with a vengeance. Suddenly, life was very different; a new normal was waiting for the three of us. One evening I was sitting in semi-darkness while Ursula and the baby were sleeping. It occurred to me that there was nothing more I could want from my life.

A letter came from the university saying that Ursula had passed the exams with good marks. The past year had been good for her. She sent off her application to the University of Hamburg.

One evening, we settled on Angela as the name for the baby. We were both admirers of Angela Merkel and her role in dominating European politics after the end of the Cold War and in maintaining Europe as a champion of peace and prosperity. We hoped that the baby would agree in due course and that, for once, peace and harmony would be the norm for her generation.

For the next several months, three-hourly feeds from the breast were the main priority, with clean diapers ranking a close second. Angela's domain was a crib on Ursula's side of the bed. I was in charge of dinner and breakfast and did most of the shopping.

It was a strange period for me. There was deathly silence about the hunt for me or any other culprits. I kept checking the world to make sure. The world seemed to have forgotten the nuclear attacks in favour of worrying about the economy that was struggling to recover from the sequence of shocks. Debates were raging about how and when to go green and whether or not greenery should be coupled with a transition to a more egalitarian society. The case for a wealth tax was very much on the agenda, but this was conditional on a system having near-total financial transparency, coupled with the abolition of tax havens and with measures to harmonize the effective tax regimes across jurisdictions. As usual, the EU was in the vanguard. China had the will, and the means, to ensure central control of its economy at all levels, from the individual wage earners to the mega-corporations. Between the EU and China, they accounted for more than 50% of the world's GDP and could collectively set the agenda for a new financial order. I lived in changing times but regrettably would not see the outcomes.

Spring was in the air, and there were decisions to be made. Angela was at the crawling stage and delighted in rearranging the books on the lowest shelves. She was beginning to exhibit personality and could tell us when she was not happy.

"I think I'd like to remain in Innsbruck until mid-summer. By that time, Angela will have had her vaccinations, and she'll begin to eat proper food. There'll still be plenty of time to get settled in Hamburg and get ready for the start of the semester in the Department of Psychology." Ursula had a plan, and I liked it.

It was my turn to explain myself. We had decided that I would leave a couple of weeks before Ursula so that she could hand back the keys. We would concoct a story that I had been called away to a sick relative in Torino. After my departure, Ursula would leave a forwarding address to a mythical relative in Karlsruhe. When in doubt, lay a false trail, we decided.

The plan was to find my way north through the EU to Ireland. I would use an old identity card from the time I had been with the IAEA. Scotland was now independent and had become a member of the EU. It had just ratified a provisional extension of the Schengen Agreement. Getting to Ireland should be straightforward, most likely by ferry. From Ireland, there were ferry connections to Scotland. The border to what was left of the UK was likely to be even more porous than that between Ireland and Northern Ireland. There were places where the border was within easy walking distance of Hadrian's Wall. Many years ago, Hasina and I had walked one summer about 40 kilometres along the Wall, and I knew there were several locations of easy access from either side of the Wall, from one watering hole to another. Once inside the UK, travelling was just a matter of finding the right buses.

"You're going back to your roots, aren't you?" said Ursula.

I thought about that for a while and then said, "Not really. I don't seem to have any roots. But I lived in the UK for many years, and they were the happiest and most productive years of my life. There are many memories from those years that will comfort me as my days run out."

My next check-up, possibly the last one, was in mid-May. The pains had been more bothersome. I feared the worst. The results were not encouraging. One of the kidneys appeared to be dysfunctional, and the stomach lining was under attack. The specialist had a sombre message. He thought I had no more than a year left, and the ending would be increasingly painful. We had a discussion about pain management. I explained that I was planning to leave Innsbruck and return to a place from my past life in order to feel at peace during the final months. The specialist nodded and said he understood. I think he might have run into this kind of situation before.

"Would a morphine pump be a suitable way to ease the pain?" I asked him. After all, the primary cancer was hard up against the spinal column, and I could possibly manage with small doses. I wanted to remain mentally functional for as long as possible. He said that he needed to consult his colleagues and would then get back to me. He called back the next day and said I could come in for an assessment. The consensus seemed to be that a morphine pump could be implanted in the abdominal cavity with a catheter running to the spinal column. Relatively small doses of 1 ml injected morning and evening would leave me mostly pain-free and with my mental faculties intact. The reservoir would be sufficient for eight months before needing to be topped up. The operation was routine, but I would need to remain at the hospital for two days in order to make sure that there were no complications. I was entirely agreeable. A booking was made for the following week.

The procedure was straightforward. I could press a sub-cutaneous button to get a dose when it was needed.

"What happens if I press the button several times?" I asked.

"You go to sleep and don't wake up," was the answer.

Then, came the difficult part. I had to tell Ursula. She took it much better than I had expected. She had got used to the idea that I was leaving and that I wanted to meet my end with dignity and in solitude.

We settled on the second week in June for my departure from Innsbruck. Ursula would stay for another month. These dates were conditional on events beyond our control. I began to destroy evidence that might suggest that I had been hiding in Innsbruck in recent times. All the motion sensors were collected and smashed to the point of being unrecognizable. The debris was then deposited at several different rubbish collection stations. I collected all paperwork that could possibly be of interest to a search party. This was then incinerated in the backyard. My redundant personal belongings were either burnt or deposited at collection points for reuse by others. When the time came, I would be carrying the remainder in the backpack, which had been my trustworthy companion for nearly three years. This was how my life with Ursula and Angela was going to end. Once I had left, Ursula would do a deep clean of the cabin before handing back the keys.

The final two weeks were difficult. We were metaphorically and physically clinging to each other and wishing that time would stop. Even Angela seemed to sense that there was something in the air. The silences were heavy, and her gurglings were subdued. When I was going to pick her up to check the state of her diaper, she grabbed my thumb and would not let go. I went to the bathroom and wiped away the tears.

The days went – one by one. The moment came when I was standing by the door holding the backpack. There was a final embrace, a last sob, and a plea for remembrance. At the gate, I stopped, turned around, and waved to Ursula sitting on the doorstep with Angela on her lap. Then, I turned around and walked down the hill. I did not want them to see the tears running down my sunken cheeks.

* * *

The journey began with a day-long bus ride to Paris. There I stayed overnight before catching an early bus to Cherbourg. The ferry to Dublin left in the early evening. As expected, my old ID card from my days in Vienna did not attract any interest. Arrival was at lunchtime the next day, and there was time to find a hotel for the night.

Once the Scottish independence referendum was won, and it was certain that Scotland would join the EU, a direct ferry connection between Dublin and Glasgow had become available. I booked myself on to the first available sailing and found myself in Glasgow a day later. The fresh air must have been good for me, so I saved the morphine for another day.

I spent a day in Glasgow being a tourist while finding out about buses going south to Carlisle. In an outdoor shop, a nice man told me how to cross the border and find Hadrian's Wall. He even sold me a map that showed the paths in the area. The next day, I headed south on the bus to Carlisle. After a night in a B&B, I got a taxi to drive me down to the beginning of the trail and then began walking east on an easy path. By mid-afternoon, I had completed the first day, as suggested on the map. The weather was good by the standards of Scotland, so I decided to press on for one more day. I felt surprisingly well and wanted to make the most of what was likely to be my last serious walk. The next morning, I was beginning to run out of steam. Over breakfast, I was told by a group that was coming the other way that there was just a short walk out to the east-west road where a bus would come along every hour. The bus would take me close to Newcastle. That evening I was tucked up in a nice soft bed close to the main bus station. It was just another day of bus travel to Oxford, and I would have come full circle.

I had known all along that I could not stay in Oxford. While Oxford was my favourite place, it was a small town; I could not stay there for more than a few hours without being recognized by someone. Before leaving Innsbruck, I had logged on to several real estate agencies in the Oxford area to find a bolthole not too far away from the city centre but well away from where I would be recognized. I was partial to the Thames. There was a stone cottage for rent in Lechlade-on-Thames that seemed to be near perfect for my purpose. I made a tentative booking by e-mail and announced my arrival before the end of June. A quick phone call to the realtor was enough to be told that I was expected. Then, I discovered to my great surprise, that our dormant bank account with Barclays was alive and well. Hasina and I had left a few thousand pounds to deal with finalizing various standing orders. Unfortunately, it was of no use to me. I had changed my euros into pounds in Newcastle to pay for the monthly rent and some groceries. Someone at the real estate office agreed to meet me at the bus station with the keys and then drove me to Lechlade. Apparently, there were only two buses per day, and I had missed the last one.

In the evening, I had settled in after a fashion. I could just about see the Thames between a couple of other houses. It took me a few minutes to find the one and only grocery shop and to fill up my plastic bag with staples to keep me going for a day or two. I guessed that the cottage had once belonged to a farm and been used by the workers. The main house of the farm, complete with a thatched roof, was still there, being guarded by a large black dog. A big tractor and a muddy Land Rover suggested that some farming was still worth doing.

That evening the farmer and his dog came over to introduce themselves and possibly to check me out. I described myself as an author who was looking for peace and quiet to finish off a monograph on the political philosophy of the EU. Now that the UK had left the EU, this was the perfect place to look at the EU from the outside. Also, I had access to the exceptional library of the university further down the river. My farmer friend muttered something about the most stupid decision ever and left me to it. I gathered that he meant leaving the EU. Later that evening, he came back to check that everything was OK. I assured him that I was fine but asked about the internet. He said it was not blindingly speedy, but it should be available in the cottage and in the converted barn. He explained that the farm made more money from holiday lets than from working the land. The last two years had been bad because of the virus and the war, and Brexit had not helped. The nuclear attacks might be the final straw. I made sympathetic noises to the effect that we were over the worst.

Ursula and I had set up encrypted reciprocal e-mail accounts. In addition, we had agreed on meaningless code words for sensitive information. I sent her a message that I had arrived safely on the banks of the Thames and that all was well. She responded that she was missing me, but Angela was being an angel. I hoped that the GCHQ had better things to do than wasting supercomputer time on decrypting gibberish messages between a stone cottage in Lechlade and a bedsit in Hamburg.

I went through a phase of feeling desperately lonely and despondent. Memories were surfacing from the days with Hasina, the time when we had walked the length of the Thames and how special our lives in Oxford had been. I wished there was a way to know where she and Eden were and how their lives had been since we parted. I felt better about Ursula and Angela. Their lives were on track, and they were as safe as was possible in a chaotic world.

I decided that I had to get a grip and make some use of my

remaining months. Having a good look at myself and my life seemed to be the place to start. Walks along the river, here I come.

What was it that had made me into the person I had become? How much was due to nature, and how much was nurture? Given that I had never known my parents, much less what inventory of genetics I had inherited, that did not get me very far. What about nurture?

Memories from my earliest childhood were few, fragmented, and made little sense. I remember walking along a dimly lit tunnel holding on to someone, but I had no visual memory of who that someone was. Then, I remembered a circus with elephants performing, but again there was no memory of another person. Another fragment had me sitting next to a female child on a hillside amongst heather in full bloom. Was it possible that I had a sister? Yet another had me watching a wartime movie from the projector room, but there was no projectionist. One vivid memory was set underground when there was a great explosion nearby; a fluorescent light fixture had fallen down, and there had been a bleeding arm. It seemed that until the age of five, I had no visual memory of an adult. The first adult I could visualize was a grey-haired couple taking me to school, but they did not seem to play any further role in my life. I do remember walking back and forth to school and being worried by a large dog and by older pupils who might give me a hard time. I think reading and writing came easily to me. I also remember being thoroughly bored most of the time and that I usually retreated into my inner world.

Half-way through the second year in elementary school, I came down with a bad cold that turned into pneumonia. The doctor came, declared me to be fragile, and told me to stay in bed. I recovered and went back to school. The pneumonia returned, and I was taken to hospital, where I stayed for three weeks. I got home for Christmas;

I think I was still with the grey-haired couple.

Early in the new year, pneumonia got me again. This time it was serious. I was sent to another hospital run by a religious order. Maybe prayers and godliness would have better luck with me. Within a week, I went into a coma. I was quickly wheeled to a single room in case I would not make it through the night. During the third night, I woke up and looked at the crucified Christ illuminated in the corner. I thought I had died and gone to another place. There was a strange person sitting by my bedside. I never saw him again. Then, I blacked out once more. Two days later, I regained consciousness. The nurses proudly announced that they had put me on intravenous antibiotics and that must have done the trick, or maybe it was their prayers that had pulled me through. Later, I asked about the strange man. They said he had turned up and had claimed to be my father. They let him sit by my bed.

I remained fragile until spring. One gloriously sunny day in May, I was allowed out. The blinding light, fresh air, and the noise from the city were overwhelming. I had been given my life back again. By this time, my previous notional family had decided that I was not worth the bother, and I was sent off to distant relations in the North.

The North, and the new family, were good for me. They decided that benevolent neglect was what I needed the most. As well, the new school was a great improvement for me. I think the teachers might have been warned that I was a difficult customer.

During the year, I finally realized that there were two internal voices that were talking to me. One was the rational me, and the other was the fearful and irrational one. During the year of being more or less left to my own devices, I think I gained some insight into myself and acquired the beginnings of dealing with the two voices. I needed survival skills, having survived the encounter with illness. I needed to come to terms with my situation and deal with the world as it was. During the fifth grade, I discovered reading and books. It came about because I knew that I was not any good at relating to people and to the society in which I found myself. I thought that I needed to understand both, and books might help. There was a small library attached to the school, with four walls of shelves and more books than I had ever seen. I began on the top left-hand side and read my way, shelf by shelf, reading one book per day. At the end of the year, I had learned a lot about people, societies and ideas.

I caught up academically with what had been missed during the year lost to illness, then established a working relationship with my host family and faked being an acceptable social animal. The exams at the end of elementary school went well. The teachers and my "family" probably patted themselves on their backs for having salvaged the damaged goods. It could have gone so much worse. The two voices remained with me for most of the rest of my life.

I was sent away to high school in a big city. It was a disaster for me. I thought the material being taught was either trivial or useless. There were some good teachers, but several were worse than ordinary. I kept reading whatever I could find but steered well away from the syllabus. The report cards kept saying that I was a difficult pupil. The standard refrain was that I needed to pull myself together. Little did they know that I was trying, but high school was not the place to do it. Half-way through the final year, the French teacher took pity on me. I think he saw me as a challenge. I ended up spending an hour per week in his office while he tried to understand the way my mind worked, and I tried to work out what he was trying to tell me.

Some months before the final exams, I caved in, stopped going to the library, and ploughed through the syllabus at high speed. The exam results were not wonderful, but they got me into the university in the capital. I had no idea what I should study. The protestant work ethic came to the fore, telling me that one should work on one's weaknesses. Therefore, I signed up to do physics. The rest, as they say, became history. It seemed to me that, in hindsight, something had been terribly wrong with the nurturing in the early and critical years of my life. It also seemed that I was left to deal with it by myself. By the time I reached university age, I was able to present myself as a tolerably functional person. It was only when I met Hasina that I finally came to terms with my personal demons.

* * *

My soul-searching went on for several long and slow walks during the summer along the upper reaches of the Thames. In the end, there was one question that remained unresolved. Did what happened in my earliest youth predetermine my actions in later life? If I had experienced a tolerably normal childhood, would I still have joined Qadeer Khan to change the world and played my part in inflicting death and destruction on an unimaginable scale? The best answers I could come up with were the effects of the two voices that had been with me for most of my life. One voice spoke for the rational person who would follow a relentless and dispassionate path when confronted with a problem. When I lost the only family I had ever had to Raja, global warming became an all-consuming problem that had to be solved. The other voice spoke for the person who responded to the sight of Hasina and Eden weeping by the splintered stump of a mango tree on the hillside in Chittagong, where my family had lived and died.

I resolved to use the time I had left to write an account of my life. Then, it would be for others to pass judgment.

The next six months became a race between the cancer and my

ability to average writing a thousand words a day. Toward the end, I had to rely on the morphine for sleep, and I would write during the lucid few hours when the dose was wearing off and before I needed the next shot.

In the early summer, the last one I was going to see, I could feel that the end was coming. I had sent the manuscript off to the publisher that Hasina and I had worked with over the years in academia. They would know what to do.

I was sitting on my favourite bench by the bank of the river. My Sunday morning morphine shot had not yet worn off. There was a feeling of peace. There was nothing else for me to do except enjoy being alive for a few more days.

Then, I noticed a group of three walking upstream along the towpath. When they came closer, it suddenly struck me; it was Sheila, Stephen and their son! They looked at me, and I looked back. Our eyes met and locked on. I knew that I had been recognized.

They had stopped. Stephen and Sheila were looking at each other. I got up and walked back to the cottage and locked the door.

* * *

The evening had come when I would press the hidden button three times. The merciful sleep would come, and I would not wake up. In the halfway house to oblivion, there was time to say farewell to Hasina and Eden and to Ursula and Angela. Please, world, be good to them.

Postscript: I Am Hasina

If you are reading this, you are in possession of a second or later edition of my husband's story of his life. A while ago, I came across a copy of the Saturday edition of the *Times* newspaper; it had been abandoned by a visitor in a café. The review section had an article describing the content of the book that you have just read and a thumbnail sketch of its author. After a period of thinking about what the reviewer said, I felt that I should add my voice to the debate about the justification, or lack thereof, of my husband's acts. After all, he is no longer with us and cannot explain or defend himself beyond what he has written. Furthermore, I know more about him than any other person. You might think that I am biased when I talk about the man I lived with for many years and who is the father of my son. I like to think that I have a reputation from my scholarly days of being the author of several works that have been praised for the dispassionate, factual and unbiased analyses of political events in our time.

No woman or man is an island. We are all children of our times. It is impossible to truly disconnect oneself from whatever is happening around us on the microscale or on the macroscale. Usually, most of us can only change things on the microscale. Most of us are confined to do our best to make the world a better place for the small number of people that we can personally interact with. There are very few who can change the world on the macroscale – but more often, such change is for the worse rather than for the better. My husband has had an impact at both ends of the scale. At the personal level, he was a saviour of lost souls. He once told me that he would like his epitaph to read *Largely Harmless*. At the time, I think he was referring to the microscale.

For many years, we were an unremarkable middle-class nuclear family in Oxford. We were fortunate to spend most of our time inside a parallel universe where intellectual pursuits and scholarly rigour were valued above all else.

Then came Raja, a savage tropical storm, and the sea took our parents away. Only two splintered mango trees remained where we could shed tears. The grief lasted a long time and became the trigger for thinking about global issues that really mattered. Before Raja, my husband had spent his time and energy on nuclear technology and on related issues, and I had tried to make sense of the politics on the Indian sub-continent.

My husband became obsessed with the science of global warming. He read the early scientific papers and found that most of the predictions made 15 years ago had come to pass. I delved into the politics of global warming and found it thoroughly dysfunctional. It seemed to be a classic example of the frog in the pot of water being heated. By the time the frog realizes there is a problem, it is too late. Something had to be done. Tinkering around the edges of business as usual was not going to be sufficient.

Then, we met Qadeer Khan in Rawalpindi. My husband had known Khan for many years during his time with the IAEA in Vienna. He and Khan spoke the same language and understood each other. Khan had given Pakistan the nuclear bomb as the means for Pakistan to be a truly independent nation after the partition and the humiliating loss of Bangladesh. Khan saw himself as the saviour of his nation. Once the nuclear deterrent was in place, he began thinking about global warming and came to the conclusion that the greatest threat to the people of Pakistan was global warming. The three of us corresponded and met over several years while our views matured and coalesced. The financial crash of 2008 focussed our minds on administering a shock that would put an end to the current world order and thus allow a new order to emerge. The pandemic and the war in Europe were fortuitous for us, and we began to think seriously about how we could re-enforce the instability arising from the global pandemic and the war. We realized that, uniquely, we combined the scholarly understanding of global warming with the analytical insight into the dysfunctional politics of the day and, most critically, the means to make change on the macroscale. Judicious use of nuclear weapons was available to us. We were not intent on gratuitous violence and destruction – but we wanted to dislodge the system from its present equilibrium state and then through a metastable one, into a new stable state where global warming would be recognized as a credible threat to human survival.

I am now the sole survivor of the group that planned and inflicted the shock, and I can see the outline of a new and better world. Millions died, but I believe and hope that posterity will agree that our actions were necessary. We were simply the tools that pulled the trigger. The old temple was a monument to false deities, where all of humanity was being readied for sacrifice. We pulled the temple down. It is for the next generation to do the rebuilding of edifices that celebrate nobler ideas and better lives.

My husband sent Eden and me away so that we could be safe and so that we would know the answers. We have new identities and have been to places where we cannot be found. I pray that Eden will grow up in a better world. One day, he may know how that happened and that his father was one of its creators. I hope that I will also see that happen.

My husband was on the run from the wolf pack during the last three years of his life. I am glad he teamed up with Ursula and became the saviour of a lost soul. Angela will be his final act and epitaph. I wish that Eden and I could meet Ursula and Angela, but I understand that is impossible. It is a comfort to me that, in the end, he chose the time and the place to die. I feel within me that he will rest in peace.

Please be kind to his memory.

Printed in Great Britain
by Amazon